CHAPTER 1

Voices come to me in the darkness, and prey on my weary heart.

"Eo nahkeh nahiih."

All I wanted was rest, but all I'd get were those words. I'd been blindfolded for weeks, and starved. Things had gotten to the point where I would have welcomed death, and yet the voices still wouldn't leave me be.

"Why are you so eager to die?"

Evil knows when I'm alone. When I am, it rests above my ear; there it speaks secrets, churns riddles, and trickles hot breath down my neck. Everyone I tell thinks I'm crazy, and I can't blame them. I'm forced to keep my head down, and bear with what haunts me, *every, single, night.*

"You know what will happen, why hide?"

This thing, this voice? It was fate itself, I think. You wouldn't be wrong to call fate the god of my people. There runs a belief in their doctrine that fate could never be defied, so, here's where I'd prove what I really was; a true fool. I'd hold out hope for a miracle, I'd try to defy fate, or gladly die trying...

A void of shadow stood around me. My abductors had been leading me for awhile, and at long last their footsteps ceased. I had no more strength. When someone nudged me from behind, I went crashing down.

On the ground, a silk-like hand graced me. It worked

it's way down my face, and yanked away my blindfold! Ere ensued the first time I saw her; a certain young woman with pale blonde hair. Her skin glistened, and her dress was just as regal. I laid on my belly, and looked to her for answers. She didn't look back, instead her eyes flew beyond me.

"You fools!" she cried, "What were you thinking!?!"

"Our expedition held some... complications." said a scruffy voice.

"Loshki! Don't you dare try to pass this off!"

"My lady, this girl-"

"Silence!" she cried again, flailing her arms, "Get out of my sight before I hand you back to those sadists as retribution!"

Quiet ensued. My gaze stayed on the woman, who seemed intent on putting Loshki to death with her eyes. He must have backed down, because I heard footsteps leak away from behind, then there was the creak of a door, and I heard it close. Right after, the woman descended alongside me. She went straight to the binds behind my back, and set me free! She pulled me up, off my stomach, and to my feet.

"It's no simple thing to forgive such senseless acts." she said.

Regret trickled off her tongue... but real or fake, I couldn't tell.

There was no use trying to read her, so I decided to play dumb. "Still, I'm thankful for your kindness! I'm very, very thankful!"

"Of course..."

She took me by the hand, then looked to my eyes. Her eyes were soft, and kind, but I could tell there was something hidden within them.

"You must be hungry. Shall we see to that, my dear?"

"That would be wonderful, thank you!"

I used to think I was thin before, but that was nothing compared to the skeleton I was now! I was desperate for anything she'd give me. She led me by the hand, and through the room; it was laden with silks, fine tapestries, and all sorts of regal frills. She sat me at a table, and then she started to give requests to a servant for all sorts of foods I'd never heard of.

I snuck glances in the meantime. Something about the paintings strewn about was really tipping me off. I could swear I'd seen them before, but that couldn't be the case, right? In the midst of my confusion, a servant laid down a tray of sizzling hot, fresh food. Another two were right behind, and they each did the same. Saliva started to beam from my mouth, and my eyes went wide.

"Eat, young one."

My stomach roared. I was too shocked to eat, despite how much I wanted to.

She brushed away at my long, pitch black bangs, and gave me a little smile. "Is food uncommon where you come from?" so she said, "Please, my dear, eat."

Was this some sort of test? If so, then I was eager to fail in glorious fashion! I clawed at the table, and flooded my mouth with it's bounty. Nobody seemed surprised when I started to choke, especially the woman, who had a goblet of water at my lips in mere moments. A good minute of gagging ensued before I could breathe again.

"It only makes sense you wouldn't have the sort of food you deserve, where you hail from." so she said.

My eyes stayed on hers. I wanted to try one more time to see if she'd tip her hand.

"You're right!" I said, "I really didn't, but I wish I had!

LAIT YUMEMI

Food from there isn't nearly as nice as what you have, miss...?”

“Miyune, but you can call me *Miyu*.”

My eyes couldn't decipher *anything*. Only my ears were getting me anywhere. “It's a name I used to go by...” she said, “once upon a time.”

Something was amiss with those words... but what? Usually I was good at this type of thing, so it surprised me when I couldn't get a read on her.

“Well then, Auntie Miyu, thank you for dinner! It's spectacular!”

“Of course, my dear.”

I wanted to make use of the momentum I had, so I kept talking. “I'll serve you well, Auntie Miyu!” I said, knowing *well* they hadn't taken me to make me a slave, or anything so simple.

“Serve me?” she laughed, “As if! If anything, you could serve me by being the sister I ever wished to have.”

Her deliveries were convincing, so I couldn't blame her for trying.

“What is your name, my dear?” she asked, breaking me out of thought.

This must have been her way of playing dumb, because there was *no way* she didn't know *precisely* who I was.

I broke my act of innocence in front of her for the first time, albeit just for a second. “I'm not eager to keep my name...” I admitted, “Kehah! Kehah is my name!”

I wondered if my name sounded weird to someone of her tongue.

“*Kehah?*” she said, raising a finger, “Then from this day henceforth, may I know you as my dear 'Kea Leestel'?”

What '*Leestel*' meant was beyond me. Still, anything was better than retaining my surname. I hated my bloodline, all the scars that painted me from head to toe stood testament to the sort of character my family had.

"I really do like the sound of that, thank you."

"And how old are you, young one?"

As if she didn't already know...

"Fourteen." I told her.

"Ah, a fine age. That is still more than young enough to experience the world in a way the aged cannot understand. That in itself is a blessing."

Her words had a rhythm to them that made everything she said sound good.

I nodded, smiled, and went along with her little game. "Yes, very true!"

"Such energy." she sighed, a grin embroidered onto her face, "That'll suit you well with us."

Yes, I could only hope it would... because whether I liked it or not, I was stuck with her for the foreseeable future. Could I run? Of course! I was adept, swift enough, I could probably escape! Except, in a place I did not know, there wouldn't be much of a point. Where could I run to? So yes, I was all but bound to whatever fate she had in store for me... and yet the last thing on my mind was giving up.

CHAPTER 2

Miyune did more than just treat me to dinner. She gave me a pair of night clothes, left me alone to bathe, and waited patiently outside in the meantime. I emerged from the bathroom, to find her seated with a small cloth and a pair of slippers.

She looked to me, and smiled, then rose from her seat. "If you would, take my place, Kea."

I sat where she'd been, and then she dropped to a knee. What was going through this woman's mind? Out of anything she could have been doing with her time... why did she choose to spend it drying my feet? She took the slippers, and put them on me. They felt soft, and wonderful, and were probably the best slippers money could buy.

"Are you alright, truly?" she asked.

"I-, yes, yes! I'm just a little tired."

I'd really had no clue what to say...

"Then let us see to that."

This didn't seem as simple as her just using me, and yet I couldn't imagine it was any other way. I was no commoner back home, which meant she must have had a purpose for taking me. If she pawned me back off to my people, the first thing I'd do is search for death, because there was no way I could endure my old life any longer. I couldn't let things get to that point.

She led me to a room drizzled with dark chocolate furniture; and frosted with tempting silk sheets, of which rested upon a king-sized bed. Flowers were strewn about, which explained why the room smelled so good. I gawked, and dawdled, around to the room's center, where Miyune caressed me on the head.

"Do you like it?" she said.

"This is wonderful! Is this room yours?"

"No my dear, it is yours."

What in God's name was the point of all this? Fears aside, I relished the idea of living in a room like this, if just for a little while. She smiled with reassurance. Her subtle chuckle was an indication she'd picked up on my distrust. I was nothing if not a convincing face, so this surprised me. I didn't have a reply for her. In turn, she nudged me towards the bed.

"Do you like this shade of red, Kea? It just screams *Sohalian Noble*."

...Sohal? I'd heard of it from forbidden texts! That would make where I now resided the World of Unraveling; Lathine. *Nobody* back home would have *ever* dared kidnap me, so I'd known from the beginning my abductors were likely otherworldly. Still... I'd never thought something like this could ever happen.

"Sohal... Hadia, Elratheo, Dial, and Milkar? Are those the nations of Lathine?"

Miyu raised me an eye. "You are quite knowledgeable, my dear. I bet you even know what lays beyond Lathine."

I wasn't sure whether she was referring to some place beyond the waters of Lathine, or of the other worlds that laid beyond.

"I don't think I do. I'm sorry I'm not very knowledgeable, Auntie Miyu!"

Again... I'd honestly had no clue what to say.

She kissed me on the forehead, and left things be.

"Would you like to rest for the night, my dear? You must be exhausted."

That sounded good to me. If she left me alone to "rest", then I could poke around and maybe learn a thing or two.

"I'm very, very tired, so I think that's a smart plan!" I said, throwing in a yawn for good measure.

"I hope you do get good sleep, Kea. Find a maid should you need anything, and do feel free to call for me."

"Of course, Auntie Miyu, thank you!"

She made her way to the door, and departed without another word. There I laid, all alone, in the most comfortable bed I'd ever had... and yet sleep was the last thing on my mind! I let a quarter of an hour go by before making the leap to my feet. I was paranoid she might have been waiting on the other side of the door for me to act, hence why I waited so long. My little feet tippy-toe'd and tappity-tapped up to the door, then my ears flew against it. With any luck I could confirm the presence of a soul, or better yet; the likely lack of one.

There was... nothing! Or nothing I could hear, at least. I wagered there was no harm in gambling, and talking my way out if things went poorly. I opened the door, and took a quick peak down both sides of the hallway. Sure enough, there really was nothing! I was all alone! Or so I thought.

A familiar presence made itself known, and a shiver ran down my spine. Something started to tug at my soul, something sinister. An air of malice went around my neck like a noose.

If a maid should come wandering my way, I'd say something to the tune of *"I'm thirsty, may I please have a drink?"*

Yes, I was sure I could make people go away... but what

I couldn't make go away was the *shadow,* which was now ready to take shape in *this realm.* It had followed me as long as I'd lived. Sometimes it took the shape of a specter in the shadows, and other times it took the form of fire red eyes.

Left or right? Left or right... how about left, I guess? Honestly, it didn't matter which way I chose. All that mattered is how well I went about traversing which path I did choose. Luck proved to be with me, and Miyune's hallways were lit with nothing more than candlelight. Candlelight, and torchlight, was about all I'd had back home, so I knew how to make use of them. I'd watch the way they ticked around corners, and use their hints to detect oncoming movement. Deciphering hidden presences with a lone flicker was second nature to me. Also, I was small, so I could get away with popping my head around corners if I needed to. I know that sounds stupid, but it was true.

I had no real plan, besides gathering *any* information I could. What I found first was a beautiful study; decorated with reds, vibrant dark oak, and plush furniture. It was lain to the brim with books, and scrolls, which were more than enough to lure me in. A certain light from above also intrigued me, it was seeping in from an overhead window.

I went under to see what was causing the light, and what I saw couldn't have left me any more confused. We were underwater, I think? I wasn't sure what to make of the dark blue sight, or the great white lantern that hung in the far away distance. I stood around like a clown for the next ten minutes, trying to make sense of it all.

When at last I kicked from my daze, I started rummaging around the study. Like always, I was cautious not to leave anything so much as a *hair* out of place.

"History of Lathine – The Unraveling" so read a book.

This sparked my interest. I'd heard of the Unraveling of Lathine, albeit only from forbidden books in my homeworld. All knowledge not of our own doctrine was deemed wicked, and therefore knowledge from the other worlds was deemed most wicked of all. I went to work, brushed off some dust, and began to plow through the massive tome. I was curious to see if the so-called *"wicked"* teachings my father kept sealed away were accurate.

"Ere begins the day when Fell King Mararuuthos of Raloia began his wrath. Henceforth swooped the nation of Lathine, crushing his reign to dust, and far too much with it."

There was no way I could finish the book anytime soon, so I made the snap call to skim for tidbits of importance, and key facts. In the end, I was rather disappointed. All I found was the same old facts I'd already known about the Unraveling of Lathine! Though, I guess that in itself was a good thing, because now I knew the knowledge I already had could be relied on.

I continued to raze the library. All I came up with was other books of irrelevant history, and useless tales. Without any good reason to stay in the study, and hold out luck for something big, I passed on, and made my way further through Miyu's labyrinth. Attendants and servants were easy to evade, but those cursed eyes... that was another tale entirely. It wasn't possible to lose the eyes. Throughout the night, the eyes only furthered their materialization into the realm. Their fierce glow kept getting stronger, and they kept inching closer, *and closer, and closer.*

I ended up finding a kitchen, the dining hall, a few elegant restrooms, and... a locked door? I fumbled around with the doorknob, and hoped to work some magic, but alas, I couldn't. With nothing to show for, I cut my losses, and gave up. I was already on my way off when fate spat something my way. A sound met my ears... a faint sound. I couldn't make anything out from it. I went back, and pressed my ear against the door.

One last time, I heard it, the same indistinguishable sound. Where had I heard it before? Honestly, I had no clue, but for some reason, I started to feel anxious at the thought, and my hand started to twitch. Without any way in, I was forced to move on.

Not long after, I peaked around a corner, and saw two men guarding a door. I'd wager it was the way out. On the flip side, the furthest way I could go in the opposite direction led me to another blocked off door. From the shadows I saw a lone attendant sitting by. She must have been at the wait of Miyune. That would make it Miyune's bedroom, right? That was the last area for me to explore on the ground floor.

I waltzed my way up to the second flight, where there proved to be even less of interest. Story number two was nothing more than a collection of guest rooms, and a room for lounging. Here I would have thought there was nothing to the upstairs... if I didn't try the last door that I did. Yet again, I found a locked room! There really was no way out of here.

I decided to call it a night, rather than give the eyes any time to get closer, or risk the prospect of being caught. By now, the power of the eyes had grown strong. They emanated a red aura from behind that illuminated the path ahead, making it appear as if it were drenched in blood.

I went straight back to my room, and didn't dare take another detour. There wasn't a reason to keep bumbling on with no way out, and nothing to be learned, right? I may as well rest in the meantime, for when a pivotal time did present itself, wouldn't you say?

Darkness reigned. I laid in bed. Ere began the voices, the laughs, the breaths that ran down my neck, and the spider-like hand that tickled through my hair. Whispers ran out, one after another, and echoed into my ear.

"Kehah..." they said, one and the same, "Kehah, do you wish to die yet?"

"We will help you..."

"Are you ready to die?"

I was thankful to know that the spirits would vanish by morning, as was the norm. I just had to endure a little while longer.

"Just open your eyes... we will help you."

"Just open your eyes."

CHAPTER 3

Morning rolled around.

"I take it you enjoyed breakfast?" Miyu proclaimed.

I set another plate out of the way, and fell back into my chair. Here I'd thought nothing could outdo what her cooks had done yesterday!

"Shall we move on?" she asked.

"Move on to what?"

"I thought I would take you to see town, to enjoy the fresh air. Have you ever been outside, Kea?"

"Outside of what?"

I didn't understand what she'd meant, and visibly showed it. Pity was engraved in the smile she gave me.

"Well then," she said "you're in for a treat."

She grasped me by the hand, and led me through her home. Soon after, we found ourselves at the door that two men had been guarding the night before. Now, neither was there! My heart buzzed. We walked along, Miyu opened the door... and something struck me down, something unlike I'd ever felt before.

My face tasted the ground, and I went into a daze. A moment passed. I came back to my senses, and realized I was grasping at my eyes. My eyes were burning! Their searing pain was quick to ease, so my grip began to loosen. I could make out Miyune on a knee alongside me. She set her soft hands around my shoulders, which helped to settle me down.

Disgust left her lips... but at herself, not me. "I should have known." she hissed.

"Known what!?!" I cried.

"That you would wilt in the light."

"Is that what it was!?!"

"Yes, my dear. Just stay down, I'll make this right."

I caught sight of her motioning to a servant, then the servant left. Soon after, the servant returned with a black piece of cloth I couldn't get a good look at. Miyune took hold of it, and placed it over my head. It was a veil! Now, the whole room looked lightless.

"How can you handle a light like that?" I asked.

"Because my dear, it's clear you've never touched the outside world."

Miyu opened the door, and again came a blinding light, but this time, I could manage. A cold air accompanied the light. Was it the cold that made the air smell so different? Was this what she meant by *"fresh air"*?

I walked out of the room... and into something unlike I'd ever seen.

Miyune led me a short distance, and then through a gate. I was left in awe at how the room we were in went on far as the eye could see. There were no walls, no limits! I spun in wonder some dozen times, and reveled in the playful warm light from above that tickled up and down my tiny frame, lighting up my bone white skin. My eyes looked to the light, and were met by an endless body of water. Miyune was quick to notice my interest in the twirling blue above.

"Have you ever seen the sky?" she asked.

"The sky?"

"Yes dear one, the sky."

"It's not an ocean?"

"Not quite, my dear Kea, not quite."

"Auntie Miyu?" I said, as she led me on by the hand, "Where does it all end?"

As she replied, I took in the sight of countless people walking every which way. "As far as we know," she said, "it goes on forever."

"*Forever?*"

She leaned into my ear, with an aura alike the whisperer. "Call me a collector of secrets, Kea. What I will tell you is this; I believe there's more out there than we know. One day mankind will tame the seas, and see the dark truth for themselves."

"Dark truth?"

"The seas are rampant, and that's Lathine's greatest blessing. We could never hope to see the secrets they house."

What was that supposed to mean? This woman was all kinds of trouble. She continued to lead me by the hand, while I gave a look at every person that passed our way. They were all calm, and orderly. Some seemed a little dirty, and some a little thin, but that was the extent of anything amiss. This place was a far cry from where I'd been raised, from a place where all people were stained in grime, starvation, and blood. Albeit, the nation we were in, Sohal, was said to have some starvation and blood of it's own.

A hulking man showed up in a flash of light. He walked beside Miyune, and continued along with us. Neither him, nor her, acknowledged one another with their eyes.

"How fare you today, Loshki?" Miyune said.

"Good, but not as good as you, it seems. Enjoying a change of pace?"

"Yes, I've only ever needed someone to share these

times of peace with."

Miyune looked down at me, and smiled. "I can share these time with you, can I not?"

"Of course!"

I got a good look at Loshki, and marveled at his physique. He had muscles on his muscles! That must have been why he seemed to be Miyune's right hand man. You wouldn't even notice he was about average in height, because his arms, chest, and thighs, were just so hulking!

"Have you formally met my dear Kea?" Miyune asked Loshki.

Still, neither looked to the other.

"*Formally?* No."

Not *formally*, but still otherwise? I bet he'd led my abduction...

"Well, now we have!" I cried merrily.

"It's been scheduled, your highness." Loshki said to Miyune.

My eyes snuck a peak at Miyune. I wanted to gauge her reaction. She seemed unsurprised by whatever Loshki's words meant.

Miyune waved off at Loshki. "Thank you, that will be all."

Loshki left without another word. Miyune continued leading me to who knows where.

"You seem to have a thing for sweets, and cakes." Miyu said, stopping the both of us.

"Yes..." I said, getting distracted, "I really, really, really do!"

Something beautiful scented the air. My nose took me over to the source, where I found a merchant at a booth, selling all sorts of sweets.

"Lady Miyune! I haven't seen you in quite some time!"

the merchant said.

"Yes, I have been quite the recluse of late," she grinned, "it is really quite sad."

Again, Miyune leaned beside my ear. "Pick something you like, today is a day for you."

As excited as I was to try something out, what I really wanted was for this woman's warmth to be true. It was too hard for me to believe it was, even if I could tell she genuinely was enjoying this.

With a snack in each our hands, we continued through town.

"Auntie Miyu?" I came to say, "Is this how you like to spend your time?"

She gave a real smile, right as the stretch of road we'd been on ran out. In fact, not only had the road run out, but so had town, and all it's buildings. Something tall, and green, flooded far as the eye could see! To think, my own home had been nothing more than total darkness, and brick...

"Is this grass?" I asked, plucking a piece.

She sat me down, and the both of us laid back. All the greens were soft as cotton!

"Yes my dear, it is."

For some reason, she lost herself to thought. At first, I was more than alright with that. I relished the idea of having time to myself, except my lust for answers was just too great.

"How does the sky and the bright lamp stay afloat?" I asked.

"The sky and sun." she corrected me, "That is simply the nature of their ways."

I'd heard of both, while reading forbidden books... but only now did they make sense. Before I could speak again, she came out with words. She must have known what I was going to ask, because she pointed to the sky.

"Do you see those white, fluffy objects?"

"Yes."

"Those are clouds, Kea. They go hand and hand with the sky."

Interesting! I enjoyed learning, and was more than happy to lay back with Miyune; to watch the sky dance, and the clouds glimmer.

It was her who broke the silence next. "Many things change, but this is one of the things you can always count on."

Whatever that meant was beyond me. She didn't even seem to be talking to me! It was like she was thinking aloud, or recounting something from the past. Soon after, the bright part of day passed. What ensued she called *"sunset"*. We were on the verge of heading back to her home, when a hulking figure appeared, yet again.

"My Lady." Loshki greeted Miyune.

"Has it gone ill, Loshki?"

He went silent. His lack of words seemed to say everything she needed to know, and her happy glow faded into something a little more stern.

"I'll see to it at once." she said.

She then turned to me. "Kea, I'm sending you with Loshki. He will take you back to the palace, is that fine?"

"Of course!" I nodded.

Miyune got up. She shared whispers with Loshki, and then left.

Loshki turned to me, arms crossed. "Shall we get going, My Lady?"

I nodded. "Yes, I think we should."

Loshki led the way, and I followed at his side. With any

luck, I could get an answer or two from him, because I wouldn't get as much from Miyune.

CHAPTER 4

"Loshki?" I said, as the sky grew dark, "What's that, in the far off distance?"

"Stars, Master Leestel."

"Aaah... so that's what stars are."

I could tell he found me amusing. "Get used to them," he said, " and me too, while you're at it. I serve the whole of Lady Miyune's house, which you're now a part of."

"Is that so! That's very, very interesting!"

It seemed like there was something he wanted to say when I cranked up my energy... but chose not to, for whatever reason. There must have been loads of things that were off limits for him to say.

A little silence passed, which I was quick to break up. "What do you do for Miyu?"

"I'm just the Captain to her guard. 'Really nothing more than the muscle of the operation, you could say."

The *"muscle of the operation"*? Now if only I knew what the *"operation"* was, but he kept choosing vague words, so I couldn't get anything insightful. He walked me back to the palace, and I realized how great it's fortifications were. Miyune's home, her incredible palace, had an enormous wall all around it! There were also armed men on top of the wall. They looked down to us, and then opened up the gate at seeing Loshki.

"Captain." a guard greeted Loshki, when we walked in.

"Captain, and young Lady Leestel." Loshki corrected

him, "Do well to remember her."

Loshki led me through the glistening courtyard, and back into the palace.

"Any more use of me now, Lady Leestel?"

I looked up at his towering frame. "I'm good now, thank you, Loshki."

"Well then," he said, cross armed, "I guess I'll be off to accompany Lady Miyune."

"Alright, that sounds good!"

"Speaking of company; you'll be without hers or my own for the next few hours. Let an attendant know if you need anything, they serve you now."

I had to suppress my excitement. Several hours alone was a lot of time to work with!

"Okey doke, that's fine!"

He faded away. My thoughts went to the room an attendant had been sitting in front of the night before. If it really was Miyu's room, then there shouldn't have been anyone in front of it anymore, since she was gone, right? I scurried through the palace, and made my way back to the room. Turns out, my hunch was right! Now, there was nobody at the door! I crept along, and nudged the door open...

There wasn't a soul to be seen, so I entered. That was when the eyes took faint shape; ever did they stay in the corner of my vision.

Words licked their way into my ear. "*You are so quick to doubt.*"

I wish I could have denied the voice, but I couldn't, because it was right. Consequently, it was hard for me to focus on the moment at hand.

As the eyes burned behind me, I did my best to survey Miyune's room, which was like heaven incarnate. My reflection even shone in the marble floor underneath! There was also a crystal chandelier, a well draped bed, shimmering curtains, soft furniture... and most incredible of all, a dizzying array of lights. Lights danced all over due to the shine of the night's sun, which dripped from an overhead window, and reflected through colored vases.

I bore down, snapped out of awe, and started making rounds through the room. There was nothing of importance lying in the open, so I went to the drawers; I was on the verge of giving up and shipping out, when I saw a little something glistening in the depths of one of them. I grabbed for the object, which turned out to be a key!

Laughs trickled from under my breath. I flew out to the locked door from the night before, where I'd heard faint sounds. I put the key in, and twisted, to no avail! My feet took me upstairs, to the second locked room. Again I tried the key, but this time, it worked!

With an ominous creak, the door inched open. My heart raced at the prospect of what might lie inside. I always expected something sinister when I opened a locked door, and yet this room was anything but so. There was nothing more than a desk, and a large cabinet. I scratched my head, and walked to the cabinet. My little fingers opened it up, to reveal an endless stream of papers. I picked one off the top. What could be on the papers? What could be so important?

"Ere after years, Lord Cedleana," so it read, "*Exact* has come into your possession. What information it holds will soon be yours. We have disposed of the last man in your path according to your wishes. Please now, look well upon your faithful servant."

What I would learn, is that "*Cedleana*", was nothing

more than an alias. Miyune was loaded with aliases. There was also someone called the *"Unsaid One"*. I found that person in specific interesting. It seemed that Miyune answered to whoever the mythical Unsaid One was.

Miyune had a palace worth a Queen, a guard worth a Queen, and servants worth a Queen; now it made sense how all that came to be. She had made her fortune off schemes, and corruption. I would wager she was one of the most prominent people in Sohal by now, if not Lathine as a whole.

I made sure to put everything back the way it had been, and lock up, before returning to Miyune's room. I put the key back where it belonged, then got out of the area.

That might have sounded like all I did, or even could do, but that wasn't quite the case. I stopped by Miyune's library, and began to scour for maps. There was a clock in there, over a dead fireplace. From the start of my scouring to the finish, the needle moved about an hour. At the end of the hour, I came up with what I was after! I stuffed a map of town into my pocket, and determined myself to learning it thoroughly.

How did I know the name of Miyu's town in the first place, you might ask? Well, in the locked room, I'd made sure to memorize the address all the letters for Miyune had been sent to! We were in a city called *"Sciruthon"*. I also got a good map of nearby areas, which I stuffed into my pocket too. Learning both maps might mean the difference between life and death if I ever fled, so I had every intent of getting the both of them under memory.

I think that was good for a night's work. Miyu seemed to be the patient sort anyways, which meant I shouldn't rush too much. I went to the dining hall, got with one of the maids, and had them start rolling out sweets. If this was the one chance I'd ever get to be a glutton, then there was no way I wasn't taking it! I was thin as a straw. A little fat would have gone a long way to helping me out, so I saw this all as a win win. Near the end of my conquest at the table, a door opened. I looked back, and saw Miyune!

"You think like me." she said.

I gave a little laugh. At this point in time, I thought I was an impressive little devil. Still, I was sure to sell off my laugh as an agreeing one.

"Yes, I guess we do!"

She walked along to the table, and motioned to an attendant. "Please pour me something," she said, "anything."

Miyu took a seat opposite of me, while the attendant hurried off. She didn't pay me much mind, which made me uncomfortable. Now, don't think I was an egotistical maniac craving attention or anything... it's just that she seemed *too* patient with this game of ours. What was she hoping to get out of me? Why couldn't she just beat the answers she sought out of me? Or, was she holding me for ransom? Again, I'd rather die than be sold back to my people.

"Are you alright, Auntie Miyu?"

The attendant returned, and set down a glass of luscious red. Miyu started to fiddle it around with an outstretched finger.

"Of course, my dear. I had nothing more than a little matter turn ill is all."

"Oh! I'm sorry, Auntie Miyu! What matter was it? I hope it wasn't too important!"

"Not at all, my dear." she said, taking a drink of wine, "I have an important dinner tomorrow with colleagues. I had wished to enlist the talents of a certain sweet toned songstress to keep us entertained, is all. However, there is no basis for I to say that she will in fact participate."

"That's unfortunate!"

I drifted off for a second, and thought about my own talent of song. Either she picked up on what was going on in my head, or she already knew.

"I do not wager you have a talent for song, my dear? Or yet might you?"

Lying was something I wanted to flee from, and if she already knew the answer, well, then sneaking around the question wouldn't do me any good either.

"I do, as a matter of fact, but who am I to say if I'm any good?"

"Even if you aren't, all that matters is that you enjoy the art. Tell me Kea, do you like to sing?"

"I do!"

"Then you must let no soul take that from you. Come, let us hear you."

What she'd just said is how I'd always felt about singing. Still, it felt good to hear someone agree with my sentiment. My songs had always been used for rituals, dark prayers, and all sorts of torture sessions. With such bad times in mind, I'll admit, that I struggled with keeping my love of song from getting spoiled.

"*Ah naheo neh kahsahs neo meesh zahlah*

Ah rooiih lahsah gahme soo fah kehl liihreen

Ah ooyoo ehmihn yaiih eon dahiih nayeh"

Claps blazed from the attendants at standby. Applause leaked all the way from the kitchen. A bewildered spark lit every pair of eyes I saw. That was all no surprise.

What surprised me was Miyu's lack of awe. She was too comfortable, too relaxed.

"That was truly incredible, Kea." she said.

It dawned on me how her emotions never changed. She always had the same sense of calm to her; save for the one time she went off on Loshki, which I bet had just been an act.

"Thank you, Auntie Miyu."

"Of course, Kea, that was simply remarkable. Now then, I do not suppose I could interest you in joining our little banquet tomorrow, could I?"

I nodded. "I'd like to join you!"

"You are absolutely sure? You might find it boring."

"Yes, yes! I really want to!"

"Alright then. So you wish it, so it shall be."

Quote unquote *"banquets"* with *"colleagues"* was probably the place where she got most of her dirty work done. There was no way I could pass up the opportunity.

CHAPTER 5

"Do you still feel comfortable with this, Kea?"

She kept asking me that, so I'm sure she had a reason.

"Yes," I said, "yes of course!"

That ended up being the last time she asked. I could only wonder what had been the point of being so insistent. Soon after, guests began to stream into her great dining hall, and I watched them with eager eyes. Not a single one could be seen without fine garb, perfect posture, and excellent etiquette. I couldn't understand how Miyu could still look so far and away superior. She was like a goddess; from her shimmering hair, to her glistening hands. In comparison, my own skin was pale, and my hair a bland mess.

Miyu rose up to greet her guests. "Would you like to join?" she said.

"Yes, of course."

We went out towards the crowd, and the crowd began to flock around her. That night, Miyune would go on to introduce me many, many times over.

"This is my dear niece, Kea." so she would say.

We'd agreed to parade me around as her niece, so that's just what we did. Time passed, people downed drinks, and appetizers faded. Miyune stayed the center of attention through it all, and her gravity didn't cease until courses began to roll from the kitchen. Only then did the guests find seats at the table. Etiquette and vocal constraint was nothing new to me, so I felt comfortable being in the midst of high society. I'd kept out of mingling for the most part, thus far, being more than content to observe. My mouth nibbled at good food in the meantime, and that's when an old woman paid me mind.

"As for your niece, she is simply adorable."

"Her brilliance is celestial. That is the way of my house." Miyune said.

She was so confident when she said things like that. Excellence seemed like a doormat to her ways, and what she could achieve.

In turn, the older woman replied, sounding a little backed into a corner. "I can certainly see that, Lady Miyune."

Everyone replied to Miyu with such reverence. It was clear she was the head of all these pieces.

"You can see for yourself why faith is ever vested within me. I accept nothing less than excellence." Miyu said.

"Yes, I can see that... I am utterly impressed."

"To see your empire for myself is inspiring." a man said to Miyu.

"Truly I say to you, this is nothing compared to what will become."

Miyu raised a goblet, which hid a soft grin. She must have caught sight of the peeks I was taking, because she turned to me.

"I hope you do not feel left out, young one."

"Of course not!" I replied in a cute tone, "I am having an excellent time!"

"I really can't say enough about what a delight she is." someone said of me.

Miyu raised me an eye, with a sly grin I'm sure nobody

else could have seen. "Well then, Kea, would you be so kind as to honor us with a song?"

If I went on too much, I'd get too into my singing, and probably never stop! I decided to just roll with one tidbit at a time, and take things from there.

"*Ah ooyoo ehmihn yaiih eon dahiih nayeh.*"

Everyone around me lit with awe, even before I finished the first verse. My lips continued to sing, and I ignored the guests reactions for now. Ignoring things while I sang was simple enough, nowadays. In times passed, I had to be able to ignore *every* and *anything*.

"*Ee vah zehn sah yoon uhiih fehl*"

I had to...

"*Veo mahsah iihneo keonoo oh hikiih sasuh*"

That last verse left everyone bright eyed, so I stopped. Stop while you're ahead, and all that, right? I ended up in dead silence, which made me uneasy. Did they hate my language? I didn't blame them if they hated everything about the world I'd came from. All the bruises and gashes I'd had from back then were healed by now, so I guess I felt new ones were long overdue.

"Is that the old language?" a guest cried.

Miyune nodded. "It is so," she said, "dear Kea is one of the wonders of our world."

"I can see that... but here I'd thought the old language had faded into history?"

Miyu's grin stayed put, and she took another drink from her starlit glass. "It's more common than you'd think."

"You really are the magician we hear you to be." a new man said.

Miyu chuckled. "You are only beginning to understand. Now then, for the matter we all came here for..."

"Your games with Hadia are dangerous." a man said.

"That only depends on whether or not Lord Keras sees them as a danger, and feels the need to act in a corresponding manner."

"Precisely." the man replied, "Lord Keras is not the sort of man to play around with."

"Lord Keras is the last thing on my mind." Miyu boasted, "I have met him before, on several occasions. I can tell you with *absolute* certainty that I will have him licking my shoes when all is said and done."

The man's face grew sour, and his eyes furrowed into the floor. "That's blasphemy!" he cried.

"If you would hear the words from my lips and show faith, so be it. If you doubt, then you have no place in this operation, it is really that simple. I pray the spirit of wisdom befalls you by night's end."

Miyu exude an aura of confidence that nobody could deny.

"I've called this dinner tonight only to know who, or who will not follow me." she went on to say, "I ask nothing more of those who follow me than what they already do. I will handle Keras myself."

Keras must have really been something, if ill talk against him was considered "blasphemy". People shoke their heads, and stressed over the decision at hand, and I swear most of them started to beam sweat.

"My Lady, turning Lord Keras to our will..." one woman said, "how can it be done?"

"With a certain amount of charm, and a few visits on my part."

"You would visit with him? You actually believe he'd have an audience with you?"

"You don't believe I can? Tell me now, do you doubt

my will or ability? Come now!"

This was all it took to put the woman in her place.

"No... no, I don't doubt you."

"Good, because I will personally *guarantee* you that Lord Keras will be aligned with us by the end."

This all sounded good to me, because I knew my songs could be useful in Miyu's conquest. Furthermore, the more she flaunted me around as her gifted niece, the harder it would be for her to sweep my disappearance under the rug at a later date, which might discourage her from trying.

Yes, I'd just joked about serving her well two days ago, and yet, my ability to do just that might make me too valuable to pawn off. Unlikely? Yes. Possible? Also yes. There was no harm in trying.

Dinner continued, and Miyune kept the topic of their *"operation"* off the table.

Miyu did not resurrect it until the night hit it's end.

"Once again I thank you all for your attendance. Now, before you all leave, I only ask a notice from those seeking to leave the order."

She started to look around the assembly of nobles. Nobody dared speak a word.

"Anyone?" she asked, looking again, "Nobody?" she said, continuing to look around.

I can't imagine anyone would want to be the first one out, so I wasn't surprised when *nobody* opted out.

"Well then!" she said, "It looks like many will prosper from our mission, many, *many* indeed."

They began to take off right after, leaving Miyu and I alone yet again.

"You were very attentive through the whole dinner." she said to me.

Yaheen! It dawned on me that she was more cunning than I'd first thought.

"I'm a very curious person," I said, "I just really love to learn!"

"Yes. You are much like I was, my dear."

Again, she lost herself to thought. Before I could poke to see what was brewing in her head, she snapped back to the draw.

"I know what you want; you want to see the world, roam forests, climb mountains, feel the sands between your feet. You want to see the glimmer of life, am I wrong?"

She had me dead in the water. I don't think anything she'd said wasn't right on the money.

"Well, yes." I croaked, "I am very interested in seeing the world."

"That is quite fortunate, Kea. I have a friend I wish to see." she said, "He fights in the Legions, but I wager you have yet to hear of those, am I not wrong?"

Zvah. She really was quite the magician when it came to conversation. Rather than reply, I tried to think of a way to break her momentum. Unfortunately, I failed miserably, and couldn't spit a word.

She took the conversation back over, because of my silence. "The *'Legions'* is a famed series of events in Sohal, one that turns the art of swordfaire into a *'team sport'*, shall we say?"

I guess there was nothing to do but give her the responses she wanted, and let her rag doll me around... She was just too quick to every draw.

"What teams fight?" I said.

"Many famed cities in the land of Sohal have a team, or, *'Legion'*, of their own. Battles are held all throughout the season of Senitheera, with each city vying to become champion of the year."

Something about her felt different, like a hidden gear had clicked into place. I couldn't pinpoint what. She just had an overall shift in aura, I guess?

"Have you any familiarity with the lands beyond Sohal, my dear?"

"No, just the names."

"Then we will have to venture to those too someday."

She was always so smooth, and collected... Her suave felt more deadly to me with every passing second.

"I'm excited for you, Kea." she said, "I'm very excited for you to see the land."

A grin wrapped around the side of her face. Her perfect posture made my *fourteen years* of etiquette training look like a joke. Even *the inflection in her voice* was all too perfect.

In the end, she was treating me better than anyone else I'd ever known, and she did intended to show me the land. I guess I couldn't complain much... *yet,* at least.

CHAPTER 6

"The carriage is ready. Do you wish to leave yet, My Lady?"

Miyu shook her head. "Not yet, Loshki. Take the company to the outskirts, we'll meet you there shortly."

"As you wish."

Loshki went over into the corner of the courtyard, where rested a stable. In the meantime, Miyu took me by the hand and led me out.

"Do we have something to do first?" I asked her.

"I thought you might want to pick a treat for the road. You seemed to really like those sweets you tried a few days ago, did you not?"

There was warmth in her words. I smiled at the feeling. "I did." I said, "That's very kind of you."

"Of course, Kea, it is not a problem."

She took me out to the same seller from before, and let me pick a small pouch worth of things to try. Afterwards, we walked until we were out of the city's limits. We ended up not far from where, just a few days ago, Miyu and I had gone to watch clouds pass by. Now, we saw a handful of men, just as many horses, Loshki, and a horse led carriage.

"You'll enjoy this, Kea." Miyu told me, as she lead me to the carriage.

Loshki dropped the back of the carriage, and I was left stunned at how beautiful the inside was.

"Hop in, give it a try." Miyu said.

I did as so. Inside of the carriage was soft as a cloud; due to a plush, red, wooly fabric, that ran all across it! There was also little throw pillows, which I went ahead and tried out. They made for a perfect fit under my head. I even spotted blankets to go along with them; they were rolled up to save space!

"You'll get to lay in comfort while you watch the world go by." Miyu said, "Are you excited yet?"

"Absolutely!" I cried.

Miyu took half of the carriage, and I took the other half. Loshki took control of the reigns, and we started to ride off. I'd never imagined hills could be as great as I'd see, nor mountains quite so tall. Forests never ended, and even little ponds made for bigger bodies of water than I'd ever seen before.

What could have possibly been wrong with my world; that it could be nothing more than brick, and endless corridors, while a world like this existed? It was amazing just to smell how fresh the air here could be, and how much it changed with every place we went to.

It only took a few days to reach our destination. Miyu brought me to an inn, and we stayed there for the night. Breakfast that next morning proved inconsequential... Loshki brought it in for us. Afterwards, we left the inn. Once we got outside, I saw more people at once than I'd ever seen before. Every street was packed from end to end! Miyu led me through the dense crowd. As we kicked along, I snuck peeks behind us, to see that Loshki wasn't far behind. He didn't stay close enough to be obvious, but still stayed within reach should anything happen.

After awhile, I tugged at Miyu's sleeve. "Auntie Miyu?"

"Yes, Kea?"

"Is the arena outside of town?" I said, "It would have to be, to hold all these people, right?"

Miyu chuckled, and pointed over the buildings in the distance. "Very perceptive, Kea. We're almost there, just be patient a little while longer."

We walked another minute or two, and what we saw didn't disappoint.

Thousands upon thousands of spectators could be seen prancing, mingling, and scattering around! A great row of stands formed a box, that reached high into the heavens; said box held openings in the corners for people to pass in and out of. On the inside of the square outline formed by the stands was a great dirt circle; no doubt where the combatants waged battle. Miyune led me through the grass that resided between the great dirt circle and the stands.

In an instant, Miyu snapped our momentum.

"My, my..." she said, turning to an armor clad man with short, muddy blonde hair, "...Lathimian?"

Unlike Loshki, this man's height and muscle was nothing noteworthy. Still, he had enough going to be a fighter, even if physique was never going to be an asset. He'd need more raw skill than the average man, though. This man, "Lathimian", as Miyune had called him, looked up and past her as he spoke.

"Let's not pretend this is a fluke encounter." he said, seeming a little hassled.

Miyu went and ran two fingers down the side of his face. "Mmmm? What has you so tense, Lathimian?"

Don't ask me for any insight on what was going on between them, because I had none. This seemed as good a time as any for me to go barging in!

"You must be a very, very talented fighter!" I said.

I started to tug on Miyu's sleeve. "Auntie Miyu! Where does he fight for? Where is he from?"

"Cavala, young one. As for the latter question? It is not my place to say."

A smile painted Lathimian's face. "That's never stopped you before."

Ouch.

"I suppose not." Miyu admitted.

Lathimian looked overtop me as he spoke. "You could call me a spy... or something like that. I fight in the Legions in my spare time."

I smiled with big, fake eyes, that shone like stars when I saw them in the mirror. Miyu would probably pick up on what I was doing, but I didn't care.

"You two must have met while you were on a mission!"

"You've been especially keen today." Miyu said.

She continued on, before Lathimian could speak. "I was rather helpful to you, Lathimian, was I not?"

Lathimian let a grin that alluded to something much more chaotic. "Yeeeees, I couldn't agree more. I'd say you were the heart of my mission; my shining star."

"You were the heart of my mission?" I think that was his way of saying his mission concerned Miyune, and her empire. That was the impression I got, at least. I'm sure her schemes put her on bad terms with the King of Sohal, and it's knights. His wandering eyes turned to me, but never met my own. Instead, they continued their habit of looking overhead, or beside, whomever he was speaking to. In this case, they looked overhead me. I found it eery, and I don't think I'd ever seen anything like it.

"I don't believe we've ever met." he said to me.

I nodded. "I don't think so. I don't think I've met anyone in this world!"

Miyu cut in without so much as a hair of desperation, or panic. "She is from a *special* place of her own."

How Lathimian and I would work around her was beyond me, so I prayed he was very, very good.

"Where are you from?" he asked, "I'm always looking for places to visit."

"I don't think I could go back even if I tried, but Aunt Miyu would know!"

I must have been too happy with what I'd considered a good choice of words, because I missed the fact that Miyu had been mouthing something. I only saw a split second of movement in the corner of my eye as she finished. I guess whatever she'd said didn't matter, because Lathimian had a big smug grin on his face, and you could tell he hadn't bought anything she'd said. As a result, my respect for the man flew higher than it ever had for any man before. It was sad to think that a lone minute could net someone an achievement like that.

Miyu waved off at him. "Farewell, Lathimian."

I mimicked her wave, and played up a high pitched squeal. "Farewell, Lathimian the knight!"

How cruel a thing fate is... that it would bring us three together for no purpose, other than robbing each other of knowledge. That was the reason Miyune had gotten the scenario going in the first place, right? I followed Miyune on, and we got good seats on ground level. She'd reserved them in advance, which was apparently something you could do with the sort of power she had.

My curiosity was quick to boil over. "Is he good at fighting?" I asked.

It appeared like she wanted to speak well of him, but it also seemed like she didn't have many good tales to fall back on.

"To be in the Legions alone makes you quite a fighter; but against others from the Legions, he is somewhere around average. He is very gifted with the defensive form Thadiir, and he is a natural born playmaker, but beyond that, he is not much. Cavala is lucky to have him, regardless."

Could I do anything with this information? That was the real question. Our wait for the event to start was anything if uneventful; even if what events occurred were forgettable. Well dressed nobles came from left and right, all for the chance to speak with Miyune or wish her well. It wasn't until the event began that the annoyance of a parade subsided. Both teams sent a man out, and the fighting began. I'd never thought something as straightforward as sword fighting could be so complex. Miyune kept trying to run me through all the rules of the event, and how tactful it was; but I just couldn't get a grip on it. I watched the fighters on the field, followed the scoreboard, and called that good enough.

Awhile passed, the head judge at last came to call "For Cavala, Lathimian!"

Lathimian ran out with a wooden blade in tow. Each fight was held in a white circle, that sat at the heart of the great dirt circle. Lathimian took up a stance opposite of his opponent inside the white circle, and the judge gave a calling for the fight to begin.

"By Lathine, commence!"

True to what Miyune said; Lathimian went straight to the defensive. His footwork was impressive, and his willingness to wait for his moment spoke to a level head. He was forced into the end of the white circle rather quick, which was bad, as stepping so much as a foot from the circle meant defeat.

Finally, Lathimian kicked in opportunistic counter strikes. Each blow he threw was weak, and cautious. It seemed like his priority was not jeopardizing his defensive stance.

All it took to win a match was a lone hit, which meant Lathimian didn't have to be flashy, and you could tell he was alright with that. At the same time, I think he was so defensive because he had no offensive skill to fall back on. He was on the slender side for a fighter, and not exceptionally quick, so it made sense.

Blades continued to soar around. Lathimian's enemy played confident, and all but dared him to lash out on the offensive. Lathimian couldn't slip out of the corner, so instead of trying to blitz out, he decided to slow down the pace of the fight. Things slowed with every passing second, until both fighters stopped throwing blows entirely!

They stared each other down, and the crowd fell to silence. Tension rose, and people tumbled to the edge of their seats. At long last, Lathimian's enemy lashed forward! He got into a deadlock with Lathimian, and then shoved him out of the circle!

The head judge leapt forward, pointed to Lathimian, and called out to the crowd. *"Out of circle, victory to Inolta!"*

"Pity..." Miyu mumbled.

"He looks skilled, but a little raw." I said.

"He does not have the same experience as other fighters." Miyu said.

"It shows, just a little."

"Trust the words I speak to you; he will be special once he finds himself."

"You're probably right."

"I've wishes to see him again after the event, as a matter of fact. It is not often we get to see one another."

I could stand to learn a thing or two from Lathimian, which made the idea sit well with me.

"Absolutely," I said, "that would be fun! Let's do it!"

She stroked my hair, and combed the mess of strands. "Cavala holds dinners for the team after each fight, so we will attend the banquet. I have not attended a Legion banquet in quite some time."

What I would do in the coming hours caused one of the greatest ripples Lathine would ever receive... whether I knew it or not.

CHAPTER 7

Lathimian's team, Cavala, battled to a hard-fought loss. Afterwards, Miyune led me through town, to a building almost as large as her own palace. At it's mouth stood two guards, who proceeded to welcome us in. Miyu, knowing the way, led us onto a great dining hall. It was weird that someone of the stature I was back home could feel starstruck; I recognized some of team Cavala's fighters, and marveled at their presence. At their sides was family, by the looks of it. What rounded out the rest of the attendees was nobles galore.

Being a Legion fighter was a big deal, that much I knew, and yet even they couldn't come close to matching Miyune's prestige. Nobles started to flock around Miyu from the moment we walked into the dining hall. She greeted them all, and half an hour passed before we could take another step forward.

A familiar voice sighed. "Well, this is about exactly what I thought would happen." it said.

Both of us turned around, and saw Lathimian! He'd swapped out his armor for something more casual, and he'd also cleaned up. I was surprised how sharp he could look.

"Why the pessimism, Lathimian?" Miyu asked, "Don't you care for old friends?"

Miyu had a devilish grin. You could tell she was having fun with this. You could also tell Lathimian wasn't pleased about this whole ordeal.

"I'm the suffer alone type." he joked.

"That makes two of us." Miyu said.

She kept her voice down for what she said next. "You know I hate gatherings."

Lathimian grinned. "'Can't say that counts. You make a living off them, after all."

"No, I suffer through them for spare change. I could live a thousand years off what I have now." she said.

She threw a finger to her mouth, and mumbled out thoughts. "Excluding investments, of course... I could live forever off those."

"We get it, you're rich."

Miyu chuckled. Even though Lathimian was having none of it, she just wouldn't give up. I could only imagine what business she had with him that was so important.

"I-..." Miyune started to say, when a noble took to introducing themselves.

Lathimian slipped away to a table for food. I waited by at Miyu's side. All of a sudden, a little crowd began to swarm around her.

"Auntie Miyu?" I squeaked, "May I please get something to eat?"

"Of course, my dear. Take care."

She was busy, so I felt comfortable waltzing over to Lathimian. Luck was with me, I managed to get beside him in line. He noticed me, but didn't pay me any mind. We each got a plate, and finally got far enough in line to start grabbing food; that was when I spoke, but not with the dumb kiddish voice I usually ran out. I spoke to Lathimian with my real voice, which had grown quite dark. My true voice had become twisted after fourteen years of torment.

"You know about Miyune."

He raised his eyes, which must have meant he was surprised. "Unfortunately."

"I need to know," I said, keeping my voice low, "what's she after?"

He didn't outright reply. No doubt he thought it was unsafe to talk with me. I couldn't blame him. He must have thought I was just another piece to Miyune's puzzle.

"I'm not her niece, and I'm not with her out of choice." I said, "If you're worried about me blabbing; don't be. Telling her about this little chat would hurt me worse than it ever could you."

He mumbled something to himself that I couldn't make out. "That depends on what you want to know." he went on to say.

"Then let's play a game of 'yes or no'." I said, deciding to go first, "Is she the sort of person to do things without reason?"

"Dead no."

"Yes or no, does she do things without dark reason?"

"No."

"Yes or no, does she do things out of charity?"

"No."

"Yes or no; if she chose to keep someone with status close to her, could there be a chance she wasn't after anything?"

"Dead no."

"How did you two first meet?"

He clicked off one side of his mouth. "I wouldn't mind a few answers of my own."

"Have all you want." I said, "I don't care."

"Yes or no," he started, "is she holding you hostage?"

"Yes."

"Yes or no, are you royalty?"

"You couldn't possibly know that."

How on Lathine could he know that!?!

"I'll take that as a yes."

It dawned on me that he'd been keeping a close eye on Miyune as we spoke. Every time her eyes shifted towards us, he made sure to ignore me.

"There's nothing she can do to you here." he said under his breath, while picking out food, "I can free you if you want."

"Can you punish Miyune?"

"No, Loshki will just take the fall," he said, "him or someone else."

What was Miyune thinking, messing around with someone that was so on to her schemes?

"Then I can't leave her yet," I said, "I have too much to figure out."

There's no doubt in my mind Miyune's plans for me were the long lasting sort, so I felt comfortable being with her a little while longer.

"Gambling you can outsmart her isn't going to end well." he said.

"She's not that good."

He clenched his teeth off one side of his mouth, and looked away.

"What do you do?" I asked him. "What do you mean when you say you're a *'spy'*?"

"I work in the shadows for King Neromas." Lathimian told, "I've been tasked with keeping an eye on Miyune a few times before, that's how we met."

"The King knows about her and *still* isn't doing anything?"

"I wish things were as simple as they should be, but Miyune always has someone lined up to take the fall. She also has the might to sink Sohal's economy in spite if we get drastic, so we have to be careful; there's no telling what she might have hidden away for such a day."

"I-..."

He cut me off. "Go back to your act."

I did just that. "Mr. Lathimian! What's this food here?"

I hadn't noticed until now how close Miyune had crept.

"She seems to take a liking to you." she said.

"All girls do."

"Be that as it may, I'm not surprised."

Miyu turned, and gave me a warm rub on the head. It was soothing how her soft fingers weaved through my hair.

"You seem to know your way around, my dear. Would you like to help me choose what I should eat?"

"Yes, of course, Auntie Miyu!"

She waved off at Lathimian one last time, and we went to get her a plate. I didn't see Lathimian again in the dining hall after that, which really didn't matter... since Miyu was glued to my side for the rest of the night. It's not like there was anything I could have gotten away with saying to him.

All that really matters is that finally, after fourteen years of being spurned, I might have finally found someone I could count on. I could only do so much on my own, but Lathimian was certainly the sort of person who could help me. My only hope was that fate would bring me back to his side one day.

CHAPTER 8

Awhile had passed since the Legion event, and we'd long since returned to the city of Miyune; Sciruthon. From the time of our return onwards, things never felt the same. Miyune stopped flocking to my side, and parading around with me every day. She had me around to sing at banquets, and took me out to snag treats and watch the clouds one lone time... but that was it. Today in particular, something just wasn't right. She hadn't been treating me much like a child; in turn, I let my act fade some.

We were sitting around the table for dinner. It was just me, and her, until an attendant brought a bottle of sparkling red. Miyune very much enjoyed the brand, and as did I. I won't deny that I had a bad habit of relieving my worries by stealing drinks. She poured herself a glass, took a drink, and then extended her arm out to me.

"A very fine drink from Hadia, Kea. Do try some."

She must have thought I really was just a dumb kid... a dumb kid that was about to get hammered, and spill all their secrets! Joke's on her! I grabbed the glass, and downed it in one gulp.

"This is very good grape juice!"

"Yes, I know." she said, shifting her eyes ghoulishly upon me, "I can certainly see why you have been sneaking it."

Of course she knew...

"Oh, I'm sorry, Auntie Miyu! I just really like grape juice!"

"Please do not bother lying, Kea. You know very well what that is."

Hm... sad eyes were worth a shot. Maybe they could get me out of this?

"Are you sure super sure this isn't grape juice?"

"Kea," she said, pouring a glass for the both of us, "let's be honest with each other, if nothing else."

I drank away. With any luck, a little liquid delight would help me spin the yarn of a lifetime.

"I'm just really confused. Isn't this grape juice? If it wasn't, you wouldn't have given me more, right? Is this a test? Do I pass Aunt-...!?!"

"Kea, I'm not concerned with anyone who's greatest sin against me is stealing a little wine."

"I'm sorry, Auntie Miyu!"

In the moment that followed silence, her void eyes fell upon me.

"So, is wine...?" I said, "Wine is the-...?"

"Kea, I'm bleeding silver and gold. Wine isn't hard to replace, don't offend me so."

"I-..."

She raised a finger, which brought me to silence. "Kea," she said, "have you enjoyed your time here?"

"Of course, Auntie Miyu!"

"Good, I thought as much. Consequently, I've concocted plans to bring your family for a stay as well. Their company will only bring you greater delight."

My body paralyzed itself with fear. This had to be a bluff, right? It had to be!

"You must be excited!" she exclaimed, "Please do not worry Kea, so you wish it, so it shall be. You will be happy to be reunited with your father, mother, sister, and brother, will you not?"

Curse her... curse her, *curse her*, **curse her**. I'd had enough beatings for one lifetime, I wasn't about to take any more!

"Oh, that's very, very kind of you! They'd love this world... but I know they'd love to stay in their own world much, much more! Don't worry, their fun would just be ruined if they left home!"

Her reply was rather sarcastic, and I could tell she saw right through me. "Are those your true feelings, Kehah?" she said.

It inflamed me to hear her use that name.

"I-, yes! They're just so happy where they are, is all."

"If that is truly your wish, then so be it, my dear little Miracle Maiden."

I'd assumed from the beginning that she'd known *exactly* who I was; the foretold Miracle Maiden. Still, it enraged me how long she'd pretended to be oblivious for! If looks could kill, mine would have sent her dead to the floor. My anger was only furthered by the oh so smug grin she had on her face. She was having too much fun.

"Kehah, my dear, have I struck a nerve?"

She was so collected...

"I'm just tired!"

"Off to bed then, love. With good fortune, your family may yet be here to sing you blessings when you awake."

My people would raze this world to the ground, and both of us with it. She had to be bluffing! *She had to be!*

She waved off towards the door. "Go on, have a good rest. You are tired, are you not?"

"Well, I'm not *super* tired. I'm just a little tired, I guess."

"So then you lied?"

Could I just get off *one sentence* without being stepped on? It's no wonder why the eyes started to manifest in the corner of my vision, they always found me when I was struggling.

"Do you see something, Kea? Is it the eyes?"

My ears must have been playing tricks on me. I stopped glancing at the aura of red beside me, and composed myself.

"What were we talking about?"

"The eyes," Miyune said, "are they bothering you?"

Impossible...

"What eyes?"

Even though the eyes didn't emit sound, I could tell they were laughing. *I just could.*

"Kehah Gehnahdiihneh; the young Miracle Maiden, born to King Darotho, and Queen Veoda. You mentioned you sing, my dear," she said, "but not that you dance. Pity! You know how I enjoy your songs, Kehah. I am sure I would enjoy your dances just as much, they must go majestically with your voice."

My people weren't the sort to give outsiders information. Could that mean that the wretches of my world were already here, and had formed an alliance with Miyune? Just the thought made me suicidal. I couldn't bear to consider the idea any longer...

I did my best to bear down, and hold my stance. "Don't you know, because I've mentioned all this? I thought so, I really did!"

"No, you never did, young Princess."

There wasn't a point in denying anything, since she clearly knew all she said as fact.

"I'd rather be like you!" I said, "You're much more of a princess than me, and all your clothes are very, very pretty!"

"You are a princess, Kea, are you not?"

"Yes, I am! That's what everyone tells me, at least!"

Fine, Miyune, fine...

"Did I really forget to say all these things, Auntie Miyu? My people were nice and let you know for me, I guess! They must like being here!"

Maybe she'd slip up on what was really going on...

"Here I thought you wanted them to stay away?"

Zvah, Zvah, Zvah! Were there any words I could get in that she wouldn't tear to the bone!?! I clenched my teeth, veiled it behind closed lips, and tried to ignore the hot blood that pulsed in my chest.

"Well, I just thought I'd say *'hi'* if they were already here, is all!"

"Good then, Kehah. I will arrange for their arrival since you wish to do so. Now, off to bed, young one."

She rose to her feet, and shooed me off to bed. I couldn't go, because I was too fear stricken at the thought she might actually bring *them* here. What's worse, she started to make for the door herself.

"Auntie Miyu?" I called in desperation.

She continued to glide to the door.

"Auntie Miyu? Miyuuu?"

My whole body had started to tremble. There were no more cards left to be played, save one. My act died in the blink of an eye, and my real voice came to fruition. I was always curious what people thought when I hit them with such a sudden shift in tone.

"Miyune!"

Sometimes fear is just too much... I couldn't risk her doing what she claimed she would, even if we both knew she wouldn't. Miyu's head rolled so far back that I thought it was going to fall off. She stopped in her tracks, and her fingers lifted off the doorknob.

"So I see you're ready to end the facade, mh?"

I was surprised she knew about my knack for guises...

"Facade? I would say the same to you, Miyune of Daynore."

Miyu raised an eye, and I felt the momentum shift. She'd already shown she could beat me when she wished, so the fact she let me win this little exchange must have meant it was inconsequential.

"Should I call you Miyune Leestel from now on, or Miyune Perfana?"

"Alright, Kea. I see you have wit of your own."

Now, I think I was the one to kick a nerve. Her eyes took an ever so slight drop, at the knowledge I'd pried from attendants. Her childhood must have been as brutal as I'd heard, because I could tell this was a line of thought she didn't want to go down.

"No more *'Kehah'*?" I said.

"Only if that is your wish."

"Alright, then let's forget the name ever existed."

In reflection... I was happy this all happened. Our fake fronts had done nothing more than put us at a standstill. Now, at least we were moving forward... even if she did in fact have the upper hand. Ultimately, we had no trouble finding mutual ground.

"I am all too happy to have the real Kea wandering my halls." she said.

At long last, I was free to be myself around her... which was a load off my shoulders. She requested that I keep up my act around loyalty, and while frolicking around town, but that was it. I gladly met her on those terms.

She spared me no expense, never failed to give me

words of advice, and seemed to have no other wish but to spend all the free time she had with me. One of my great regrets, looking back, is how I didn't cherish those days more...

Yes, I worked my way into her trust, in exchange for compliance, just as a daughter does to a mother. Now begged a question for me; where should I look to find out how she knew all she did? More importantly, what she was truly after? Suspicion dominated me in those days, because I was a product of sight, and not faith, and that alone is the greatest regret of my life.

CHAPTER 9

"Kea, you understand the importance of this, correct?"

"You should already know I do."

How many times did I have to tell her this? We were in one of her carriages at the moment; it's subtle bobbing had put me to sleep for the majority of our venture. I raised an eyelid for a quick peek at Miyune. She wasn't pulling hair, or doing anything obviously anxious. In fact, her face was as calm as ever. Still, I could tell something was wrong with her.

"If you would only tell me-"

She cut me off. "Kea, 'life' is akin to a game I must win. It is also one I am more than capable of winning by my own machinations. Do not fret, and simply stay true to your act. Can you do that for me, Kea?"

I closed my eyes, and made myself comfortable on the soft, silk insides of the carriage. "As you wish, Miyu."

Not long after that exchange, I awoke before an absolutely *massive* castle. Despite only being half awake, I could still understand just how incredible the place was.

"It might even outdo yours." I told Miyu.

"Yes, it really is something."

A handful of guards stood at the gate. They banded together to give us a warm welcome, and then let us in. That was where something truly peculiar happened. We walked into the courtyard, and Loshki didn't join us! That was something you didn't see often. When Miyu and I went out, it was as normal to look back and see him as it was to breathe! Even at banquets, he could always be seen standing in the corner of the room like a mime.

Inside the great castle was a rather appealing, albeit surprisingly practical interior. There was an occasional statue, but that was about it for anything eye popping. Not long after we entered, we found ourselves before a great pair of doors. A guard stood in front of them. He nodded to us, and then opened the way!

Inside the room, I saw a man in a great fur cape. He was seated at the end of a large table that reminded me of the one Miyu had in her dining room. No sooner than we saw him, did Miyune's voice go flying out with youthful splendor. She spoke with a squeal much like the one I had when I was pretending to be a child.

"I've missed your company, Keras. More time with you would soothe my spirit!"

Ah... so this was the esteemed Lord Keras. I'd never seen Miyune expend this sort of energy. It was clear this Miyu wasn't the real Miyu. Still, her words caused something to bubble in the man's eyes. Did he have hope that through Miyune some diabolical plan would be accomplished? Maybe. Did he have hope that he'd found a partner to pass through life with? Well... that looked just as likely.

"My dear, dear Miyune," he said, "have I ever missed your smile."

His eyes turned to me. It confused me how kind he seemed for someone so corrupt. I'd done my research; this man, Keras, Lord Keras, possessed an empire of corruption even greater than Miyune's. This was the very same person she'd been so confident about getting her way with. By the looks of it, she might have already been where she needed to be with him.

"This is the young niece you write of, with the voice of an angel?"

Miyu nodded. "She most certainly is."

I dropped to a low curtsy, and let words fly. "*Veo mahsah iihneo keonoo oh hikkih sasuh Eon soo fah dahah geo tnahl oo vdiih.*"

Keras' face flickered with something other an amazement. "The old language is a curious thing for a youth to know. This is a story for you to tell one day, Miyune?"

Miyune grinned. I don't think that had went how she'd envisioned. Still, her body language continued to stream confidence, as if she could end the world with a snap of her fingers.

"Truly, I could not agree more." so she said, quick to change the topic.

At the table, her sheer warmth of speech lulled him out of a want for answers... about anything. She seemed to have her way at every step, and ere was my first meeting with Lord Keras. Miyu, him, and I, merely had dinner, then I split ways with them. A maid escorted me through the castle, and brought me to a guest room. It would be mine for the duration of our stay.

Of course, the thought of scouring for secrets did come to mind, but the idea sounded too risky. If I sunk Miyu by slipping up, then she'd *more* than sink me in return. Instead, I tried out another king worthy bed. I got a good night's sleep... and add some.

I'm not going to lie, I must have gotten a good twelve hours of sleep before something started to slither on my shoulder. It bore words that didn't pass coherently into my head, even if I knew what they were saying.

"Would you really sleep through another day?" I could

finally make out.

It took me a moment to realize the soul beside me was Miyune, which in my honest opinion was worse than if it were a spirit. At least the darker things of the world wouldn't make me wake up and pretend to be responsible. I know that's pretty sad, but it's true.

I brushed off her baby-like hand. "You should've given me notice. It can't be anything too important. You can handle yourself, I believe in you."

Miyune hissed out her teeth. "Kea, don't be a child."

"I am a child."

"You know what I mean. Kea, a day of life is a meaningful thing! It can never be retrieved. Are you truly willing to trade it away for gratuitous sleep?"

"Yeah."

"Kea, a short while will pass until this happens; but I intend to marry Lord Keras."

My head sprouted up; I hadn't expected to hear that! "Well... you chose well. Being at his side gives you power near godship."

"Kea, don't be silly."

"And here I thought we wouldn't lie to one another." I said, "Anyways, what am I awake for? Keras liked you just fine, you really don't need my help with him."

"I couldn't agree more."

I chuckled. "Alright, what has you in such a mood that you learned a sense of humor?"

Her eyes shifted back upon me. "That's wasn't a joke, Kea. I have something else in mind for you."

I refused to say a word, which forced her into continuation. Nothing good could come of this...

"Kea," she said, "I'm sending you off with Loshki. I would like you to oversee a task for me."

"Who's head do you want on a platter?"

What had seemed like a joke to me, seemed something more like truth to her. I wanted to glare, but didn't bother to. I'm sure she could already tell full well how disgusted I was.

I coughed out words. "Don't tell me that really is what you want?"

"Loshki will brief you." she said, "He's waiting outside the gate, so hurry on, Kea."

I didn't want to talk with her anymore. I got up from bed, and left the room without speaking another word. My feet rolled out of Keras' castle, and through the gate. Sure enough, there on the outside, stood Loshki at the ready! In the sunlight, he looked more the picture of manly health than ever. His muscles were enormous, and his posture was terrifying. There was just something to that glaring smirk, and those crossed arms he always had...

"Lady Leestel," he greeted me. "I hear Lady Miyune has honored me with your guidance."

Loshki was on the short list of people I could be myself around. I wasn't going to pretend to be happy.

"So she tells me too, but I guess that doesn't matter. What matters is what she told you."

"She told me *almost* everything." he said, "We'll be traveling to the northeast, which'll take a few days. We're on the hunt for a man with information critical to Lady Miyune's vision. She wants you to plan our attack on the night we take him."

Great... *just great.* What on Lathine was I supposed to know about leading fights!?! I was usually too lazy to get out of bed, let alone come up with battle plans! Loshki led me to the outskirts of town, where some two dozen men were at the ready. He took me through to the heart of the little camp, and took a knee. This brought him to my eye level. He pulled out a trio of papers, and handed them to me.

"First off," he said, "a report on the men you've been given. Second off; a layout of the town we'll be acting in, Xadiir. Third is the defensive routines and capabilities of the man's walled home, and it's protectors."

I noticed that all three papers were crammed from front to back with words. I'd have a fair bit of studying to do.

"How should I know what to do? This has to be a joke!"

"Lady Miyune thinks otherwise, and we both know you're a studious kid. She instructed me to avoid making any decisions; but that doesn't mean I won't teach you all I can. You're not in this alone."

"Miyune's crazy!"

"This is just as much a mystery to me, but Lady Miyune isn't one to act without reason."

Those words made me stop, and take a moment to think. Lathimian had said quite the same about her, when I'd spoken with him in Cavala.

"...I suppose not." I said.

I picked up my head, and looked to the men roaming around. "None of these are ours."

Loshki nodded. "Sellswords..."

"Miyune doesn't trust me with her own?"

"No, Leestel, 'don't think so. She didn't trust me either on my first assignment."

"At least you had experience by that point, I'm sure."

"That I did."

He rose up, and led me to the carriage Miyu and I had ridden here in! Now, it was littered with books.

"Can't get knowledge like this just anywhere. You could learn a thing, or two, or twenty, by the time we reach Xadiir."

"How long *exactly* will that take?"

"Two long days."

"Two days? How can I be ready in just two days?"

"'Take that up with Lady Miyune next time you see her. 'Just don't dwell on it now, 'won't do you any good."

"What would you say to me? What do I need to know to get through this?" I begged.

Loshki took a moment to think. "Leading is as much about your character as anything else. When pressure mounts, *real* pressure, we find out who we really are. That's all Lady Miyune wants to see, I think."

"Who I really am?"

I guess that made some sense... given the game of masks Miyu and I always played. I'm sure she did want a definitive read on me, but I couldn't imagine anything with her was that simple. I did myself a favor, put my thoughts out of mind, and hopped into the back of the carriage. There was no point in worrying about Miyu's scheming now. I got to reading while the company took off. I hoped Miyune knew what she was doing, and these men had the skills to protect me.

There was no way my plan would be any good, which would leave all of us in danger... in two lone days.

CHAPTER 10

Night drew near. At long last, Loshki gave in to it's heed. I felt the carriage begin to slow, and soon it came to a halt.

Loshki bellowed out to the heavens. "Pitch shelter, we leave at daybreak!"

I was still in the back of the carriage. Loshki came there to see me.

"What've you been going with?"

"Strategy Of Day's Passed." So I said, as that was the name of the book I'd been delving into.

He nodded, seeming to think that was a good choice, even if he didn't seem to think it was the best choice. He went through the stack of books I'd made. Finally, he came up with what he'd been looking for. He handed me a red binded book that had a flame encrusted eye upon it.

"Get through chapter four if nothing else."

I nodded. "Thank you Loshki, I appreciate it."

I took it near a campfire Loshki would go on to make, and divulged my night into it. I got far more reading done than one lone chapter, or even just the first four.

"The Majesty of Lathiris." So the book was called.

It concerned a man by the name of Lathiris, who had lived over a thousand years ago. I'd read of him in the past, in forbidden texts my father kept locked away. My father's personal study had held myriads of books containing history on Lathine, albeit old history. His most recent books on Lathine were still a few hundred years old, if memory served.

I had a good track record of sneaking books, and through all the times I'd ever done it, I'd only been caught once! My one time being caught hadn't come by any fault of my own, but by the will of my sister, Sehrehah... *curse her.*

That night passed away, and soon the next. I learned far more than I'd expected to in such a short time, I'll admit. We lurked into Xadiir on the third day, and came within sight of the castle of our target. I marveled at it's mighty wall, and wondered if an invasion could really be done. Loshki walked alongside me, sharing none of my bewilderment.

"Explain your plan off memory, no map." he said.

He'd been quizzing me over and over, which did make sense. What Miyune had made into a game for me; was life or death for him. It also seemed like this was his way of testing me.

"Their guard outside will be nothing more than a gatekeeper, and four scouts on the wall. We'll have a man approach from the ground, pretending to bear a letter. When the gatekeeper opens up, our man will drop him real quick. Our archers will take the men on top of the wall, then we storm in."

Loshki grinned. His grin could have meant anything, but I'm sure it was aimed at how awful my plan was.

"Sounds like my first fight with a wall." he said.

"We both know this is going to get messy..."

"'Least these are hired men, if it ends that way."

Loshki walked off, over to the men that lied in wait. He spoke with them, then they rushed past me, and got into position. I was surprised to see that Loshki didn't join them. Instead, he stood at my side.

"Her lone role for me is to protect you." he said, before I could open my mouth.

I wouldn't deny his hulking physique could make anyone feel safe, but still, I'd much rather have had him on the front lines. I'm sure putting him at the forefront would have made things run a lot smoother.

"That's a demand from her herself?" I inquired, hoping to bend the rules.

"Yes, Milady Leestel, now let it go. Tacticians can't afford to feel their own burdens. You should be at ease, if anything. 'Nothing here can bring me down, 'just a matter of whether things run smoothly, or with pitchers of blood."

Our archers formed into position. I took my eyes to the guards on top of the wall. To me, seeing all those guards proved our target had something to be paranoid about. I watched as the gate opened up, our first man entered, and then arrows launched in synch! Men began to drop off the wall... one, followed by two, three...! Loshki nudged me, and pointed out something I'd missed. One guardian stood unharmed! My eyes sunk into the back of my skull. Screams of attack echoed through the air, and bludgeoned each our ears. Our sellswords could only take care of the last man so fast. By the time they did, the damage had already been done. Knights were bound to arrive any minute. Failure burned inside me, and it took a firm shake from Loshki to get me going again.

"Leestel! Keep your head together! We're going in there!"

He pulled out an enormous blade, and nudged me on with one burly hand. We cut past the men I'd assigned to keep guard, and followed the back ranks of what men entered. In the courtyard, something shimmered alongside the moonlight from above; a collection of swords, lances, and axes, wielded by guardians of the fortress! Our men ran out to oppose them. What volume ensued killed any hopes we had left of acting in stealth.

Blood poured, and screams filled the air. Guardians fell in swarm, save for one, who managed to slip past our front line! He seemed intent on killing Loshki, for whatever reason. I distanced myself from Loshki, who walked out to meet the enemy. First blow was thrown by the guardian!

Loshki used his muscle to stonewall the blow. It took Loshki no more than a second to get hold of the guardian's wrist, and then snap it! A sickening crunch met my ears. I'd seen many horrible things, and yet I still couldn't help but grimace. Shrieks of horror bursted from the guardian's throat.

Loshki took the end of his pommel, which was sharp, and stabbed the guardian through the throat. Red spewed *everywhere.* The man fell to the ground, started to scream, and continued to spill all over. Loshki didn't even take a moment to put the guardian out of his misery.

Guilt fell onto me, and sin, and heartache for the fact that I'd led this horrible ordeal. I felt even worse knowing that I'd gone as far as to reason to myself *"It's not like I have a choice"* in the days prior.

Loshki snapped me back to reality. "Leestel!" he said, "Hold in there! We're going in!"

Loshki was covered from head to toe in blood. It bothered me that there was still nothing on his mind but completing the mission. I followed him up the castle's steps, and through the front door.

He was so determined, so fierce... which proved to be a good thing for us. He took charge, and started dishing out commands. Thank goodness he did, because I'd had no clue what to do at this point. My snap calls would have probably gotten us all killed.

"You two are with me, the rest of you keep guard!" he ordered, "We're going to the target!"

I'm not going to lie; I'd forgotten where our target's bed chambers was. That spoke to the level of skill I had as a tactician... none. My intel report had even said point blank where in the castle to look. We followed Loshki on, and he led us to a door where two men stood guard. I slammed on the stops, and waited for Loshki to do the same, but he never did!

Loshki threw a one handed swing to knock the first guard down, then he grabbed said man by the throat, and held him as a shield. Not about to slice through his comrade, the second guard snapped his wrists and stopped his blade. Loshki was all too willing to take advantage, and skewer the second guard through the heart. Right after, the first man fell dead from Loshki's iron tight grip.

Loshki's killer focus didn't allow time for remorse. He picked up one of the guardian's blade's, and bashed the door with it's pommel! Away flew the door! We looked inside to see a man huddled in his bed.

"I'll pay you double!" the man cried, "I'm begging you! You can have-...!"

Loshki paid those words no mind, and grabbed him by the collar. He dragged the man across the floor like a dog. With our target in tow, we went back to the courtyard. There, we heard the thunderous sound of horns, and iron. Most startling of all was the screams of dying men.

Fights were breaking out left and right.

"Push through!" Loshki roared, "Fight!"

Loshki flung our target into the ground, then set the tip of his blade before the man's face.

"Think of moving," Loshki said, "and you'll lose your neck."

To no surprise, the man we'd taken didn't move a muscle. Loshki went right ahead, and entered the fray of battle. It was weird to watch him fight, because he was slow, and yet his fights went by in the blink of an eye. He was quick to pull into deadlocks, then grapple right after. He'd break his enemy down in some way, then go for a finishing strike. This was how he ended four of the five knights he fought. I think the one knight Loshki didn't get a kill blow off on knew he'd lucked out, because right after they traded a few blows, said knight retreated into the night.

Loshki led our march out of the courtyard, and some two blocks down. There awaited the horses, and carriage. I jumped straight into the back of the carriage, and Loshki had the horses blazing soon as I did. He got us out of town without issue, despite having to avoid a few knights on foot. He didn't stop the company until we were long gone, and when he did, he only did for a minute. He threw our prisoner in a little supplies wagon, shackled him, and then got us going again.

Loshki kept us on the march until daybreak, and I was still awake at that point. Despite being exhausted, I hadn't been able to sleep. I was too upset, too confused...

At long last I fell asleep, and I didn't reawaken until darkness returned. Well, darkness wasn't the only thing that returned...

"Justifier..."

That was it's word of the night.

"Justifier."

It's presence added to my turmoil. I breathed in real slow, and tried to quell all the emotions within me. I felt like I'd lose myself for good if I gave in to my feelings, so I resolved to keep calm. Loshki couldn't have been far from my carriage, which made me consider opening my eyes, screaming for him, and challenging the voice this one time... except I was too scared.

"Justification is the trade of demons."

I'd been wrong to go along with Miyune's wishes, sure. I'd justified what I'd been a part of, I didn't deny that... but I wasn't a demon! Hearing that made me want to scream, because it made me think of my people. According to them, *any* thinking outside their own made you a *"servant of the demon"*. Those who questioned so much as a word had a habit of being *"whisked away"*, because they were said to have *"left the teachings of the just"*, which allowed *"demons"* a chance to take them.

Obviously, demons weren't really taking them. What happened was that my father would send his chiefest enforcers, led by a nameless masked man, and together, they would take marked ones in secret and dispose of them. This was just one of many truths I'd uncovered during my time in the labyrinth. My father was good about beckoning out self-fulfilling prophecies, which gave the mindless zombies underneath him more than enough reason to keep believing.

I kept my eyes closed, crawled out of the carriage, and plopped onto the grass below. The *presence* typically vanished when I left where I had been, and so it did once more. I opened my eyes, and took a peek around the carriage... everyone was asleep, save for a lone scout.

He was seated around a fire, paying little mind to anything around him. Fortunately, the wagon holding our prisoner was close! I made my way over, and grabbed a few things on the way.

It took me about ten seconds to get the back of the wagon down, because I'd wanted to be as quiet as possible. When I got the back down, I caught sight of the man we'd taken; he had shackles on his arms and legs.

I kept my voice down. "Be quiet." I said, "I'm a friend, not a foe."

He still seemed terrified. I took a chunk of bread I'd grabbed on the way over, and put a piece in his mouth as a peace offering. Nobody seemed to have any intention of feeding him, so I hoped my doing so would win him over. Turns out, I was right!

"Thank you..." he panted out, "thank you."

He was still mortified. I could only imagine what Miyune and Loshki would do to him.

"I'm sorry," I said, "I can't free you, but that doesn't mean I won't help you how I can."

I brought around a canteen of water I'd snatched, and gave him a drink. He downed the water like a rabid dog.

"Please, there must be something..."

"I'm sorry, but the large man, Loshki, has the key to your shackles. There's no way to get it from him."

"Please, please... please, there has to be!"

"I'm so sorry to be the harbinger of ill news... but there isn't."

Tears began to run down his face. "They're going to kill me." he said.

"I know. They probably will, which is why I've come to you."

"What do you mean?"

"I need you to tell me what you know. Please, help me!"

"If I tell you anything, she'll torture me to no end. I can't."

"She's holding me hostage too! Nobody is supposed to know that... *there,* now you can get me back if I speak, so please, tell me what you can! I'm only fourteen. I have so many years ahead of me, and no matter how bad things get, no matter how bad I feel, the truth is... *i'm terrified to die!* I'm begging you, *please help me!*"

He fell quiet, and went back to dropping tears. What hope did I really have of making him talk? My face tossed itself into the side of the carriage, and I started to hiss.

"So be it..." he finally said, "I'll tell you."

This shocked me. My eyes shot wide open, and I started bowing frantically.

"Thank you." I said, "Thank you!"

"I made the mistake of leaving my partnership with her, and embezzling the silverion we'd made together. I also made the mistake of speaking ill of-..."

Did his heart give out!?! He froze!

I shook him. "Sir...!?! *Sir!?!*"

This snapped him out of the daze he'd gone into. "I can't tell you." he said.

What on Lathine was tugging at his heart!?!

"You're going to die anyways. Get your revenge, help me, please! *I'm begging you!*"

"I can't. She'll torture me to no end if I tell you of *the one.*"

"I already know of the Unsaid One, just not details! I'm begging you; tell me, trust me!"

He pondered both sides of the coin. "His name is *Nothaniir.*" he finally said, "Nothaniir is the lord of the underworld, and only known by a select few. Lady

Miyune is his left hand, and a man by the name of Lord Keras is his right."

"Lord Keras!?!" I choked.

He nodded. "With his left Nothaniir rules Sohal, and with his right he rules Hadia. The time is nearing when he rises over both. People talk of this era as a time of peace, but only because they don't know any better. Nothaniir could bring around the second Unraveling of Lathine; that's the sort of power he holds."

"Where is he?"

"Nobody knows... and I don't even know if he is really a he, Nothaniir might be a she. Save for Miyune and Keras, nobody has ever met Nothaniir, far as I know."

"Of course..." I grumbled.

There was *no way* I'd get something as big as Nothaniir's identity out of Miyune!

"That's all I know," he said, "and that's the truth. He's as good as a ghost."

I nodded low. "Thank you... I swear I'll put this information to good use. One way or another, I'll bring Miyune down, and Nothaniir after! I won't let Lathine unravel again."

He put his head down, and went back to sniveling. I didn't bother to speak anymore; instead, I put the end of the wagon back up, and returned to my carriage. It appalled me to think that Miyune had no problem holding fear of torture over people's heads.

I'd been furious with my people since I could walk, and had always been forced to bottle what I felt. Between all the past emotions I still had inside me, and the sour feelings I now held for Miyune, I was ready to explode!

Loshki brought me back to Lord Keras' castle. We entered the dining hall, where we saw none other than

Lord Keras, and the glistening white witch herself.

Loshki leaned low, beside my ear. "Lady Leestel," he said, "wait outside."

It's a good thing Loshki had sensed my anger, and taken to action. I'd been in a bad state of mind, and would have been bound to put on an ugly display in front of Lord Keras.

"My pleasure." I grumbled.

If I had made a scene, Miyune would have probably made my life a nightmare as retribution. After all, everything I did reflected on her. A bad outburst would have put some strain on her marriage hopes.

It was stupid of me to punch the wall outside the dining hall with my little fist... I bet I couldn't have even made water flinch.

I mumbled to myself, while soothing away the flickers of pain that ran down my hand. "Kehah, you stupid, stupid girl!"

I wasn't looking to the door, nor did I turn around to see who had come to open it. Somehow, I already knew.

I cried out. "You think that's a task for a child!?!"

"Kea, you neither act like a child nor try to. To think; you spend your days sleeping away, and yet you still claim the wisdom of the aged. 'Let me make of my life what I will' so you say. Will you truly try to say that you are nothing more than a clueless child? Should you truly be treated as so? Kea, is it really so that you are clueless?"

"That has nothing to do with any of this!"

"Either way; you are of my household. No human could have failed that task. I even gave you my strongest warrior out of goodwill. Do you really think I like being without Loshki's protection? Would you really still say I did not give all I could for you?"

"How can you be so vain! You know Loshki should've seen it through! Why would you torture me like that!?!"

"Even so, I heard you fared well, Kea. I am willing to invest when I see talent. If you cannot trust yourself, then at least trust in the faith I hold."

"'*Fared well*' for a stupid kid. I'm no tactician! Don't count on me like that again!"

"That remains to be seen." she said, turning back to the dining hall, "Have a nice night, that will be all."

Anger worked magic for me, because somehow, someway, I managed to remember the way back to the room Lord Keras had given me. A certain red aura followed me the entire way there. It was startling how fast the eyes were moving today, I think it had to do with them latching onto my anger.

I got to my room, closed the blinds, and tumbled into bed. I felt mentally and emotionally dead... and there wasn't anything I felt I could do but hope a good night's sleep would amend me. I'd hoped to fall asleep before the whispers could begin, but that was a wish that didn't come to fruition. A hand began to weave through my hair, and whispers began to trickle into my ear...

"You can't hide."

"They will find you."

"They will come to Lathine."

CHAPTER 11

"Kea, please then, tell me; what better thing could you do in this world than serve at my side?"

"You're acting crazy." I said, "Murdering, lying, sending children home fatherless... what kind of a way to live is that?"

"Well then, Kehah, I only pray you understand the truth before it's too late."

I shook her off, and grinned. Whatever she'd meant, I could only imagine. Still, I decided to see her words as a threat. I took a simple take at revenge. You see, Lord Keras had sent someone on a long journey for a bottle of wine Miyune particularly liked. A few days had passed, and the person had just gotten back with a bottle of the wine.

Now, the bottle stood at the table, and Miyune had only got a lone fill of her glass. Being the lunatic I was; I grabbed the bottle, and downed it whole! When I set the empty bottle back down, she shook her head, and glared at me; as a mother would to a bad child. I got up, and left before she could say anything about it. Now... when I say I *left,* I really mean *left.* Whether by my own will, or just out of drunkenness; I went into town, bought a pony, and made my way off.

Could I keep my balance well on the pony? No. Could I move fast with it? Also no. Regardless, I'd make better progress with it than if I went on foot. I had a head start too, so that should have been all I could ask for, right? My sights were set on Cavala. Fate was with me, because it was just two towns over. In theory, I should have been able to make it there rather easy... barring I got lost.

Doubts weighed inside me, of course. I'll be the first to admit I wasn't right in the head, now more than ever; but then again, I don't think I ever was. I'd figure this all out, somehow... I was good at pushing through.

I made great progress day one. By the time darkness began to near, the town of Keras wasn't *anywhere* in sight. On the other hand, what was in sight was the middle town of my little venture! I went to the first inn I could find, and entered. Before I could even take my first step in, a voice met me.

"Where are your parents?" it said.

My eyes ticked up to see a man behind a counter.

I shook my head. "On their way, they'll be here any minute."

I walked up, reached into my pocket, and grabbed Silverion to set upon the counter. Silverion was the currency of Lathine.

"They wanted me to run ahead and get a room." I lied.

"Whatever you say." he said, "Room eight."

"Thank you."

I went into my room, locked the door, and unwound. Falling asleep was easy enough. When I came back to, I don't think long had passed. Night was now in full bloom. I didn't hear any voices in my ear, nor could I feel the presence of anything sinister. Still, something just wasn't right. I went dead still in hopes of figuring out what had awaken me; in turn, something met my ears... something faint, from outside my room.

Dim light bled underneath my door from the hallway.

I could tell there was a shadow standing on the other side. Could it have been Loshki? I guess it made sense my defiance wouldn't go uncontested. I flopped out of bed, and then crawled under. Maybe I could hide out when he barged in? I kept an eye on the light that fled in, and wondered if I was losing my touch. I took a second look, and sure enough, there did appear to be a pair of feet on the other side! For some reason, the feet weren't moving... but whoever they belonged to had to move eventually, right? I kept watching, I even started to count. Ten minutes went by, then twenty, then thirty...

At long last, I heard a voice! Even though the voice did in fact belong to a man, I could tell it wasn't Loshki's.

"Go iN, gO In..."

What on Lathine was going on here!?!

"gO in, go *IN."*

His words just kept getting more and more crazy with every passing second. Now, I couldn't even understand what he was saying anymore! Whoever it was started to pace around my door. Every step he took was accompanied by deranged gibberish. His pacing just got more and more frantic, up until the point that he started to get animalistic. All of a sudden, he pounded a *"thud!"* against my door. Out of instinct, I jumped like a cat, and ended up bashing my head.

"Kea, you moron..." I grumbled.

I'd made sure to keep my words quiet, because I hadn't wanted to give away my presence... but then again, the man clearly already knew someone was in here, so maybe being loud wasn't a bad idea? I took my hand, and banged it against the creaky floorboard underneath me. A chain reaction caused the board to shake and wail all the way to the door. I could tell the man heard it, because his mouth stopped, along with his feet, albeit only for a hot second. He went right back to acting like a freak afterwards.

After that, I started to count. He didn't leave after thirty minutes, nor did he after an hour. As it turned out, an hour was all I could make it to before drifting back to sleep.

When I awoke, I forgot about where I was, and bashed my head again. I screamed this time. "*Zvah!* Kea, you idiot!"

I rolled out from under the bed, and grasped at my head. Everything around me was illuminated. I rose begrudgingly to my feet for a look out the window, and saw that daylight was at it's peak! I heard people skittering outside my room. I ran over and listened in. What I heard was normal people talking about normal things... what they wanted to eat, what they wanted to do, dumb things like that.

I cloaked up, and left my room. I stopped by the front counter real quick, and dropped off my room key to the inn keeper I'd met the night before.

"Leaving so soon?" he said.

I didn't reply; instead, I hurried outside, and went into the stable that sat alongside the inn. My feet took me over to my pony. I was about to hop on him, when a big hand fell on my shoulder.

My words came out sheepish. "...Loshki?" I said.

I didn't get a reply. I tilted my head back to see... the man from the counter. What on Lathine was he doing, *alone,* with *me?*

"Where are you going? Your parents never came."

"How would you know?"

"Because they never did come."

He must have been the same creep from outside my door! He had a twisted smile on his face. I threw a finger to my mouth, and began to dawdle... towards the door.

"Hmmm... I can't say I'm quite absolutely sure what exactly it seems we are talking about. They were un-doubtedly with me, and that's a fact!" I said, vying for extra steps.

I snuck glances from the corner of my eye, and saw that I wasn't the only one inching forward. He was on the verge of jumping, so I took a gamble... and bolted for the door! I got a grip on the door knob, but that was all I could get before he grabbed me!

"So, you're a runner are you?"

He gripped me tight, and flung me into a pile of old bar-rels! I shrieked in pain, and looked down to a little barrel shard that had ended up screwed in my arm. I pulled the shard, and threw it away, which caused a spurt of blood to fly.

His eyes and face went full on red. *"Don't make this so difficult!"*

"You're insane!" I screamed, "IN-SANE!"

I tried to run past him, but his reach was too great! I flailed to no avail, and then he gripped me by the collar. He slammed me against a wall, which took the air out of my lungs. His raw strength forced me down to my knees.

"Here's the thing-...!" he started to say.

At that very moment, I managed to suck in a barrel shard off the ground. I thrusted it at the man's heart! He threw up his right hand, and opted to take the shard there instead; it ended up *deep* in his right hand, and caused a surplus of bleeding. He shoved me back, threw the shard away, and then we struggled. He had no issue getting both his hands around my throat.

He howled to the heavens; each word he spat put an ounce of spit on my face. *"You're going to die for that!"*

My heart started to burn. Drool waterfalled out of my mouth, along with desperate squeals. His right hand couldn't grip me well because of the damage it had taken, and because he'd made my throat slippery by lathering it with blood; with those two things in mind, I did the only thing I could think of. I flailed hard as I could, managed to budge an inch, and then dropped my mouth on his right hand. I bit as hard as I humanly could! One of his fingers escaped, sure, but two weren't so lucky...

He fell to his knees, and roared. An iron taste coursed through my mouth, and seeped from my teeth. I was fortunate he didn't sock me in the face, or snap my neck. He must have been too in shock to do anything but stare at me, and scream.

I kept biting, and biting, harder, and *harder!* When he finally fell back, I knew it was time to run. I spat out both fingers in his face, and bolted for the door. He was too dazed to do anything, so I managed to get it open with ease. What met me was something unexpected, Loshki!

Loshki looked livid... but not at me. He walked over to the man, who was still groping at his maimed hand. Loshki crushed the creep's face with a hammer-like punch. Blood splattered all over, and hit down as loud as hail. Loshki pulled out steel, reigned it into the air, and slammed down; he pulled it back, wiped it off, sheathed it, and then turned to me.

"'Lucky Lady Miyune sent me after you." he said.

"I had it covered."

"So I see."

He walked over, and used his sleeve to wipe off all the

crimson on my face, then he gave me a canteen of water to wash out my mouth with. While I was busy with the water, he took a look at my throat.

"Does it look bad?" I asked.

"You'll have some bruises, that's for sure, but you'll be just fine."

His eyes were a little wide, I could tell something was on his mind.

"Just come out with it." I said.

"'Surprised how well you're holding up, is all."

"This..." I hissed, "this is nothing. Things are so much worse where I come from."

Loshki crossed his arms, and let firm words. "I know, I saw for myself."

I could tell just from looking at his eyes that he'd seen some twisted things in the labyrinth.

"Tell me something I don't know." I said, shying away.

"Lady Miyune isn't angry with you."

I'll admit, hearing that surprised me. "I'm not sure I believe that."

"You should already know she won't blow her top, 'since she views loss of control as a weakness, and all."

"True..."

"So, Lady Leestel, you gonna' come back to us?"

Loshki was too good at his job. If Miyune sent him out to get me, there was no way he wasn't coming back with me. I'm sure he'd be smart enough to stop me before I reached Cavala, anyways, even if I did say *"no"* and part ways with him.

"I will." I said.

"Good, you'll be happy to hear I'm taking you back to Sciruthon."

"Miyune's done with Lord Keras?" I asked.

"Not quite. She's doing you a favor, Leestel. She's letting you go back before even her, and she's giving you me."

I felt like she really just wanted to get me away from Cavala. Muinflor, the capital of Sohal, wasn't far beyond Cavala, so throw that in for good measure.

"Alright... I'm grateful."

Regret writhed me over the fact that I'd rejected Lathimian's offer of freedom, some time ago. I'd been too self righteous, thinking I could stop Miyune on my own. Just where had that sentiment gotten me? Nowhere! Still, all that line of thinking did was motivate me. Had I done a lot of failing? Sure! Of course I had, I was human! Life is all about ups, and downs; I'd just gone through a down, which meant it was time for an up! Being at the palace without Miyune would be quite an opportunity. I resolved to make the best of the time to come.

CHAPTER 12

My hands were empty. Turning up Miyune's home three times over had yielded no results. Where did she keep the key for the second locked room? Either it was in a secret compartment I could never hope to find, or it was kept outside the palace. I'd been standing across the locked door for some ten minutes, until at last an attendant came my way.

"Is this the room with the extra blankets?" I said, not wanting to be open about my intentions.

"This is an ever sealed room." so the attendant said, "I don't actually know what's in there, My Lady."

"Oh... is that so? I bet Auntie Miyu doesn't go in very often, then."

"I've only seen Sir Loshki go in there."

Loshki had the key... no doubts about it. In retrospect, that should have been obvious. My newfound knowledge didn't do much to ease my lust for answers, though. When would I ever get a good chance to break into Loshki's? I didn't even know where he lived, first off. Second off, how would I ever begin to go about searching his home? He must have had a lot of attendants of his own.

I'd done nothing but search for answers since returning to Sciruthon, so I was in need of a little pick me up. There wasn't many things that I enjoyed doing anymore, so I thought that turning to good food sounded decent.

While I'm sure Miyu's cooks could have made anything, there was just some things that tasted best with a certain street flair to them. I left the palace, and took to town. I got some treats, and started to make my way to the plains. I wanted to look at the clouds, and think. Maybe some down time would help put me at ease? My nerves had never really calmed since the *"task"* I'd gone on with Loshki.

Something weird happened. I could swear I'd heard a voice! Was I so stressed that I was starting to hear things? I was sure whatever had spoken had used the *"old language"*, as people here called it... in other words, my language! This wasn't the sort of place the eyes would normally bother me in, nor the voice. I took an eye to the shadows, to a back alley where I thought I'd heard the sound from.

There wasn't anything to be seen...

It only took me a few minutes to reach the plains that laid beyond town. I set my picnic basket down, and plopped on the lush greens. Every strand of sun kissed emerald that danced up and down my skin went a long way to soothing my heart. I took handfuls from my basket, and snacked away for the next half hour... until a lack of sleep reaped me.

What ended up awakening me was a shadow. I pulled myself up to see a young girl about my own age. Interestingly enough, she had a thick veil much like the one Miyu had given me. What was wrong with her? She couldn't stop her lips from quivering, nor could she stop her hands from shaking. I could tell she wanted to speak, but for some reason, she seemed unsure about what to say.

I decided to play my part. "Hello, hello! Have we met

before! Do you want a snack?"

At last her demeanor changed, and then she sighed. "You don't have to fake around me... Kehah."

I don't think instinct had ever kicked so fast in my life. I fell straight back, and scrambled for the butter knife I had in my basket. I wasn't sure what to do, or what to say. When someone points a weapon at you, despite however small, you typically do something, right? It surprised me when she did absolutely nothing.

She just *stood there, silent.* With my free hand... I lunged forward, grabbed her veil, and then dropped it in shock.

She was exactly who I thought she was; my sister, Sehrehah. I tried to step back, but ended up falling thanks to wobbly knees. Sehrehah's flowing brunette head didn't veil her eyes like my black mess did. She had to throw up both her hands for protection from the sun.

"I... hear you've had a better life in this world," she said softly, "I'm happy for you."

I was too emotional to scream for guards. My nerves shot up, and left me still as a statue. She knew me well enough to know when I was frozen, so I was surprised to see she didn't pounce forward and try to hurt me. Instead, my sister reached down with a trembling hand, and picked up her veil.

"I see you don't need one anymore," she said, "that's very impressive Keh-... Kea."

Even though my blood started to pulse again, control of my body just wouldn't return.

"What sort of game are you playing!?!" I cried, still clutching the butter knife.

She looked away. "I've earned nothing else, I don't blame-..."

"Just get out of here, go away!"

I felt nauseous to the point of passing out. How I'd managed to return to my feet and stay there was beyond me.

Sehrehah's voice came out soft as a whisper. "I really don't blame you..." was all she could muster.

What left her was one last line of words so timid, so quiet, that I couldn't quite make them out. I think they were something to the tune of *"I was never there when you needed me."*

This was all wrong... She began to walk away, head drooped down. I could hear tears falling from her face. This girl was different from the one I'd once known, what right did I have to deny her repentance? What I wanted wasn't more of the past, but a new world entirely; a better world. If I couldn't pioneer what I wanted, if I couldn't show the sort of love and compassion I wanted, then I had no place dreaming of such a world in the first place. Maybe I'd get hurt by trying, and trusting, but I'd end up even worse if I couldn't learn to trust enough. I took steps after her.

"Sehrehah?"

It was weird to hear her cry. She stopped in her tracks, and worked her way down to a sniffle.

"I'm sorry," I said, "I really am sorry. Please come back, I wasn't thinking."

She turned around, and wiped away at what tears were left on her face. Her struggle with the blasting sun above gave me all sorts of déjà vu.

"It's fine," she told me, "you shouldn't be sorry."

Here we were, again, face to face, after all this time. It didn't surprise me that neither of us had the heart for words. In the end, it was her who broke the silence. I guess that was an act befitting for an older sibling.

"I think you look very pretty, Kea."

"I can't really take any credit. It's all thanks to a lady named Miyune."

"Even still."

What had caused her to change so much? It was weird to think that she was the same person who used to torment me.

I took the next leap. "How did you end up finding me? How did you escape?"

"I don't know how you managed it all those years... but they crowned me as the Miracle Maiden. I had to leave, I couldn't do it..."

"Do you see *them?*"

"Them?"

"Nevermind, forget it..."

I couldn't believe my father would actually do that; try to throw the mantle of *"Miracle Maiden"* on someone else! She seemed to pick up on what I was thinking.

"They're all crazed," she said, "all of them."

"I'm sorry you had to go through that."

I could tell she was trying to convince herself the madness was over. "I'm not concerned about it anymore." she insisted, "I guess... I just wanted to see if life was treating you well, if it *really* was."

"Only time will tell. Do you have a reason to be scared for me?"

"I've heard things about Lady Miyune, is all."

I could tell she wasn't telling me something. "I need to know." I said, "Please tell me."

She fiddled around with her fingers, and licked her lips.

I'm sure she was in a tough place emotionally; so I thought I'd make things easier on her, and narrow down my question. "What happened, *that* day, Sehrehah?"

"'*Sehrea*' is fine..." she started by saying, "and... after their men snuck in and took you; that was when she arrived."

I choked on my saliva. "*That was when she arrived? Miyune?*"

Sehreh-... Sehrea, started to play around with her hair. Her lack of desire to keep going said it all.

A moment of silence passed before she could muster anymore words. "After Miyune's thieves got away with you, they shocked us again by coming back before we could send out a strike team. Her and her thieves stood by the way out, or the '*portal*', as I'm sure they'd tell you. Father went to meet her... and I don't know exactly what they said. All I know is that somehow father bartered for your safety, Kea. He counts on you being returned to the labyrinth, one day. I don't know why, but he does."

"Never! I won't allow it!"

"You should run, Kea. With enough effort, you could lose Miyune and her guard."

"How do you know her guard's been keeping tabs on me?"

"Kea... that's part of her end of the deal."

Truth made me *sick*. Stealing me for the sake of selling me off later had been my first assumption about why Miyune had really taken me, though, so at least I wasn't surprised. Still, it did hurt to think I really had been nothing more to her than a bartering chip all along.

Now it made sense why Loshki himself was always sent after me, or to protect me. All I couldn't wrap my head around was the '*task*' Miyune had sent me on. It didn't make sense why she'd have done that... so there must have still been things I didn't know.

"Father wasn't planning on your return for several

years." Sehrea said.

Those words set me at ease more than she could ever know.

"I don't understand. Years will pass? Why so long?"

"I wish I knew, but I don't."

Silence ensued...

"Will you help me?" I finally mustered.

"Of course, Kea." she said, looking dead into my eyes, "This time I'll be here for you, forever and ever on. I promise."

This touched my heart. I'd never heard words like that. I couldn't prove she was for real, sure, but something about her heart just felt right. I was sure she'd turn out to be real, absolutely sure...

Still, I won't deny I was desperate for someone to cling to. I just wanted someone who would hold me tight, and tell me that everything would be alright. We all need that one person.

"Hadia's the key." she went on to say.

"Hadia's the key?"

She nodded, and for the first time today, her sad eyes disappeared. A certain fire-like aura took hold of her instead, which reminded me of how she'd used to be.

"That's where the way to our people lies; the bridge between our world and Lathine. There's still a multitude of things in the labyrinth that father isn't telling us about, there has to be things nobody alive but him knows."

"I've snuck into his study many times before, Sehrea, but that's something you-..." I didn't mean to bring up the time she'd ratted me out, "anyways, I don't know what else there could possibly be to it all. I've been everywhere he's ever tread, ten times over. Do you mean there's secrets he keeps only inside his head?"

"Father has a secret place."

My eyes lit up. "*Yaheen...* are you sure? *Absolutely sure?*"

"I don't know where it is, but there *is* a secret room, somewhere in the labyrinth."

What should I have said to a revelation like that? From start to finish, this life was an unbelievable, confusing, unending torment.

"It's where he's hiding the truth," she said, "truths nobody can afford to know, about the many *'worlds'* we were taught of, of the Unraveling, of our place in all this, even the full prophecy of the Miracle Maiden."

"That explains why Miyune's trying to marry Hadia's most powerful crime lord."

"Is she really?"

I nodded. "Yes, a man named *'Keras'.* He lives in Sohal, but his domain is Hadia."

"That woman can't be trusted."

This new Sehrea was so much more reserved than the old one. I just couldn't link all my memories to the girl who stood before me now.

"I agree, but not just anyone is going to believe us." I said.

"That's our biggest problem."

"But there is one who might..."

"Can we trust this person?"

I nodded. "I have maps on how to get to him, but I can't get away to see him... It's not my place to ask, b-"

"Of course I will." she said, "If it's someone you trust, that's good enough for me."

My heart fluttered. I couldn't help but smile. Thank goodness! Finally, after all these years, I'd found someone I could trust, someone I could hold dear! I couldn't even accept the possibility she was fake, because it would hurt too much.

CHAPTER 13

There was only one thing I could think of that made me want to get up at the break of dawn. I hurried through town, and soon found myself in an inn. I hurried to a specific door in the inn, and then knocked. Who showed from the other side was none other than Sehrea! She hugged me tightly, then we moved into her room.

"Is this place still treating you well?" I said.

"A warm bed and good roof is all I need. You shouldn't worry about simple things."

"Still, I feel bad... I'm sleeping in luxury every night, adorned in silks."

She gave off a smile, albeit a faint one. Everything she did was so solemn...

"I still have a multitude of treasures from back home." she said, "If I sold them all, I could probably live just as well as you."

"Alright, I guess that's true."

A little silence ensued, which was no surprise. I think we were both still anxious around one another.

"Has she returned yet?" Sehrea finally said.

I shook my head. "Not yet... which must mean everything is going according to her plans, I bet."

"I'm not surprised." Sehrea said, dropping her head, "I think she's the only person that's ever pressed the King into submission."

She wouldn't refer to the King as *"father"*, which I

couldn't blame her for. I set the little bag I'd been carrying down, and opened it up. There was a never ending sea of papers inside, as well as some Silverion.

"Here's the papers." I said.

"From the room she keeps locked up?"

I nodded. "Nobody guards her room when she's not around. It's pretty easy to slip in and out of."

She started to go through the papers, and was surprised how deep the stack went.

"Won't she notice all these missing?"

"I copied them all, word for word."

"That must have taken you a few days."

I shifted my eyes around, and grimaced. "That's an understatement. Anyways, all that matters is that we get them to Lathimian."

She nodded. "I understand. I'll be careful with them, I've already memorized the route."

"That was fast, are you sure?"

"I started learning the area around Sciruthon when I heard that's where *she* lived. I already knew most of it by the time we met again."

"I'm impressed, Sehrea, that was a really good idea."

"I only wanted to be prepared, should you have wanted my help."

All I could do was smile... I didn't know how to express my gratitude.

"Kea, I'm telling you," she said, "let's make a run for it. Let's *both* of us go after Lathimian."

"It's too risky. Besides, Miyune is betting on having me for a few years anyways; you said it yourself. We shouldn't rush, we can wait for our time."

"Lolagis was the best horse money could buy. Nobody will catch us if we dart in the night." she said, referring to a horse she'd bought upon coming to Lathine.

I still found it surprising she could ride a full grown horse. We didn't even have those back home.

"I'm thankful you care," I said, "but just trust me on this."

"Understood."

"I-..."

"There's something else to today, isn't there?"

I nodded. "Loshki's schedule is pretty free, I say we take advantage."

"You want to ransack his house?"

I couldn't help but smile. I'd set this day up perfectly! For the last few days, I'd kept Loshki occupied with an endless stream of tasks. As a result, Sehrea had been able to not just find out where he lived, but to scout out a potential means of getting in. According to her, nobody lived with Loshki. He didn't even have a single attendant! Consequently, I felt comfortable working with a simple plan.

"I didn't wish to push the burden on you, but-"

"I'll do as you wish." she said, "Whatever you wish, so be it."

"He was at the castle earlier today, training the guards. Let's start by going back there."

"Good idea, Kea."

Together, we fought through fences, and back alleys. We made our way to the palace pretty quick, and took gazes at it from the shadows.

"Luck is with us." she said.

"No kidding..."

We saw Loshki standing at the gate, speaking with a guard!

"Once me and him go in," I said, "get going. Give yourself an hour, hour and a half at most."

She nodded.

I couldn't tell if this mission made her uneasy.

I tried to be comforting, regardless. "I can keep him entertained *at least* two hours, so it'll be fine."

She nodded. "Of course it will be."

Ironically, it was her who ended up trying to relieve me. "Go on," she said, "I'll be fine."

"Yes... take care."

"You too."

I emerged from the shadows, and started to walk towards the gate. Loshki didn't notice me until I was already within feet of him.

"Lady Leestel! Rare to see you up this early. Something I can do for you?"

"Actually... there is."

"Oh, and what's that?"

"Miyune's going to send me out on more missions, won't she?"

Loshki snickered, which was his way of saying "*Wish I knew.*"

"All I'll say, kid, is that you should prepare."

"That's why I came to you, Loshki. Do you have an hour or two? I was hoping you could sit down and instruct me in the library."

"'Not about whether or not I do. Even if I don't; I'll make time."

I smiled. You could always tell his deep voice meant everything it said. We went into the courtyard, then into the castle. Sehrea must have been halfway to Loshki's by the time I took a seat in the library. Sehrea and I had been raised as creatures of the dark, that's why I wasn't too concerned about how things went on her side of the mission. She was every bit the master of the shadows that I was, so I was sure she'd be fine. At worst she just wouldn't find a key, and we'd go back to the drawing board.

"Tacticians just don't start at your age," Loshki said, setting a few books down, "but if you decide it's the road for you; then take these teachings. You'll find yourself engraved in something like them one day."

"That's a nice thought..."

"I can tell even you don't know what you want, Leestel."

I shook my head.

My words weren't a ploy, act of innocence, or stall for time... no, they were the honest truth. "I have no clue." I said, "None at all."

"Then, young Master, you'd do well to learn. When it's time to make a choice, 'least you'll have foundations to stand on."

"That's a good way of thinking."

We went deep into studying. Save for the occasional glance at a clock, I did put my all into it.

Now, almost two hours had passed. I was about to speak up, when I heard something I hadn't expected. I heard Miyune's voice from the doorway!

"Kea, Loshki, how are the both of you?"

"Well." I said.

"'Just continuing her studies." Loshki followed up.

"Good, very good."

She joined us at the table, and turned to Loshki. "Give us a moment, if you may."

Loshki nodded, and left to the hallway.

Miyune's eyes fell upon me, and bled a sense of calm. "Can we talk seriously for a moment, Kea?"

"It's not like I have a choice."

"Nonetheless, I appreciate your time. You know, Kea, I really do not mind if you want to wander the land."

Those words surprised me as much as they confused me. I gave her a cautious look. Maybe she'd let up and show me what was really on her mind?

"Kea," she went on, "at the very least, a good daughter does well to tell when she would like to go out. Can you do that for me?"

She was just one big headache. Was this an attempt at pushing guilt onto me? I had no clue what to think.

"I'll try to be more thoughtful in the future." I said, unable to come up with anything better.

"I only ask you keep me informed. With proper notice, we both know well the guards can keep you safe. Little adventures do not bother me, Kea, truly."

"Alright." I murmured.

Nowadays, I felt like a weight was on my chest whenever I had to speak with her. There was just so many different angles she could have been coming from!

"I'm happy to hear that." she said, rising up, "As for me, I am rather tired from a long journey. I will see you tomorrow, Kea."

"Alright... see you tomorrow."

She left, and Loshki returned. "Anything interesting?" he said.

I shook my head. "Not really. I'm starting to feel a little tired, though. I think I'll get some sweets from town and go take a nap, if that's good with you."

"Of course. Anything you want from me in the meantime?"

"No Loshki, I'm fine, thank you."

"Then I'll head home for a break."

Yes, that should be fine... Sehrea should have been long gone by now.

Loshki exited the castle with me, then we parted ways. I cut through the shadows, to Sehrea's inn, and ended before her door yet again. I knocked, but didn't get an answer. I hadn't knocked loud, so there was no reason to overthink. I knocked a second time, much louder, and again got nothing...

"*Zvah...*"

What on Lathine could have held her up at Loshki's!?! If my next knock failed, I was prepared to sprint out to his house.

I smashed my hands against the door. "Sehrea! Sehrea!?!"

Nothing...

I hissed under my teeth, and then a barrage of swears left my tongue. "*Zvah, Zvah, Zvah!*"

It wasn't until then that I finally heard something on the other side. All of a sudden the door opened, and I saw Sehrea!

"Oh thank God..."

She rubbed her eyes, and yawned. "I'm sorry, Kea. I haven't been sleeping much of late, I guess I dozed off."

"Forget about it, I'm just happy to see you're alright."

"I'm sorry if I scared you."

"No, no! Don't think about it, really!"

I entered her room. She'd closed the blinds, so what met me was nothing but darkness. I didn't think much of it, because lightless rooms had dominated the first fourteen years of my life.

I looked to her, only able to make out a silhouette. "Any success?" I said.

"Yes. In his pantry there's a hole in the wall, behind

a bag of flour. There's a key there. I saw no locks in his home, so it must be to the room in Miyune's palace you speak of."

"I'm sure of it, no doubts."

"It'll be dangerous." she said, "Let's go after Lathimian instead... if not just forget about the key, at the very least."

"Miyune's never come close to catching me snooping. Father could never catch me either, I'll be fine."

"Still... I find it odd she has a locked door in the center of her home, where no light can pass."

"What are you thinking is in there?"

"I don't know... I just don't like it."

I'll admit, I'd never thought of how dark it must be in the last locked room.

"It'll be awhile before we get a good opportunity to make this work." I said, knowing that was likely to relieve her.

"Yes, let's be patient."

"Right, no rush..."

I wanted to see what Miyune was hiding more than anything... but Sehrea was right; this wasn't something to rush. I only hoped I'd get my chance soon. My eagerness to uncover another secret was increasing with every passing day. With luck, the room would hold an answer that made all the pieces fit.

CHAPTER 14

Awhile passed from the day Sehrea confirmed a hidden key in Loshki's home. Speaking of Sehrea, I hadn't seen her in almost a week. I'd been so busy at banquets with Miyune that I hadn't any time to see her. Miyune and I had just gotten back from something of the sort, in fact. We were now sitting in her dining hall, having a meal. That's when a door opened, what stood in it's wake made my gut wrench.

...Keras? What on Lathine was he doing here? Even Miyu looked puzzled. You could tell this wasn't something she'd planned.

"This is a welcome surprise." Miyu said, "What has brought you here, Keras?"

"My innermost wishes."

He marched beside her, fell to a knee, and presented a ring. Of course she'd succeeded, of course... Consequently, they started making wedding preparations at once. I spent the rest of the day over a book, and an endless supply of ice cream.

What was I supposed to make of all this? My heart tingled at how much more powerful she was going to get. It was crazy to think she hadn't already hit her limit...

Miyune came back into the dining hall late that night. I was still over ice cream and books.

"I have a lone request for you." she said.

"And what's that?"

"Like I said, it's only a request. You do not have to if you do not want you."

"Just say it."

"Would you sing at my wedding?"

I wonder why she was asking, instead of demanding...

"Sure."

"And would you be my maid of honor?"

It amazed me that she'd ask someone she hadn't known for long. Though, when I thought about it... I couldn't think of anyone else she could ask. She didn't have any family left that I knew of, nor did she seem to have any real friends.

"I'd be honored."

"Thank you, Kea. I do appreciate you."

Sometimes she didn't seem to be after anything, and those times scared me the most. Almost another week passed until I could finally buy out the time to see Sehrea again.

"*I hear Miyune and Keras are being wed.*" That was the first thing either of us said, and it came from her lips.

"Unfortunately..."

"What do you make of it?" she asked.

"The bottom line is; we're not getting into the locked room anytime soon."

She was happy about that. "Are we settling down in the meantime?"

"Anything but that, I was hoping you'd go after Lathimian in the meantime."

"Good idea."

I hugged her. "Just, please be careful."

"Of course. I'm not concerned about that, you should be more concerned about yourself."

She probably had a point, who knew what plans Miyu

had at the ready?

Afterwards our talk, Sehrea went on her way, and I on my own. It was incredible to see how fast Miyune could plan a wedding. She'd sent out invitations the day Keras had proposed. Very little time had passed since then, and we were already on the verge of the wedding date! Still, against all odds, she made it work.

"*The best trees are slow to grow.*" Miyune once told me, when we'd first went to see the land.

Those words of hers stayed on my mind. Her marriage with Keras just wasn't like her. She was always so patient, and yet this marriage was done with such haste. I'm sure she had her reasons, but the whole thing still didn't sit right with me. A few more days passed, and the day of the wedding arrived. I hadn't practiced what I was going to sing *at all*. I felt there was no real need to, since singing was second nature to me. Besides the exchange of vows, and rings, the only other piece to the ceremony was set to be my singing. I was honored, to say the least. It was quite the compliment for someone of Miyu's stature to ask such a thing of me.

Now arrived the beginning. Lord Keras made the walk out to the altar; it was draped with a white as pure as clouds. Lord Keras looked powerful, and dignified. I'm not going mention much of him, because of what came next. As if I really needed to say who or what took the show... I'm sure you could have guessed the answer yourself. I'll give Miyune credit, even I couldn't help but marvel.

Miyu's skin glowed like stars, and sunlight beamed off her hair as it does off glass. These things in themselves would've been enough, and yet she still found a way to go the extra mile. Her dress must have been worth a fortune; it was also a white blinding enough to get you intoxicated just for staring too long. She also had a glimmering necklace made of crystals and silver, which was accompanied by her finishing piece; a *gorgeous* light-weight crown that weaved in and out of her hair, as do little branches through a thicket.

All and all, it didn't matter that her resources could have made almost anyone looking stunning, because she used them to transcend into something else entirely. She was less a person, and more a goddess.

Soft music played in coordinance as she walked down the aisle. I wager few people noticed because of how stunning she looked.

Loshki leaned into my ear. "Keep your head." he said.

I shook off my daze. "Of course, of course."

Honestly, I only meant to repeat words when I was pre-tending to be cute. Except, times like that were so fre-quent that I'd started doing it out of instinct.

On went a little speech by the officiator, and soon, the wedding vows. With my part about to be up, in such a perfect wedding, with an enormous crowd, you'd think I'd be nervous about messing up, right? Well, you'd have been wrong if you thought so. Public speaking, er, sing-ing, couldn't have been any more routine to me. An endless sea watched as I walked up to the altar. At the forefront of it all, I stood alone. Miyune, Keras, and the officiator, had already taken seats in the crowd.

"Ah naheo neh kahsahs neo meesh zahlah."

It's funny how routine something could become. I got lost in thoughts every time I sang, and yet I could still hit every last note on key. This was by far my largest crowd since the last time I'd chanted for a ceremony in my homeworld. I guess it was only natural to think of what those days had been like, while lost in thoughts...

In front of me was a crowd of well dressed nobles, and fine mannered people. An image flashed of the past, of what my people would have looked like. They'd have been stained in blood, markings, and shreds that barely deserved to be called "clothes". There was so much light here... whereas my home had been as dark as the night, all the time.

"*Soo fah ziihf neh kahehn fiih ah sahn vliih fah beo.*"

I kept my eyes closed while I sang. I'd always done that back home, because I'd never wanted to see the mutilations, tortures, and sacrifies, that went with the ceremonies I chanted for.

It was nice to hear a thunderous roar of applause. I could say for certainty that my gift of song would hold up in any world I went to.

People began to mingle, and go to the tables for food, with the exception of Miyu. She went out to meet me part way down the aisle. Nobody was watching, which made me wonder why she did what she did next; hug me. She didn't give me a quick, or loveless hug, but the sort I'd always wished my own mother would hold me with.

"That was beautiful, Kea."

I went into a little daze. It was hard for me to know what to think of her.

"Are you alright, Kea?" Miyu asked, snapping me from my daze.

"Yes, Miyu... thank you. I wish you the best in your marriage."

She smiled, and stroked away the mess of hair that had flown in my face. "Thank you, Kea. Now, come sit with us; I've arranged the dinner to your liking."

"Thank you, that sounds nice."

She led us to a small table. Keras wasn't at it yet. We were the only two there, and it was already brimming with fresh appetizers. I couldn't help but start pigging out, because she really had arranged the dinner to my liking! Life was such a confusing thing... how could I ever begin to know right and wrong, light and dark, good and bad? What I'd always been spoon-fed to believe was bad didn't seem so bad after all.

In the midst of my pigging out, a shadow emerged. My eyes shifted over to see a middle aged, well shaven man. There was also a young boy alongside him that was about my own age. Only naturally, Miyu and I put our eyes to the well shaven man. We'd expected him to take the lead, but in the end, it was the young boy who led the way.

"Lady Miyune, and the young second Leestel, right? I'd wager a round on it if I was a little older!"

Whereas my energy was fake, this boy's was clearly real; you could tell because every word he said made you want to shove a pound of cotton in each ear.

Miyune grinned. "Did our garb give us away?" she joked, as if she hadn't just been the center of the entire event.

From a wide smile, to a little grin, the young boy mumbled under his breath. "No, just the anti-social table."

Alright, I'll give him props... that made me giggle, and Miyune too.

"I think what my *foolish* nephew meant to say," said the man, "is that the elegance of house Leestel speaks for itself."

In turn, the man gave his nephew a sharp glare.

Miyune tried to ease his embarrassment. "Do not fret. I

enjoy a certain bluntness of speech. Few people have the bravado for such a thing."

"Now," Miyune continued, bearing down with purpose, "it's a pleasure to meet you as well, Febrithien; the Potent General."

Was... this really one of the famed three Generals? Second to none other than the royal family? This took me off guard. General Febrithien even seemed to be surprised that Miyune knew this.

"I'm just a man, with a wish to bring some goodwill into the world." he said, "*'Febrithien'* has a fine ring to it, but *'Potent General'* works too. 'Gotten used to it by now."

Miyune turned to me, and spewed her silver tongue. "Milord, General Febrithien, is both greatest of the Generals, and possibly the greatest to ever fight."

Febrithien seemed to be flattered by the thought, albeit too humble to let it stand. "The real greatest would have to be Vesoleth; what he did is the stuff of fairy tales. Still, I'm honor-..."

"I would comfortably say he is the greatest to ever fight!" the boy cut in, "'Least until his nephew takes the title. With the blood I hold in my veins, it'll be easy work."

General Febrithien reared his head at the boy. "I'm waiting for you to take Muinflor four times, Caiphas. When you do, then you can come back to me with that outlook."

Caiphas shook his head. "Ah, that'll be easy! In fact, I'll go a step further and win it five times!"

Miyune raised a glass of red. "To each their own, so I say. If you have the will, so it shall be."

General Febrithien nodded, and before he could say another word, Lord Keras emerged.

"General..." Keras said, "it's been awhile."

Both their faces got tense. By the looks of it, they'd had some squabbles in the past. Either way, General Febrithien chose to dwell on the present, and put his best foot forward.

"So it has. That said, congratulations on such a special day."

"Thank you, General. Please enjoy the festivities."

"Of course, thank you."

Febrithien turned to me, and said something that shocked me. "*Dee fehl loon.*"

That was... broken old language. It meant "*She is alright*".

Sehrea made it safe after all! Progress must have been abundant, for a *General* to be sent here as a mere messenger!

"I only know a few phrases." he said, "'No good, I bet.'"

"No, you're good, but I think you meant '*Deo fehl loon*'."

I smiled, and he smiled back. Febrithien and young Caiphas passed on, which left me the fun task of playing third wheel... great. I was fortunate, because Keras and Miyune were entangled with one another, so they didn't ask me to pay them any mind. I went ahead and ate until I could eat no more. This was about as good a feast as I'd ever had... if not the best. I slouched back, plump and tired by the end. Only then did Miyune pay me some mind.

"I appreciate how you've dealt with us boring old people for so long. Go have fun, my dear."

"Thank you."

...Without another care in the world, I skipped along. A giant smile wrapped around me from cheek to cheek. It felt odd being so full, and so at ease; to really feel like everything was perfect! There was a chance this was genuine peace, but I really doubted it. I think it was just the bottle I'd snuck from the party-wedding-thing's supplies working some magic. In fact, it was working a *loooot* of magic. I went to the plains on the other side of town, where nobody would see me.

My bad habit hadn't come to life like this in quite awhile. I guess I'd just felt pressured because Miyune had gotten one step further in her plan. At some point in her plan, she was bound to send me back to whence I'd came, which was a terrifying thought.

I finished out the bottle, and laid out as good as dead... I felt really, really, really, *really* good. I could only imagine how long I ended up being asleep for.

Nothing feels quite like sleeping in tall grass, on a perfect eve's day! Today, there was a warm, but not fierce sun! A kind, but not frozen breeze! It was like sleeping in the clutches of paradise itself! I would have been asleep a lot longer, if not for the shadow that plopped over me...

"Young Master Leestel," it said, "it's time to ship up."

"We're leaving?" I asked, rising like a sloth.

"Yes, young Master." Loshki replied.

I wasn't sure what he said next, or anything else that happened. Wherever we were going, I had no idea. I crawled into a carriage with his help, and fell back into a blissful slumber.

CHAPTER 15

I was back in bed when I awoke next. I slouched up, and saw a shadow in my door... it was Loshki!

"Let's get up and going, young Lady Leestel." he said.

"*Yaheen...* what's happened?"

"'Not my place to say. Lady Miyune and Lord Keras want to see you immediately."

"Really," I grumbled, "can't it wait a few hours...?"

My head was still spinning, which made staying on my feet a fun task. I was sure Loshki would see through me either way, so I didn't try to correct my wayward steps, and gladly accepted his hand when he offered it. Loshki led me on, and we ended up in the dining hall. Inside sat Miyune, and Lord Keras.

Why did Miyu have such a big smile?

"There's my dear, tired child." she said.

Something about the situation seemed humorous to her.

"Feeling better, young one?" Keras asked.

He had a big frown on his face. Loshki looked quite stern as well. Why then, was Miyune so at peace?

"Peachy!" I cried.

"No need to act around me." he said.

"Force of habit."

"I can only imagine."

Ere the eyes of the gods reigned upon Loshki and I. We followed onwards, as angels of the dark, and awaited the words of our masters.

Keras looked to my right. "Loshki, I trust in your record, and Miyune's confidence, by delving this mission upon you."

Keras looked to me next. "It will be in Hadia, which will be a new experience for you."

My distaste was slow to arise, because of the hangover. It took a moment for my head to get going. Keras had said Hadia, right? What on Lathine was so special to them about Hadia? I guess I'd get to see. I was so infatuated with the chance to learn that my anger subsided. Instead, what replaced it was genuine anticipation.

Yet again I was given a list of papers with information, and told to roll with them. Our travel to the border was inconsequential. There's not much to note when traversing Sohal, since the terrain all seemed to be the same. It's just an endless sea of plains, and mountains, with an occasional forest thrown in.

"Loshki," I came to say, "Is all of Lathine like this?"

It made sense all of Lathine was the same, since my homeworld was all the same.

"For the most part it is, young Master; from the Great Castle of Muinflor, out to the far houses of Elratheo. Only the barren wastelands of Milkar offer any drastic difference."

"That reminds me, speaking of other nations..." I said, looking over a paper, "why did Miyu and Keras wait so long to go after our target?"

Loshki leaned back against a tree, and crossed his arms. I was sure I'd sparked something.

"What are you saying, Leestel?"

"The reports you all gave me said that our target was in Dial for quite awhile. Why didn't Keras and Miyune go after him sooner? I imagine you guys would've never found him if he went all the way out to Elratheo."

"Dial is quite a way's away too."

"Hardly any further away than the south, or Hadia, really."

"Like I said; a way's away."

He walked off, got the men going, and got us back on the road. He never brought the topic up again, nor did I bother to, since I couldn't imagine he'd tell me anything anyways. That begged the question; why did Miyune and Keras have such little taste for Dial? I could understand Elratheo, since it was on the other side of Lathine, but the lack of presence they had in Dial was perplexing.

"Like I said, all of Lathine is the same." Loshki went on to say, a few hours later.

I called out to him, from the comfort of my carriage. "Is this Hadia?"

"That it is, Leestel."

So far, it looked the same as Sohal. I took a long look around, and ended up noticing something peculiar.

"Why are we avoiding towns?" I said, "Why are the men splitting up?"

"'Don't want to take any chances. If we don't split up, border patrol could catch on to us."

"I see... all the more reason I shouldn't be leading this."

"There's something I'm meaning to tell you about that, Leestel."

"What's that?"

"Don't worry about it now, we'll get to it soon enough." Ominous...

"Just this one time, can we go through town?" I asked, "I want to see what Hadia is like."

"Fair enough."

We went through. Whereas buildings in Sohal were usually little more than sturdily built, the buildings in Hadia looked like art! People seemed to take pride in flowers, and banners that flew in a cool day's breeze. Players of instruments littered the streets, merry men flew left and right, and there wasn't a beggar to be seen; neither was there an excess of grime, or buildings soiled with rot and holes. Here I'd thought Sohal was incredible, and yet Hadia seemed twice as great!

When we stopped for the night, later on, only then did Loshki pull me aside.

"Keep this between you, me, and Miyune."

"Alright."

"Keras is rushing into this, there's gonna' be bumps in the mission."

"Great..."

"I'm not sure what Lady Miyune is after, but what she said to me is to make any changes I see necessary to your plan."

I sighed in relief. "Good, at least we have that going for us."

"Still, I'm not writing the whole mission out for you."

"Of course."

"Your safety comes before anything else. If you feel you need to run, or hide, then I need you to do that. I'm going to give you a pouch of supplies to hold onto, should the worst come to worst."

"Um... alright."

"We don't talk of this to Lord Keras. Lady Miyune intends for you to take all credit if we succeed, consider that a gift."

"Why?"

"I don't know."

...The town we'd passed through was no fluke; every town with the exception of our destination proved to be just as merry. It was a slap in the face when we arrived at our destination, which seemed to be one of the few fortified, military areas in Hadia. Seeing such a change in atmosphere was discouraging. No amount of heart and vigor could keep them from the truth; that they still had no choice but to be realistic, to build up defenses, prisons, and weapons of war.

"Lighten up, Milady. How many times do I have to tell you, 'least you have me?"

"I'll admit being a little weak-minded of late." I said, "It doesn't help I'm not a good tactician."

We walked through the shadows of night, to a great stone prison that stood nearby.

"*I'll admit,* this plan ain't half bad. You cut yourself short, Leestel."

I sighed, and only got a few words out. "You're just trying to-..."

His steps stopped cold, and a chill went down my spine. Was someone on to us? My own feet stopped, and I froze. Had something already gone wrong?

He looked to me, and I back at him. "Kea," he said, "it's time you learn to push fear from your head. What matters isn't failing, or succeeding; what matters is learning, and opening yourself to the prospect of failure. If you can't do that, then you'll never learn, and I know you're better than that."

I grinned, and couldn't stop... there was conviction in his words, and a certain warmth.

"It's all about controlling the only thing you can; yourself." I said.

"That it is."

"I understand... thank you, Loshki."

"I'm just doing my job."

A good metaphorical slap in the face always did me well. Loshki was right; as long as I made sure to play my own cards well, I'd be fine.

We lowered into the shadows, which gave the others a moment to prepare. With armor we'd looted from Hadian knights, our men worked their way into the jailhouse. It was a pretty big place, so hopefully they remembered the layout from out intel. In retrospect, that's something I should have had Loshki go over with them more. My plan was for them to feint as fresh recruits, which seemed to be working thus far. We didn't hear any screams, or clashing blades after they went in. That must have been good, right?

Ten minutes passed, and I thought nothing of it. Since the building was pretty big, it made sense awhile would pass before they came back out. Twenty minutes went by... and then the doors opened! Out came two knights, except not our own.

"Is this a good sign?" I asked.

"Too early to tell."

Twenty minutes turned into thirty, and the same thing happened. Up opened the doors, and out came two knights!

"We're sending in two more men." Loshki told me, "If something doesn't come of it, we're calling this off. I don't like this 'much as Keras does."

"I couldn't agree more, even I can tell something's not right."

Two more of our men went out, dressed in Hadian armor. They knocked, and were promptly let in.

"Is there something else I could've done?" I asked.

"Keras should've paid off a guard to kill the man for us. 'Don't think there's much different you could've done."

After another twenty minutes, two Hadian knights returned into the fortress. Five more minutes passed before those same knights came right back out. Loshki motioned to everywhere our men were hidden, then led me away.

"This is all wrong, we need to-"

A muffled scream hit our ears. Loshki shifted us under cover, dropped me to the ground, and pulled out steel. He spun to his left, and deflected a blow from a man I hadn't even seen!

Loshki choked the man into submission, and roared to the heavens. *"Attack!"*

He let go of the man, who fell down dead. Screams echoed through the night, along with the clink of metal! Sounds of pierced flesh, and draining blood met my ears. Loshki pulled me up, and then we ran away from the jailhouse. We ran within sight of the horses, and then something else came into view; a half dozen enemy soldiers! We were about to double back, when some of our own started to seep from the shadows.

Loshki kept his voice down, so the enemy wouldn't hear. "Secure the horses!" he said.

Both sides clashed, but rather than join in, Loshki chose to lead me safely along the outside.

Like always, there was a lone man that broke through. Loshki deflected a strike, socked the man in the face, then pierced him in the stomach. Loshki left the man to writhe in agony, and continued to lead me on. I hopped into the back of my carriage, then Loshki knocked the horses for everything they were worth.

I turned back to see our men diminishing, and one

enemy soldier in particular reigning supreme. Said soldier put a twisted feeling in my heart, because he was even larger than Loshki! In fact, drastically so! He held an *enormous* shield in one hand, a *gigantic* blade in the other; and was clad from head to toe in *thick* armor.

He was blocking off two of our men's way to the horses, so the two rushed together to try and bring him down. Hadia's largest knight blocked a swing with his blade, then skidded the other man away with his shield. In a cunning cross up, he struck at the second man with his sword, then smashed his shield into the first man, causing an explosion of blood. In turn, the second man gave up on fighting, and tried to rush past the Knight of Hadia! It turned out the giant's reach was too great, because he lunged out... and sliced through one of the man's legs. It never got any easier, hearing cries like what ensued. I turned away, thankful for how fast Loshki could lead horses.

"That man's a monster." I said to both myself, and Loshki.

"He's also an issue. Keras messed up, that's no ordinary knight!"

"Who is he?"

"A High Captain in the Hadian military. He's Mermadak; a solid tracker, a brilliant tactician, and an even better warrior!"

"Can you kill him?"

I didn't get a reply. He continued to push the horses harder than I'd ever seen before, which said enough. When I turned around next, I saw dozens of horses riding after us... some friends, and some foes. There was a forest, not far away. I wager if we could just make it to there, we'd be fine...

CHAPTER 16

We were deep in the forest when at last our horses came to a halt. In that moment, I was left with nothing but silence... and soft birdsong. I looked from the back of the carriage, to lush scattered greens, to the fallen trees of yesteryear, and to the mighty trees still standing that clustered every which way. A sparkle of white trickled from above, from a strong moon that illuminated the road around us. This was the first time I'd ventured into a forest, because Loshki had always led me around them in the past. Undefiled nature was quite the sight, I only hoped the beauty it held would survive the night; avoiding fragments of flesh, and crimson stains from what may yet follow.

Weighty footsteps made their way back to me. "We're taking a moment's rest." said Loshki, "Stay in the carriage, the enemy's still nearby."

"Shouldn't we keep pushing through?"

"'Easy for you to say, riding back there in comfort. A tactician has to consider all their men."

"What sort of men get tired from riding-... oh."

"That's right, Leestel. Anything living has to be seen to, don't forget that."

"I-..."

"No time for chitchat, stay there."

He walked away. I heard him get animated with some of our few remaining men. Heated words sent the birds to the heavens, leaving a blizzard of fallen leaves in their wake. I couldn't make anything out of the men's argument... until someone finally had a point to make.

"The Unsaid One will not be pleased!" a man yelled, "He'll kill us all!"

It sounded like Loshki struck the man... "Get a grip! He won't kill you, but 'don't get your act together now and Mermadak *will!*"

"What makes you think Nothaniir will be so understanding?" I heard someone say.

I think I got a hearing boost due to how piqued my interest was.

"Lady Miyune and Lord Keras will shelter us from him," Loshki said, "that's a guarantee."

"Fair enough... if you're sure they will, then I can't doubt."

Nothaniir? I hadn't heard that name since I'd pried that one man in Xadiir for information, during my first mission with Loshki. It seemed like what the man had told me was true; Miyu, and Keras, did in fact answer to the mysterious Unsaid One... Nothaniir. It was terrifying to think that there was a dark presence strong enough to bend Miyu to it's will.

Something faint went off... that's when the talking stopped. Footsteps echoed around, and the horses began to kick. We went on once more, with night as our veil, and harsh wind as our greatest adversary.

"Shouldn't we have lost them hours ago?" I called out to Loshki.

"We probably did, but even that doesn't mean we're safe. Give Mermadak a target, and there won't be rest 'till he's put it down."

"But how could they catch up to us!?!"

"It's unlikely, Leestel, but I wouldn't put it past them. They know the land better than us. "

Hearing him so pessimistic was off-putting. His bad karma was bound to hex us. Such pessimism proved to be well founded, and soon after, we heard screams from behind.

"Riders! Archers!"

Loshki hissed so loud you could hear him from the back of the carriage. He didn't take an impulsive action, and instead just kept going. He seemed to be taking one last shot at losing the enemy in the tree line. It's good we moved as fast as we did around the next corner, because Hadia had been moments from slewing us with arrows! Or perhaps, they had hit us after all... I felt the carriage slow down, and come to a halt. Had the arrows hit after all? Next thing I knew, Loshki was at the back of the carriage. He unlatched the tail, and pulled me out.

"To the bushes! Get down!"

I did what he wanted, and bolted.

"Keep south if I die!" he said, darting out to fight.

Loshki couldn't really die, could he? Him and Miyune were like gods, so just the thought of one being slain unsettled me. Being alone with someone as brutal as Mermadak was an ill thought, which meant I had no choice but to go south, try to fend off nature, and get back to Sciruthon, to Sehrea, if Loshki did die.

All the allies of Loshki, and all the men of Mermadak, were now on foot.

Arrows continued to fly, and weapons started to singe the air. Loshki didn't go after stray knights; instead, he set his eyes upon someone far more important. Mermadak's eyes looked to Loshki's with a fiery gaze of their own. It was no secret to anyone, I'm sure, just who the two captains at work were. Mermadak brushed off at his men, and in return they created a path for him. Loshki gave a haughty tilt of his head, and then his men did the same. Both groups were rather small, and about equal in numbers, so I'm sure Loshki knew he'd have to confront Mermadak sooner or later.

Mermadak and Loshki continued on the open road to one another, swords drawn. Tension got so strong that I could feel it running down my face. At long last, the great blade of Mermadak rose for the first strike! A shockwave rippled through the night, and Loshki let an enormous grunt. You could tell deflecting so much power even took the wind out of his sails.

Mermadak slung out fireworks, and Loshki started backtracking. Even I could tell Loshki was moving for the tree line, which must have been why Mermadak swung with such urgency. There was no way such a claustrophobic area would do someone as bulky as Mermadak any good. Loshki succeeded on his conquest to the tree line, albeit doing so didn't sway the flow of battle much. Every strike thrown was still coming from Mermadak's hands!

My footsteps after them were phantom-like. Loshki started sending off careful parries, but didn't dare to take the full openings he received. Mermadak seemed all too willing to take a bruise, if that meant getting Loshki within arm's reach. All that kept Mermadak from charging in was the neck aimed feints Loshki kept making. It wasn't until the trees died down, that fate chose which life it held dearer. Mermadak got Loshki out into an area with little plant life, and even fewer trees. What's worse, Mermadak kept inching closer to Loshki after every exchange.

Mermadak looked like he was about to put his shield to use on the offensive end. Loshki seemed to feel the same way, because he kept taking glances at Mermadak's shield hand. There was no way to disengage, and run, so Loshki bore down, and tried to blitz his way out! A succession of strikes shot from his hands like arrows. One of his swings even caught the giant, and nearly tripped him! Loshki used an opening created by the strike to land a hearty blow inside the protection of Mermadak's shield.

That would have been the end if Mermadak's armor wasn't so thick. Mermadak screamed, and then pushed right through the pain. Before Mermadak could retaliate, Loshki gave him a harsh elbow in the chest! Mermadak stumbled away, and Loshki followed him with a barrage of blows. Loshki stepped close, to get a savage blow on Mermadak's left thigh, and so a "clink!" ruptured the heavens. Mermadak, now off balance, decided to throw his weight forward! Another ear piercing "clink!" echoed, and again birds were sent cackling for safety. Thanks to good footing, Loshki managed to stonewall Mermadak's shield bash, albeit at the cost of having his blade sent skittering away.

Mermadak stumbled forward, and went for a life ending swing. If not for his only weakness, slowness, it would have worked. Loshki grabbed hold of Mermadak's wrist before the swing could be laid, then landed a left hook. Mermadak acted right away, and again slammed his shield forward! Loshki roared a scream that was as throaty, as it was pain induced. It was unbelievable how far he was sent!

I started rummaging around the forest floor, fast as I could. By the time Loshki could rise back up, Mermadak was already on top of him! Loshki had regained his sword, sure, but that was his only silver lining. Mermadak brought his shield high, then went to slam it down! Loshki acted quick, and propped the flat side of his blade on his left forearm. He pulled up to a knee for added power, but still got slammed to the ground when the shield fell. A blood curdling sound of metal against metal cursed the air. It was incredible to see Loshki live the exchange!

I crept around to the front of the fight, just in time to see Mermadak drop a quick swing from the hip. Loshki was forced to cushion the blow with the armor on his right wrist, because his sword had been blown away during the shield strike. That trick kept him alive, sure, but the blunt force trauma it brought looked unbearably painful. He would be forced to do it again when Mermadak went for the next blow... and even if the next strike wouldn't kill Loshki, I was sure it would seal his fate.

I jumped out of cover, and threw a stone as hard as I could! It made a sharp "thump!" against Mermadak's face. He staggered to a knee, and spat a vial of blood between his teeth. This forced him to throw up his shield, and try to get a grip on what had just happened. Loshki didn't reach for his sword; instead, he chose to scramble away, grab hold of me like a sack of potatos, and start booking it. His tattered breaths and winces of pain dominated my ears, but weren't loud enough to drown out the weight of Mermadak's steps. As quickly as the steps of Mermadak started, so they also ended; he was no fool, and well knew he didn't have a chance at catching us on foot.

For some hour, I got a good faceful of every green in the forest. We didn't stop until Loshki's breaths got so bad that I thought he was going to die. We hadn't heard anything since Mermadak gave up on us, so there was no reason to think rest wouldn't be alright. Everything had gone *dark* anyways, thanks in part to the monstrous trees that loomed above.

"That was brave, kid." Loshki panted out.

"I threw a rock in the dark, that's all it was."

"Doesn't matter." he said, still laboring, "I still owe you one, Captain."

"Thanks... I just hope Keras and Miyu are as positive when they hear we failed."

Loshki looked upset. "I've never failed her..." he hissed, not wanting to use Keras' rushing as an excuse.

"I guess this is just an average day's work for me." I said, "It's probably rare when I don't fail and upset her."

He seemed to find this amusing. "Then you'd be surprised, if that's how you really feel." he said.

...I wish he'd gone on more, but he didn't. Not demanding him to was one of the biggest mistakes of my life.

CHAPTER 17

Loshki's knowledge on survival was limitless. Things like slaughtering animals, starting fires, pitching shelter? Child's play! I enjoyed our time in the wild more than I probably should have, and lingered a bit longer than Loshki had intended.

Getting away from the mire of humanity was wonderful. I loved whistling winds, and the way they tickled through the trees. I loved the chirp of the cicadas, and the echo of rustling leaves high and low that blended together in melody.

I'd made sure to bring the pouch Loshki had given me, which gave us some extra food and water.

Several days passed. We stayed solely in the wilderness, until Loshki at last deemed a return to society safe. Even then, we only went in for what supplies we needed, and then we faded back into the wilderness.

Not long after, we ended up back in Sciruthon. When we got into Miyune's dining hall, Loshki's first action was to drop to a knee. Loshki didn't say a word, which told Miyune all she needed to know.

"Did I..." she began to say, "or did I not say this was not a thing to be rushed?"

"What do you mean?" Keras croaked, "Loshki! What happened!?!"

"I failed."

That was hardly the whole truth, so I looked to Keras,

who was now mortified.

"Our intel was inaccurate." I said, "More guards patrolled the city than should've, and High Captain Mermadak was also present."

"Mermadak!?! That-!"

Miyune cut Keras off. "There's nothing more to be said of it, love. What's done is done, now we must look to the future."

Lord Keras didn't have Miyune's ability to push emotion aside. His face was steaming red.

"Tell me something, Loshki?" Miyune said.

She seemed to find this all amusing.

"Yes, My Lady?"

"Did you get to fight him?"

"I did... if not for Lady Leestel's intervention, I'd be dead."

Lord Keras wasn't amused. "You tell me a *child* did what you could not?"

"I threw a rock from the shadows, before Mermadak could get a deathblow. There was nothing to it." I explained, "No matter who you sent, they would have fallen to Mermadak's blade."

Miyune giggled.

Keras got irked, and shot her an eye. "Is this so simple to you?"

"Yes, yes it is. Summon your best force and go to Hadia. You have no lack of time, so use it wisely."

"Yes," Keras muttered, "yes..."

Silence went by, and Keras started to think aloud. "I will go to Hadia. This will get ugly..."

"*Now*," Miyu said, "you have no other choice. Go, see to this."

Keras rose to his feet, and lost himself to thought yet

again. "I'll make preparations at once."

"Off now." Miyu waved, "Do not waste time, everything depends on this."

"So it does..."

Keras left the room with a sour look on his face. What could be dire enough to make someone as powerful as Keras worried? Could it be that he had to answer to the Unsaid One, Nothaniir? What had the man we'd been sent to kill know that could be so problematic?

Loshki bowed to Miyune. "My apologies."

She motioned for him to rise, and he did as so.

"This was not your failure, but the failure of Keras. Thus, now, it is his problem, and his alone. As for you, my faithful servant; you did as I asked, you protected my heir. I command you to go home, and rest. I command you to drown this event from your memory. I command you to be clear headed when I call upon you next."

"I thank you for your grace, My Lord."

Loshki left, and I wondered if Miyune had forgotten about me. She hissed under her teeth, took the glass she'd been drinking from, and hurled it across the room!

Once it shattered, a glistening array of pieces fluttered through the air. No doubts about it, she had a lot to vent! There was a bottle of wine at the table, so I decided to join her for a dr-... I mean, out of the goodness of my heart.

"What are you thinking?" I asked.

She didn't have an answer, which made me anxious. Maybe she wasn't so high and mighty after all... maybe these were the sorts of weaknesses that made her inferior to a *"Nothaniir"*, or someone of the sort. Still, it baffled me to think there could be anyone greater than her; that was just a thought I couldn't accept.

"Kea, what does life mean to you?"

"What does life mean to me?"

"If someone asked you what it meant to live, what would you tell them?"

Was she reaching out to me? No... no, she couldn't be. She had too strong of a will, she didn't need my help... right?

"It's about marking yourself with love." I said, "You can't fool yourself into thinking it isn't possible, or fool yourself into thinking you can't start a new trend. Good isn't a miracle; it's the product of each and every one of us. Kindness, true love, and the right thing, are *always* possible."

"Beautiful, Kea, but it's evident we have different understandings of life."

"How would you define it?"

"As a question for vindication."

She was... content to leave it at that. Instead, she filled another glass of wine. I left it at that too. There was no reason to think I could get anything out of her she didn't intend to say.

After a little while, I broke the silence... shattered it, really. "Marrying Keras is a part of your quest for vindication. I don't even think you like him, let alone love him."

"I respect you more than you could ever know, Kea. I know that sounds stupid, but it's true."

I wasn't sure what to say.

"Have you ever known true love?" she asked.

"True love?"

She grinned. "Sometimes I get lost, and wonder if such a thing exists. I wonder if any values exist."

"What you understand is the physical, the things you

forge by your own hand."

"Yes."

"That's understandable, that's most people. You shouldn't worry about good and bad, you should worry about living with a soft hand, and a kind heart. If you have faith, it'll all come to you in time. *Trust me.*"

She took another drink of wine. I don't think she knew what to say. It didn't seem like she even knew if she wanted to say anything. She was genuinely unsure, I could tell, I just wish I knew why.

"Would you sing a song?" she said.

I could tell that was a request, as opposed to an expectation, or demand.

"Of course..."

I opened my eyes, and began to sing.

"Ah naheo neh kahsahs neo meesh zahlah"

She looked sleepy...

"Ah rooiih lahsah gahme soo fah kehl liihreen"

Her father was a horrible man. I'd always had a level of sympathy for her, as a result.

"Soo fah ziih neh kahehn fiih ah sahn vliih fah beo"

I wonder how much she was hurting on the inside. Being too hurt to let others in really runs you down.

"Ah lahiih koh yaiih... ahn dkah zluh seev"

He'd beat Miyune's mother in front of her.

"Toorah fehl koh liihnaiih neo zahlahvah mohtah ohpreh"

Then he'd beat her too.

"Lahsah ehreen giihlan froolash npah giihlan ehreen rooiih."

Was Miyu asleep...? I'd zoned out while singing, and hadn't noticed her closed eyes until now.

She was slow to open her eyes. "Thank you, Kea." she said, "Please, go make something of your day. Do not let me keep you any longer."

"Alright... thank you, Miyu."

"No, thank you, Kea. Go have fun."

I did just that. I went to do what I thought would be the most fun in the world; seeing Sehrea. She must have been back by now... still, that thought wasn't reassuring. Only seeing her face would reassure me. I ran fast as I could to the inn she always stayed at. I went to the same old room of hers, and pounded it's door to no end.

"Sehrea...?"

"Sehrea?"

"Sehrea!"

"Sehrea!?!"

Floorboards creaked on the other side, and then the door opened. There she stood, good and well!

"I was beginning to worry." she said.

"About me? I've been too busy worrying about you!"

I entered the pitch black room, and hugged her tightly. She hugged me back, and then closed the door.

"How did it go with Lathimian?" I said.

"Wonderful. I really believe we can trust him."

"That's a relief to hear."

"Did you get our message from General Febrithien?"

"It was sort of hard to miss."

"Good. Anyways, things are getting serious for Muin-flor. Miyune and Keras' marriage irks them. They're not dumb, they know this is something to keep an eye on. Now that I went and spoke with Lathimian, who spoke with them, well, now they're going to act even sooner. Lathimian's going back to Muinflor soon, they're readying a force for him to investigate with."

"Really!?!"

"Yes, Kea. Lathimian wants us to go to Muinflor. We'll be safe there. I feel we should go."

I didn't know what to do anymore, because I was reluctant to leave Miyune. I sensed a lost soul, and wasn't sure if it was right of me to leave it alone.

Sehrea sensed how unsure I was. "Staying here is asking for fate's cold hand, Kea."

"I know..."

"Let's go..."

"Not yet."

"What's stopping you?"

"I-... let's, get into the last locked door. We should figure that out first, you know we can. It might mean all the difference for Lathimian, and Febrithien, and the King... and the whole nation."

"Kea-..."

"We have to, just this one last thing."

She nodded. "If that's how you feel, Kea, then I'll help you. I'll help you no matter what."

"Thank you."

Yes, we'd go after one last secret... because I needed all the time I could buy. I didn't know what to feel anymore. Selling Miyune off as nothing more than a witch just didn't feel right.

CHAPTER 18

"You called?"

I was surprised to see how casually Miyune had dressed today.

"I wanted to let you know I've sent Loshki away on another mission."

"Alright." I said, "I'm sure we'll be fine until he gets back."

"Of course."

I walked over to the table, and took a seat. An untouched bottle of wine stood beside her, which was weird to see. She fiddled around a fork that stood over some breakfast she'd hardly touched.

"Is there something else?" I asked.

"I will be gone for two, maybe three days as well."

"Ah? Is that so?"

"As for you," she said, "I want you to stay in Sciruthon. Rest, have fun, do whatever you'd like."

"That sounds wonderful, Miyu, thank you."

It seemed like there was something else she wanted to say.

"What is it?" I asked.

"Oh, nothing much... I was only thinking it would be nice to let go, and watch the clouds as I once would."

"That does sound fun."

"Would you like to join me, one more time?"

Just the thought touched my heart.

"Of course, that sounds nice."

First, like many moons back, we went and got treats. Afterwards, we went out to the plains. My heart was pulsing as badly as it had been when Mermadak was on our trail. I was distraught... just so very confused about everything I'd ever known, about everything I'd ever felt. Should I have trusted in my heart? My head? Sehrea, Miyune, Lathimian, Loshki? What should I have trusted in?

"Rabbit."

"Huh?"

"That cloud," she said, "it looks like a rabbit."

"It does! And that one, to the right... it looks like a horse!"

"Very good, Kea, very good."

Before we knew it, the sun had already made most of it's daily trek across the horizon. Clouds wisped together, and blocked out most of what light remained.

"I've always felt it tragic how fast these days of peace fleet away." Miyu said.

"I couldn't agree more... I enjoy talking with you about sweets, and silly things."

"Those are the only sorts of things a kid should have to worry about, Kea; in an ideal world, at least."

"I really do wish these sorts of days lasted longer..."

"This was always my favorite thing to do as a child, with my friends." so Miyu said, "Time flies, it's the one thing I can't will to my fist."

My eyes turned to her. You could tell she really did enjoy this. A soft smile was on her face, and her attention was solely on the heavens. While looking to her, I caught sight of an emerald green necklace she always kept tucked inside whatever she was wearing. It was a run down old thing, and yet, she *always* wore it. She *always* concealed it, so rarely did you ever get this good of a look at it.

"Miyu?" I said.

"Yes, Kea?"

"If you don't mind my asking, what's so special to you about that necklace?"

She pulled it out, and looked to it as if it were pure crystal. In reality, it was nothing more than a standard, cheap, emerald green necklace.

"Don't mind me," I said, "if it's something you don't want to talk about."

She chuckled, sighed, and then smiled. "I-... fret not, Kea. This was simply my mother's. It's the last thing I have to remember her."

"You loved your mother?"

"Yes, very much so... How I wish things could have been different for her. Truth be told, she would have had a better life had I never existed."

"I'm sure it can't be that bad."

She sighed, and then looked back to the heavens with desperate eyes. "I'm sorry to say you are wrong, my dear. My birth took my mother down a path worse than death. I wish more than anything that I'd never come along, and that she could have had her happily ever after."

"You give her a happily ever after by living the life she would have wanted you to live. You're very fortunate to have a parent that truly loved you..."

She turned to me, reached out, and started to take gentle strokes across my face.

Her soft hand was relaxing to feel, but at the same time, unsettling. Touch was something that I was still trying to come to grips with, because I'd been so used to getting beaten back in the labyrinth.

Keeping my emotions in check was something I'd increasingly been having problems with. I turned away from Miyune, and let out a few anxious tears.

Figures she knew what I was hiding... She sat up, pulled me up, and then wiped away my face.

"I am here for you," she said, "I really do mean it."

How could I ever trust her? How could I ever know if it was okay to trust her? How could I even know if it really was okay to trust Sehrea? Everything continued hitting me at once. I clenched my teeth, and did my best to stop tearing up. Miyu put her arms around me, and held me close; as a mother does to her child.

Who knows how long went by, until I finally pulled myself together? There wasn't a single fiber of my being that wanted to pull from Miyu's grasp; in the end, it was her who pulled away. She wiped away my face one last time, pulled my chin up with a finger, and then smiled at me.

"Please forgive me for bringing such thoughts to mind, Kea. Shall we go back to watching the sky?"

I nodded. You always knew you'd had a good vent when your eyes were so rotten with tears that they'd started to burn. I laid back yet again onto the cushion that was nature. We went back to talking, and making shapes of the clouds overhead.

Shades of blue soon faded into orange and red, and then shades of orange and red led way to blacks and purples.

"I love the dark of night, nowadays." Miyune said.

"What draws you to the night so?" I asked.

"The fact it's a reminder."

"A reminder?"

"Yes, it's a reminder to rest for the day to come, and keep fighting. Sunset works in tandem; it works to show the majesty of what might be attained with the will of your own two hands."

"That's a nice way of thinking of it. I-..."

We heard footsteps from behind. "Greetings, My Lady. Preparations have been seen to."

Miyune nodded, and so the knight of her guard left. "I guess I must be off then." she said.

My head throbbed, and flamed. What should I have said, what should I have done? Even in the moment, I knew I'd miss out on something if I didn't speak up, and pour out my heart.

"I appreciated this time with you, Kea." she said.

"T-thank you... I had fun too."

She walked on. Every time I tried to call out to her, my throat went soundless. I guess I was too scared to care, too scared to trust... too *stupid* to act with my heart. In retrospect, I'd have given anything to go back to this moment. If only I'd been a better person, things could have been different, *so much different,* for *everyone.* I continued to watch the sky, until after what she called *"sunset".* Only then did I return to the palace.

Attendants swarmed me when I entered. "Please ask of us anything you need," they said, "especially while Lady Miyune is gone."

"She already left?"

"Yes, and Sir Loshki too."

"Alright, thank you."

I'd probably never get another chance like this. I left the palace, and went out to Sehrea's inn. I found her in the same old room as always.

She yawned, and chirped a little smile. "This is a surprise to be sure, but a welcome one."

"I'm sorry, did I wake you?"

"Please don't worry on my accord." she said, yawning again, "You seem on edge. What brings you here, Kehah?"

"Miyune, Keras, and Loshki, all left for different tasks. All three are long gone."

This snapped her tire away. "Is that so?"

"It is. I've already instructed Miyune's attendants to take an early night's rest, so this is the *perfect* time for us to take Loshki's key, and act."

"Yes... it's possible we'll never get another chance like this."

"Right! That's what I'm saying!"

Darkness was in full bloom. We skittered out to Loshki's home like two black cats. Sehrea led me to the back of Loshki's home, which looked like a garbage center!

"Do we break in the back door?"

She shook her head, and started moving garbage.

"We go down here." she said, uncovering a hole, "It's a crawlspace that leads under the home."

"Alright, then let's do it."

Again, she shook me off. "There would be no good reason for two to go. Stay here."

"Alright."

I let her go down, and do her thing. Soon after, the back door opened.

"See?" she said, "Nothing to worry about."

I smiled, and entered Loshki's home. There's no doubt in my mind Miyune paid him well, so I was surprised to see how practical he was. His house had no flair to it at all; in retrospect, I shouldn't have been shocked, given that's just the sort of person he was. While I was busy being awed, Sehrea worked her way into the kitchen. She opened a pantry door, pushed aside a heavy bag of flour, and reached into a small hole behind it. Out came a key!

"It's really that simple?" I asked.

She let a soft smile. "It really is."

We moved through town, quick as we could, up to the palace's wall.

"Kea?"

Her words had caught me last second. I skidded to a stop, and turned back to her.

"Yes?" I said.

"You said everyone is gone, right?"

"Yes, do you think they're not?"

"No, I bet they are... that's why I'm curious about something."

"What's that?"

"Would it matter if I went in with you?"

That request surprised me, it was an idea I'd never considered.

"I don't see why not." I said, "Actually, if you wanted to, I'd really like that."

"Like I said; that room you'll go into must be dark. Something about it doesn't sit right with me, so I want to be there with you."

I hugged her, and smiled. "Thank you, Sehrea."

"Of course. I'm here for you, I mean it."

I'd sure been hearing a lot of that lately... Together, we went up to the guards at the gate.

"Ready to go back in?" one asked.

I nodded. "Yes, I am!"

They let me in, and paid Sehrea no mind. They just thought she was a friend of mine, I guess.

"It looks even greater up close..." she said of the palace, when we got into the courtyard.

"It's funny you say that, because it feels twice as great once you actually get in."

Sehrea proved to be much better than me at keeping level headed. Once we got into the palace, she didn't stop, or get dazed with awe once! Miyune's home was incredible, which made that all the more impressive. We pilfered a candle on the way, lit it, and then ended up at the locked door soon enough.

"I don't like this, something isn't right." she said, biting her lips.

"I know..."

Sweat dripped down my little fingers. I put the key in, twisted, and ere flew a foul air. I creaked the door open, *very* slowly open.

"I can't see a thing!" Sehrea remarked.

"Neither can I."

There *literally* was no light to work with in there!

"I think we should go back. Let's go to Muinflor, and let Lathimian figure this out."

"Not when we've come so close..."

I took the first pair of steps into the abyss, and Sehrea followed right beside me. We couldn't make out any more than the steps that laid before our feet.

"I've never felt this anxious in the dark." I said.

"Me neither..."

This place was like one of the dungeons back home. I felt unwell when I made the connection, and started to get dizzy. My headache was worsened by a noxious, moldy smell, that only got greater with every step we took into the dark. It was unthinkable such a lightless, grimy, smelly place, could be hidden in Miyune's palace.

After a little while, I heard Sehrea's footsteps stop.

I looked back to her. "What's-...?"

That's when I realized how far down we'd walked. Now, you could barely see the top!

"I don't like this." Sehrea said.

"I don't either..."

It felt like we were just saying the same things over and over again. That was just our way of venting fear, I guess.

"We don't have to do this." she squeaked.

"I know... but I can't help myself. I have to know what she's hiding."

My vision started working magic, thanks in part to the candle Sehrea held. At long last I saw something... a certain faint light at what appeared to be the bottom. I heard Sehrea take an anxious gulp; it was good to know she saw it too, and that I wasn't just crazy. My feet were heavy as lumber, so it was hard to keep my footsteps going. Still, where there's a will, there's a way. I dared not go to the light, and yet here I found myself, getting closer, and *closer...* I couldn't imagine going any further alone. If not for Sehrea's presence to keep me calm, I would have broken down and fled. Regardless of whatever I pretended to be, or acted like... I really was just a little kid, in a big, big world.

Down, past the steps end... something laid near a candle. Sehrea threw a hand onto my shoulder; if not to protect me, then because it made her feel better. I couldn't even swallow my saliva right... it barged hard down my throat. I took hold of the hand on my right shoulder, and held it firm. We continued down... slow, and steady. It looks like I was a true fool, after all, because I'd just had to doubt Miyune, and walk down into that cursed place.

I turned back, and looked to whence we'd came... you

couldn't even see the top of the stairs anymore! All I could make out was Sehrea's fiery silhouette, and the candle at the bottom.

Again, Sehrea stopped in her tracks. "Kea?" she said, with a quivering tongue.

"Yes?"

"Loshki left early this morning."

"Right."

"That means the key to here was sitting in his house for half a day, at the least."

"Yes, naturally..."

"Then who lit that candle?"

I couldn't help but squeeze the life out of Sehrea's hand. We both went dead still, locked our eyes into the distance, and tried to make out what laid near the candle. Little by little the pieces came together; what rested near the candle was a man! I couldn't tell whether the man was asleep, comatose, or nothing more than a dead corpse. We worked our way to the bottom of the steps. Now, I could tell the figure was in chains; the chains looked to be so tight that I assumed the man had already died of poor circulation. His wrists and legs were covered in ghastly purple stains.

Sehrea's voice echoed. "The passageway goes even further..." she said.

I looked beyond the man. Turns out, Sehrea was right, the passageway did go on further!

First thing's first. *"Hello?"* I called.

Sehrea's grip on my shoulders was borderline painful.

"He... llo?" I said again.

"Are you... alive?"

"Hello!?!"

It seemed like the man was dead. In the midst of my

first step down the passageway, he suddenly twitched! I shrieked, while Sehrea jumped.

"Sir, are you... going to live?"

He ceased to move anymore. A knot warped my stomach. A pain laden groan met our ears, which I recognized as the indistinguishable sound from many moons ago. My eyes shifted, and took a look back at whence we'd came. Even with adjusted eyesight, I still couldn't see the top! *I couldn't see it!*

Sehrea jumped, which caused me to spin back around. I saw the figure begin to arise; it's movements were beyond slow. This moment was when fear took me... the one that zaps your strength, and makes your body disobey you. We watched the living dead rise in a painstaking manner. None of it's bones rose right. Every move it made was accompanied by a bestial cry, or soft whimper. It's face turned to me... and I swear time itself halted. My heart exasperated at the face I saw, and my blood fumed. When time returned to it's proper place, something other than shock and fear took hold of me; anger, *raw* anger.

"Miracle Maiden!" he cried.

CHAPTER 19

"Miracle Maiden!" he cried again, "By Darotho, spare thy servant!"

Darotho was no ordinary name... it was the name of my father, the reigning king of the lost people. This man before Sehrea and I was none other than my father's old advisor. He looked as drained as anyone I'd ever seen, and just as thin!

"Miracle Maiden! Save-...!"

I didn't let him finish. I lashed forward, and kicked him back.

"Your days of lying are over and done!"

Sehrea grabbed me before I could lunge forward again. I tried to break from her grip, but she was too strong.

She spit coarse words into my ear. "Kea, we need answers! Trust me!"

I snarled, and tried to breathe. "Alright... alright."

Sehrea turned to the advisor. "What do they want?" she said.

My blood boiled. I couldn't keep calm like her. She took a strong grasp on my shoulders, and moved me behind her.

Our father's old advisor clamored to his knees, and came up with lifeless words. "I was brought here before even you, Kehah."

I couldn't contain myself any longer. "What would they want with a-...!?!"

"Kea!" Sehrea shushed.

"What do they need from you?" she said to him, "What do they need from us?"

"They keep me for the same reason they keep you two; because we make valuable hostages. When did they take you, Sehrehah Gehnahdiihneh?"

"I left on my own accord."

"The demons will find you, Sehrehah Gehnahdiihneh. If you would only let thy servant free, we could return in peace. Let the thinking of demons control you no longer, you-..."

I shrieked. ***"Peace!?!"***

"Let's speak of that no more." Sehrea said, to the both us.

"They made you..." the advisor said, "the Miracle Maiden in her wake, didn't they?"

Sehrea had no reply; the fact he knew such a thing without being told infuriated me, he must have thought he was *oh so* smart!

"None of that matters. Now, I would like you to tell me what happened, *that* day." she said, "Do you know anything I've yet to learn? That's what I'm wondering."

"They... killed the portal guards, then the strong man with hair the shade of death led by stealth. He killed my guards, one after another. Almost single-handedly, Death took them. He beat me for knowledge. I gave him the most valuable thing I could in exchange for my life... if this is even a life, anymore."

"You gave them Kea?"

"Correct."

After all those years of tormenting me, it looks like he'd finally done something right. His selfishness had freed me from the world of nightmare. His words also made me realize just how dangerous Loshki was. I couldn't imagine how *anyone* could fight their way into my world, and come out alive with the Miracle Maiden in tow, no less! That said something.

The advisor crawled towards us, and we got to see what had become of him. His arms, and legs, were little more than bare bone at this point; if you said there was still flesh and skin on them, you'd only be technically right. None of the decrepit, tortured, starved people back home, could hold a candle to what my father's old advisor had become. He could have fallen dead at any moment! It made me squirmish to know Miyune and Loshki could be as brutal as *anyone* back home.

His bones crunched as they slid against the coarse brick floor. Now that he moved closer into the light... you could see what had become of his fingers. Some were void of flesh, now nothing more than raw, defiled bone.

Crunch, crunch...

He continued to work his way towards us. His hands bled as he did so.

Crunch, crunch, crunch...

I wasn't happy, I wasn't sad... I wasn't anything. All I knew is that I wanted to watch him struggle, because I'm sinful. After all the beatings, after everything... how couldn't I want to watch him struggle, here, at his end? How couldn't I want to watch true karma unfold?

He stopped. I guess he was spent of energy. Desperation rang in his eyes, along with the last bit of his life that lingered. I was about to give a crazed laugh, but that was before he crawled beside the candle, and caught it's full shine. I got to see just what had become of his face. I wailed, and stumbled back. Two holes sat where his eyes had once been.

"I am a creature of the dark." he said, "That's all I am."

This man *really, really* could die at any moment. I tried to calm down, and gather information.

"***Tell me...*** just tell me-"

He cut me off. "I am a creature of the dark... servant to the King. The blonde woman will not have my loyalty, she will not buy us out as an army."

"An *army?!?*" I choked.

Sehrea broke in. "Please, tell us-"

The advisor cut her off. "Neither will she buy my truths... and neither will you, you disgusting **wrenches!**"

I almost vomited out of anger. I didn't care what confusion wrapped around the head of whoever found him... or even if it led back to me in the end. I didn't care anymore! Enough was enough! I leapt forward, intent on doing something no human should ever have to do; kill. All the abuse ended here! Forget morals, forget answers, forget anything worth caring about, I was done with all of it!

I skidded across the ground, and lunged forward. I was a step from putting my hands around his throat, when I saw his own hands fly up... no, not his hands; his claws. His finger nails had grown disgustingly long, well, at least, which of his fingers hadn't been beaten down to the bone. His fingers that were nothing but bone, he'd sharpened like knives. I threw my hands up, so I could grab his wrists before he could stab me, and then... I zoned out.

What was the thing I was feeling? Something hot was gushing on me, something that burned like sunlight. It was blood, I think. I guess my head was keeping me from getting scared about bleeding out. I guess I was afraid to die after all. Sehrea pulled me away, and I came to.

Wait... I wasn't bleeding, the blood on me wasn't my own, and it clearly wasn't Sehrea's.

Cries began unlike anything I'd ever heard. Within a terrifying, dim hole of horrors, there I was, with one of the greatest traumatizers I'd ever known. Here was a man that would terrify me to no end back home, and even find his way into my nightmares all the way out here. Now his eyes were gone, replaced with darkness and smeared blood; even some of his fingers were gone, replaced with gangly, sharp bone. Despite everything, despite all of it, he managed to top it all, one last time...

He cried out in pain. His demented screams only got more horrific as he did his deed.

He was...

He...

was...

ending... his life...

by clawing out his throat.

Blood deluged all over. Frozen in shock, the only thing that kept me on my feet was Sehrea's guidance. I couldn't move, I couldn't even close my eyes. Despite how much I tried, I couldn't do anything! From mere feet away, I got to see everything, *everything,* that spewed from inside the advisor.

Sometimes everything hurts so bad you can't cry, other times you cry so hard that you can't do anything but keep crying. Yet some times still, you ended up where I was now. I cried as hard as I could, and screamed as loud as I could... but no sound left my lips, and I *still* couldn't move.

Sehrea was just as motionless. We watched as he kept doing the deed. I don't know how he was alive at this point, and whether it was by freak luck, or demonic might. He started to scream, and convulse, at the realization death wasn't reaching him. I could only imagine what sort of shock gripped him. He must have expected this to be a quick and easy way out...

I couldn't stop shaking. In fact, I'd never shook so hard in my life. How Sehrea kept so still was beyond me. My shaking got *even worse* when he took his claws, and delved into his own chest. Blood popped like a balloon, and squirted out to us. His face crushed into the ground, leaving another pool in it's wake. At long last he was dead... stone cold dead. I thought I was about to die from shock, because I fell to my knees, my stomach churned, my vision rolled, and my eyes shut...

I couldn't have been out any longer than a few seconds. "...Kea? Kea!?! KEA!"

Sehrea pulled me back to my feet, and that's when I heard it; deep throated wails from further down the hallway. I shot more soundless screams. Sehrea yanked me to the stairs.

Someone, something, **was with us.**

A pair of footsteps echoed from down the hallway, and that's when my feet failed me. I fell into a panic. Sehrea grabbed me as tight as she could, and started to drag me up the stairs...

CHAPTER 20

Something was with me...

My shaking got worse with every tenth of a second that passed. No light was reaching my eyes, so I must have still been in the abyss, right? Where was Sehrea? I tried to scream, but still couldn't. My head hurt, and confusion ruled me. I couldn't make anything out, and went into a full on panic.

God help me. What on Lathine was going on here!?! I couldn't cry, all I could do was shake. I wasn't sure what I should have tried to do, since I couldn't see. *Did I still have my eyes!?!* I was moments away from giving up, and trying to claw my own throat out.

A voice fell over me, "Kea...?", and put it's arms around me, "KEA!?!"

Sehrea? She continued to shake me, but I wasn't sure why. It took a good minute for something to break the darkness around me, and that something was my sanity. I opened my eyes, gasped out, and must have been an awful sight. Saliva was running down my chin, snot was running down to my lips, and my entire face was wet with tears. At long last I'd completely snapped.

"You're good, you're safe." she said, holding me tight, "It's alright."

We were in... my room! I staggered away, fell to the ground, and tried to breath. My tongue abandoned me, and all that came from my lips was gibberish.

"Calm down, calm down... it's alright, Kea, calm down, just breathe."

She put her arms around me, and gave me time.

"That wasn't worth it..." I said, with words like a whisper.

"No, no it wasn't."

"What on Lathine," I panted out, "was down there with us?"

She shook her head. "I didn't stick around long enough to find out."

"Good call."

Getting back to my feet was difficult, my nerves had shattered my strength. "Let's go..." I choked out.

"There's no need to ru-..."

"No, Sehrea, we need to go. I have to go. I can't do this anymore."

She came to my side, and kept me steady. "Then that's what we'll do. Lathimian will be happy to see us."

"I hope so."

My heart continued to beat like thunder, my footsteps were still heavy as stone. Sehrea had to help me out of the palace. She let go once we got into the courtyard, and I began to walk by my own strength. I didn't want to give the guards any impression something was wrong. We pushed out of the courtyard, and moved to the shadows, where Sehrea was quick to take hold of me again. She helped me out to her inn, and into the horses' stable that accompanied it. On the inside rested her horse; a beautiful dark steed by the name of Lolagis. Before leaving town, we rode Lolagis to Loshki's house, returned his key, and locked up. We didn't want to give Miyune and Loshki anymore reason to go after us than they already had, hence why we thought it made sense to return the key.

There wasn't much to note of our travel to Muinflor. It went smooth, and we managed to avoid getting lost. In fact, we didn't lose our way once! Combined, Sehrea and I had almost all of Sohal memorized, so I wasn't surprised.

...From far away, we saw towers that touched into the sky, and a tall stone wall. Sehrea kicked up Lolagis into going even faster, and put his raw speed on full display. A trail of green blades fluttered in our wake.

Right on the verge of the gate, I cried out. "This place is colossal!"

We hopped off Lolagis, and Sehrea pointed to a structure in the distance. It was incredible how prominent in view the structure was, despite being a long way's away!

"What on Lathine is *that!?!*" I said.

"It's the great arena of Muinflor. That's where the Yearly winners compete every year, for the honor of being crowned champion of the year, and a legend for all time."

"I'd kind of like to see inside..."

Honestly, I didn't know much about the Yearlies. All I knew is that they were the one event greater than the Legions.

"Me too." Sehrea said, "Maybe we can go to this year's tourney."

I smiled at the thought. "That sounds nice... I'd like to, if you really want to."

"Of course. I'm good with whatever you'd like to do, Kea."

Two guards met us at the gate. Before I could think about what to say, Sehrea led the way with a persona.

"We went out to explore," she said, with a solemn energy, "but we can't remember which door we went out from. Can we please come back in this one?"

"Of course, young one." said an older knight.

He had a soft smile, and seemed to feel bad for us.

"Do you two need any help getting back home?" the other asked.

Again, Sehrea took charge. My mouth was left wide open, wordless. It was nice not having to take action.

"We can find our way back. Thank you."

"No problem."

They opened the gate, and I got my first look at Muinflor. I wanted to say it was great... but that wouldn't have been the right word; it was like Hadia, is what it was like. Roads shimmered, houses had flavor, merchants were laid about, and well dressed people moved every which way. Even animals took solace in a place like this! Stray cats threw me happy eyes, dog's rested under a kind day's sun, and horses went merrily on their way. Unlike the rest of Sohal, everything, and I mean *everything* here, was in good order.

Sehrea took me by the hand, and led me on. My memory of routes ran out at this point, so we were fortunate Sehrea had a better memory than I. We followed an endless road. Not long after, something arose in the distance. Not one rooftop could be seen that was great enough to drown out what we saw! We ended up walking around a house, and it was there that our path ended. We found ourselves before the great castle of none other than Lord Neromas himself! It had to be!

"This is really where Lathimian wanted us to go?"

"Yes, Kea. He says King Neromas wants a word with us, and that we'll be safe with him for the time being."

Getting to meet a king had no effect on me, which

made sense. I was a princess after all; not just a princess, but the revered, foretold, *"Miracle Maiden"*. It's not like I didn't have status of my own. I didn't feel particularly special just because of a title, which is why meeting other people with high titles or power didn't nerve me. On the other hand, marvelous buildings, and beautiful plains? Things like those always made me drop my guard. I gawked at the castle of the King, while Sehrea approached the guards.

A guard spoke before she could. "Seh... Seh?"

"Sehrea."

"Ah, yes, that's it! You'll be happy to hear Lathimian is in the building as we speak."

Sehrea turned to me, lighting with a rare burst of energy. "Did you hear that, Kea?"

"I did," I said, "that's good!"

The guards opened the gate, and one of them led us into the courtyard. I was surprised to see how plain the King's own courtyard was! It was just a blank slate of dirt, a little stable... and a door in the near left corner that led underground. My inner adventurer was *begging* to get inside the door, to see what King Neromas could be holding underground. That would have been an awful risk to take, of course, but the idea was still inticing. Oh... also, there was a brilliant staircase up into the castle, which served as the one elegant thing the castle had going for it. It was pure marble, and shimmered like starlight. It looked so out of place, that staring at it for too long gave you a headache!

We walked up the steps, and into the castle. The inside was how you would have expected from the outside; simple, but powerful. It's flooring was a thin wood with loads of glimmer, and there was some decorations on the walls, every now and again, but that was about all to note. Our guide led us to a door that stood parallel to the one we'd entered in. He motioned into the door, Sehrea thanked him, and then we entered. What we saw was a room much like Miyune's dining hall. At the room's end sat a handful of men.

A familiar, short haired, dark blonde man arose. "Theeeeere's my favorite two people."

Sehrea smiled, which was odd to see. "It's good to see you too."

We walked over to him, and he to us.

"Done with Miyune, Kea?"

"Now I am."

"'Figured you would be soon. 'Been there, done that, wouldn't rate very highly."

I didn't bother to hide my true being; whether from him, or the others around the table.

"Tell us what breeds that glare, child." a man said to me.

He sat at the end of the table, and bore piercing eyes. His elbows were up on the table, and his hands were webbed in front of his face.

"Miyune." I said, "She'll sink every last one of us if something isn't done."

"Grim words, for grim times." so said the same man.

He wasn't a ray of sunshine, that was for sure.

Lathimian nudged me, and motioned out to the man. "This is your lord and savior, his highness, Sir Neromas."

Lathimian looked nonchalant. His joking voice made me wonder if he was being serious or not.

"Is it really?" I asked.

Lathimian wouldn't joke around if it really was King Neromas, right?

In turn, the man glared at him. "Thank you for your method of introduction." he said, turning to me, "It's true I am king. Now, I ask that you uphold your fierce demeanor, child. I prefer it to that of *someone else's,* who we shall not name."

A few men at the table had little grins. They all seemed rather comfortable being themselves, which I liked. I walked up and took a seat.

King Neromas's gaze stayed upon me. "Tell me your story, child, I must know."

I began to tell him... I started with the day I'd been abducted by Loshki, and worked my way to the present.

CHAPTER 21

I finished my tale, and set my eyes back on King Neromas. His hands were still glued in front of his face. His eyes were still cutting like sharpened steel.

"What of your life before this," the King asked, "before what you refer to as the *'World of Unraveling'*?"

I felt heated when I thought of the past. I hated to think of the people that had ruled me. They'd controlled everything about me; from my actions, to my dress, and all the way down to the very emotions I was allowed to feel. They'd expected every fiber of my soul to be in union with them, and nothing less.

"Is there even a point to what I say? I'm sure Sehrea has already told you everything she could."

"That she has, but she is not the Miracle Maiden."

"What do you know of it?"

King Neromas dropped his hands, and we stayed locked, eye to eye. "I was trained well as a child, by my father. He raised me with knowledge, and so, at hearing *Miracle Maiden,* my memory brought me to history. There is a prophecy that faded deep into the dark."

"Do you know it, any of it?"

It turns out, he did...

"Ere will come our miracle, ere will come she.

She is death, death to the enemy.

We have been banished, we who have vanished, will return to kill ah meo ghen.

By her, we will avenge the fallen.
To her, sight will be befallen.
Praise and worship be to the savior.
May fate bless the Miracle Maiden."

I wasn't sure what to say. I'd learned long ago there was a written prophecy concerning the Miracle Maiden, so that part didn't surprise me; it's just that my father would never recount it to me, and I'd never imagined anyone else could know what it said. A silence ensued, which only Sehrea dared to break.

"The king of our people is crazed."

I nodded. "It's not about any real savior," I said, "it's about a figurehead. As long as they can hold me on a pedestal, as so-called *'proof of truth'*, the people will believe everything they're told. They'll follow the *'prophecy'* to whatever end."

"Precisely." said King Neromas, "Thirivu, the deriver of the prophecy, thousands of years passed, knew this to be true. Despite being on the verge of death, he would not accept failure. He gave all the tools your line of kings could ask for to one day accomplish the destruction of Lathine; doctrine, and signs."

"That doesn't explain everything." Sehrea said, "Our people have lived in the dark for many, *many* years... a century at least. Granted, I don't know how long they've lived for, or their origins. Why wait until now?"

"It seems because our luck is just that bad." a man at Neromas' right hand said, "We need to act, or else everything that can go wrong will. If we don't act now, we're only shooting ourselves in the foot. Reach out to Clarje, Neromas, be strong, dare to fail, give everything we can."

"It seems we've no other choice, General Tranel."

"I'm happy to see you finally agree." Sehrea said.

"I'll begin preparations immediately." another man said, who seemed intent on acting before King Neromas could change his mind.

"So be it." said the King.

In turn, the man that had previously spoken looked to Lathimian.

"I'll get with you later, Arsaphi." Lathimian said.

"Will you have me going too?" asked General Tranel.

"No," King Neromas said, "stay in Muinflor. I may have need of you."

King Neromas waved off at the handful of people around the table. "That will be all," he said, turning to Lathimian, "save for you."

Everyone he'd waved off at left, except for Sehrea and I. King Neromas didn't seem to care. In fact, he seemed to have expected as much. We were a three for one deal, by the looks of it.

"I'll turn a blind eye to my own thoughts," said the King, "and allow you what freedom you see fit."

Lathimian looked over Neromas' head while replying. "I'll do all I can."

"I will keep General Tranel for now, but send him out to negotiate with King Clarje if needed, and consider going out myself, to meet Clarje, if I must."

"I don't think it'll come to that." Lathimian said, "I'm on good terms with Hadia. Arsaphi and I will be fine, but still, I'm happy to hear you feel that way."

"This is not about my own thoughts, or feelings. Now, it's about what we're forced to do. What of the children?"

Lathimian put his eyes above Sehrea's head. "You two will stay in Muinflor, peacefully. That's still your wish?"

"Ye-..."

I cut her off. "Take us with you."

"I agree." said the King.

"Who's to say whether or not there's something we know, that you'll need?" I said, "Especially if you chance upon our people, or the way to them. You could need us."

"Thought about that," he admitted, "but I'm not concerned. I'd rather you two stay in Muinflor, away from Miyune's grip."

"I agree with Lathimian." Sehrea said, "We should let the professionals do their work."

"We should help in any way we can." I said.

"Let the children do as they will." King Neromas ruled.

Lathimian clicked off one side of his mouth, and looked to Sehrea.

"I am bound to whatever Kea wishes." she said.

"Alright... then they'll go with me." Lathimian said to the King.

"Worry not, Lathimian." uttered the King, "Your company will be great, the children's safety is assured."

I hoped that would be true... but whether or not it was, I still didn't want to leave Lathimian's side.

"Anything else for now?" Lathimian asked.

"No." said the King, "Go, bring us victory amidst a time of failure."

"I'll try."

...We woke at sunrise the next day. Lathimian led us through town, and we exited one of the gates to the north. On the outside, we saw a few dozen plain dressed men. They must have been garbed for undercover work. Among them was one of the men from yesterday. What was his name... Ar, Ar-something?

He looked to Lathimian, then to us, then back to

Lathimian. "New development?"

"Funny you mention that."

"And why's that, Lath?"

"Weeeeell, because I was hoping you could chaperone them while we're on our little adventure. You'll thank me later."

Arsaphi turned to us. "Then it's my pleasure to serve you two. My name is Arsaphi, and you can call upon me whenever you need."

His eyes were sincere, like Lathimian's. There was good people out there after all, which was something I'd never believed could be true. I'd always been taught no such thing could be true, yet? These so-called *vile people* were so much better than my own. All who did not side with my people, my father deemed vile.

Was it possible he was right, and the knights of Muinflor were evil? Could it be possible they were just using Sehrea and I? No... no, that couldn't be the case.

My people's beliefs had bred me to doubt the outside world. It made sense I was still having problems trusting. At least, deep down, I knew all the doubts I had of others wasn't from my head; my doubts were just the product of a paranoia that had been pushed upon me.

Lathimian walked off towards the other men, but as for Arsaphi, he stayed with us. A chuckle left Arsaphi's lips; he crossed his arms, then turned to us.

"We will do our best to not be a nuisance." Sehrea said.

Arsaphi grinned. "No, it's not that, it's just Lathimian. Believe it or not, I'm above him in rank."

"And he just gave you an order?" I said, amused.

"Seems he did."

Arsaphi took his sights to the company, and scoured it. "Breovit!" he finally called out.

In turn, a clean headed man rushed over. "What do you need me for?" he said, "Just name it."

Arsaphi slapped Breovit on the shoulder. "I need your focus for the venture to be on the safety of my friends here; Sehrea, and Kea."

Sehrea nodded low to Breovit. "We will try not to be a burden."

"I appreciate your protection." I told him.

His energy pierced away at the seriousness Sehrea and I had, which eased our spirits. "Don't worry about it. You two just got me out of scavenging duty, I'm the one who should be thankful."

"You feel good about following on horse?" Arsaphi said to us, "Or can I extend you a hand?"

"Rest easy, that'll be the last thing you have to worry about." Sehrea said.

Arsaphi gave Lolagis a good petting. "Good, good... adventure's upon us, steel yourselves."

Adventure... I'd always been infatuated with stories of the sort. They'd given me hope through the darkest points in my life. I think this was the first time I realized how many adventures I'd tallied for myself; not that any of it mattered, if my ending was a bad one. History, stories, and tales, were more times than not told of victors, for victors. As for the fallen, more times than not, they fell out of thought; into the black void that was time. I didn't want to fall... I didn't want my life to be for nothing.

CHAPTER 22

In stories I read, knights were always the good guys, which had been an eye opener as a child. My people had always taught that outsiders were the bad guys. Even if I was putting my hope in Muinflor, and Lathimian, I still couldn't open my heart to them. We were at day three now, which ended in the wilderness. Knights began to make camp. Lathimian set up a tent for Sehrea and I before anything else, like he had each of the past two days.

"We sincerely appreciate what you do for us, Lathimian." Sehrea said, "Thank you."

"Naaaaah, it's the least I can do."

I felt more lost by the day, by the hour, sometimes, even by the minute... by every kind thing Lathimian and the others did for us.

"Can I do anything for you, Kea?" he asked me.

Too much emotion was bubbling inside me, so my faces weren't fooling anyone anymore. Fourteen years of beatings hadn't zapped me of emotion quite like my people had wanted, it appeared. All I think they'd really done was lock my emotions in a basement, a basement that was starting to get full...

"I'm good, thank you Lathimian."

"Get me if you need anything; whether that be in ten minutes, or in the middle of the night."

"Thank you."

Lathimian went away, and then I threw myself into a

patch of grass.

"You're not alright." Sehrea said.

"I'm just confused."

"About what?"

"Everything. I don't know anymore, about anything; our people, Miyune, Loshki, Muinflor, you name it..."

She rubbed my shoulder, and spoke soft words. "For so many years you saw a world in black, and white, when in truth there's a countless array of shades, and many beyond human comprehension. Give yourself time, and don't be afraid to feel things. I can tell you for certain that time won't heal anything, but it *will* help you learn to live with pain. For whatever else it's worth, I'm here for you too, whenever you need me."

I plopped over, and rested on her side. "Is all this struggle worth anything? How can I know what's real, and what's just lies that have been drilled into me?"

"I'm not pretending to have all the answers, Kea. All I can say, is that I'm here for you, no matter what. Cast your burdens on me, we'll work through them together."

"How is it so easy for you?" I asked.

"It's not. Behind every smile of mine is someone who's falling apart. I'm not anything special, I've just managed to keep from snapping."

Maybe that was all there was to life... staying strong for those you cared about. I pushed my insecurities aside. I didn't want to subject her to my problems, she had enough of her own.

"I'm here for you too," I said, "I mean it."

She smiled. Before anything else could be said, we heard a bad attempt at a knock against our tent.

"Come in." Sehrea said.

Arsaphi emerged with a bowl of stew in both hands.

"This is easy to get sick of." he said, "Just say the word if it stops doing the trick."

You could tell he meant what he said.

"Please, don't fret over us." Sehrea ended up having to say, almost every night of our venture.

Lathimian's company was so kind... I tried to be sociable over the course of our trip to Hadia, but failed at every step. On the flipside, Sehrea fared much better, and even started taking lessons from Arsaphi on the spear. She seemed to be moving forward with her life, and that was good enough for me. Who was I to ask for anything more?

Our journey to Hadia went without a hitch. Not long after we crossed the border, Lathimian decided to stop us within sight of a town. As a result, I went to ask him why.

"I'm guessing we have something to do here?" I said.

"Aaaaaah, yes, turns out we do. You know, I'd rather forgotten about it myself."

"Somehow I really doubt that..."

He grinned. "Alright, maybe I didn't."

"So why are we here?"

"I just need to see someone."

"Alright, and who's that?"

"Nobody special, just an old friend... acquaintance? Acquaintance is more accurate. Well, it's really a mixture of bo-"

Sehrea cut him off before I could. "Someone you know well enough."

"Yes, that's him. He'll be intimidating to little ones like yourselves, but he's a softy at heart."

Lathimian gathered a little party, and went into town. I laid on my back in the meantime, with my eyes to the clouds. Reliving the days Miyu and I would share was uplifting.

Little crunches of grass trickled into my ears, I turned over to see Sehrea kneeling alongside me. She went ahead and put a necklace of flowers around me.

"I like it. Thank you, Sehrea."

"I'm just happy I have someone I can give it to."

We laid by, and watched the clouds flutter. When it was time to return to reality, we saw Lathimian's silhouette riding in the distance. I sat up for a look, and saw Arsaphi was at his left. At Lathimian's right was a certain large man, who for whatever reason, looked familiar...

"What's wrong?" Sehrea said, as I went into a frenzy.

I sprinted through camp, found Breovit, and wrapped myself around him. "Hide me, hide me, hide me!"

"What's got you going?" he said, "'Whole lot of us here, nobody's going to touch you."

Sehrea caught up to me. "What's wrong, Kea?"

"That man with Lathimian, it's Mermadak! What if he recognizes me!?!"

"We know that's Mermadak." Breovit said, "He's Lathimian's old friend."

"He'll want to kill me!"

Breovit took a knee, so he could meet me at eye level. "Lathimian's a good man. He's part of the team, and so are you. He's sure Mermadak won't be mad, let's trust him."

Breovit was so calm with me, so protective... I couldn't help but put my faith in what he said.

"Alright. I-"

"Here," Breovit said, "I'll walk there with you."

"Thank you, I appreciate it."

Sehrea looked nervous, she didn't seem as sure about

this as Breovit. Breovit shooed her away, and so she backed off.

"Don't worry, I've got this. We're all fine." he told her.

"I trust you."

Sehrea waited by, while Breovit and I went out to greet Lathimian, Mermadak, and Arsaphi. When they hopped off their horses, we were the first ones to greet them.

"The homeland treating you well?" Breovit said to Mermadak.

"Yes... it has. Breovit, I believe?"

"I'm honored you remember me."

"Of course. You were part of the last ambassador team that came to Hadia for sparring. Quite the event."

Breovit shot Lathimian a finger. "And you say nobody knows who I am!"

Lathimian clicked, and didn't say a word.

Mermadak left them be, and turned to me. "The very brave, young miss Kea. I hope we can start on a new foot."

"Of course... of course. Thank you."

He was as massive as memory protested. Despite having Lathimian, Breovit, and Arsaphi beside me; I still couldn't help but keep on my heels. Mermadak's arms were like tree trunks, and his torso like an ox's. His hair was short, and flat on top. He was a dark blonde, like Lathimian.

"Weeeeell, you two get along." Lathimian said, "Perfect! You're probably the two most important people here, so keep doing that."

At that moment, Sehrea walked up.

"Make that three." Lathimian said, "Anyways, I want us all to get on the same page. It's time Miyune, Keras, and their underworld monster were put down. Thanks to our good friend Mermadak; we have a chance. We're all still in agreement with seeking out King Clarje of Hadia?"

There were no objections, instead just a joke from Breovit. "I love feeling like I have a say."

Mermadak joined our ranks for good, and guided us on our march to the capital of Hadia; Gelliomos. He didn't hold any grudges against me, nor did he interrogate me, or demand answers. Admittedly, we didn't speak much... at least, until we were on the verge of Gelliomos. We'd have quite the conversation there.

CHAPTER 23

What was with the sudden darkness that graced the World of Unraveling? I swear the sun was beginning to dim, the moon was beginning to fade, and the bright skies of days long passed was no longer the same as what stood above my head. I felt like time was reincarnating itself, because just like in the days of old, nobody understood when I told them of the things I saw.

"Kea, the world's as bright as it's always been." Sehrea told me.

"You might just miss the dark a little." Lathimian said.

"It's no less bright than always." Breovit said.

"Maybe a little rest is all you need." Arsaphi said, "I promise it's the same, don't worry."

I laid back, and again set my sights above. How could anyone say the day's weren't getting darker?

A shadow rose over me. "Kea?" it said.

I tilted my head to see the largest of the group. "Yes, Sir Mermadak?"

"I want to tell you something."

My soul was already uneasy. His sudden desire to talk didn't help my churning stomach. Still, I wasn't about to deny him.

"Of course," I said, "anything."

"Much like Lady Miyune; I'm a seeker of secrets."

"Yes, she proudly flaunts that around." I said, taking a proper seat on the ground.

He crossed his arms, and took a seat on a rock. We'd probably be here awhile. "Are you familiar with the old temples?" he asked.

"Not at all."

"You know of the Raloia?" he asked.

"Yes, the people crushed into nothingness by Lathine."

"They, Raloia, had an obsession with temples. Once upon a time they controlled northern Lathine, and that's why northern Lathine is littered with temples."

"That's the first I've heard of that."

"Nowadays," he said, "they're abandoned. They're home to thieves, murderers, and followers of the *darker* things in existence."

"And you go to these places?"

"Yes, young Kea. In my conquest for answers of the world around us, I took my sights to a temple in Hadia. I fought through one wave of sadists after another. When all the fighting was said and done, I took a look around. There was nothing left that thieves hadn't long stolen. I was minutes away from taking leave, and that's when something happened; I was assaulted out of thin air, by *dozens* of men. They were carved up, mutilated, deathly thin, ghost white; things that mark your people, so Sehrea says."

"Those are our typical traits, yes."

"I forced them into retreat, and pursued them through the temple. I pressed them with the choice of surrender or death; most chose death, and attacked, whilst the others continued to flee. I killed every last man who was foolish enough to test me, then followed after the others. Their trail led me deep into the catacombs of the temple, where light faded from existence. I'm not the man to be caught unprepared; I lit up a candle, and made my way on."

"You were all alone?"

"Yes, I was."

"How did you find the bravery to do such a thing?"

He wasn't one to smile, but he did give the closest thing to one you'd probably ever see from him. "Bravery's something we all have, because we all get scared. It's finding something stronger than your fear, that's all bravery is; whether that something be love, friendship, honor, or yet something else. It was my lust for knowledge that outweighed my fear; thanks to that, I had something to be brave for, and so I pressed on."

"And what did you find?"

"Down in the dark, I-..."

"Yes?"

He wouldn't address me outright. There seemed to be something he wasn't planning on telling me.

"I, continued into the dark, the explorer in me wasn't content to leave things be. I followed what felt like an endless labyrinth."

"That sounds awfully familiar."

"They caught onto my presence soon enough. I ended up in one bloody fight after another, by swarms of beast-like men that never ceased. All the fighters that fought me were sickly, and deathly pale, bar none."

"Exactly like my people."

"I was forced to retreat. When I returned with a small army, days later, we searched the temple from end to end."

"And what did you find?"

"Nothing, not a soul, not even the bodies of the men I'd killed. It was like I'd fought phantoms. Some doubted my sanity, and for awhile, even I did. Part of my involvement with you all is to sate my own demand for answers. I have to know where Miyune and Loshki got you from."

"Did you ask Sehrea?"

"I did, but the place I speak of is different than the place she emerged from."

I didn't know what to say. Camp began to move, which cut our conversation short.

"I wanted to tell you that story at least once," he said, "make of it whatever you will."

He went off, and prepared to leave; in turn, I did the same. Lathimian ended up seeking out Sehrea and I.

"Just a few of us are going from here." he said, "You two still want to join?"

"Absolutely."

Sehrea looked to me. "Whatever Kea wants to do, we will."

Lathimian was all too willing to oblige. "Sounds like a plan."

Only him, Sehrea, Arsaphi, Mermadak, and I, went into Gelliomos. Mermadak led us through. You could tell he was familiar with the capital. He led us to a beautiful palace, whose towers reached into the heavens.

"This is the Castle of the King, home to His Majesty, Lord Clarje."

At the gate, guards bowed with deep respect. "Lord Mermadak, it is an honor to greet you again." one said.

"Thank you, good men. I am here with Lathimian, and Arsaphi, of Sohal. We have matters to discuss with the King."

They nodded, and opened up the gate. "May it go well with you."

Mermadak led us through the courtyard, and into the palace. He spoke with a knight, to learn where King

Clarje was, then led us to said place, which ended up being a study. We entered, and saw a man that looked like a king in every sense of the word. We also saw a young boy with him, who was about my own age.

"May you give us a moment, my son?" said the man.

"Of course, father." replied the boy.

On his way out, the boy gave Mermadak a quick hug. "Mermadak!" he cried, "It's been quite a while!"

"It's good to see you as well, Elezor. I'm sorry to say I have no time for sparring, but you have my word I'll make time soon as I can."

"Good, my friend, we always enjoy your company."

Behind us creaked the door, and departed the boy.

"My King, it is good to see you."

"That it's so soon again is what concerns me." replied King Clarje.

King Clarje turned his attention around. "Lathimian, you are a good man. I'm happy to see you."

"Thank you, sir."

"I look forward to a time we can meet under better circumstances."

"So do I."

Last but not least, the King's eyes turned to Sehrea, and I, then back to Lathimian.

"Family?"

"Friends."

"Very knowledgeable young women." Mermadak said, "You remember my *story* from not long ago?"

"Yes, the prison defense?"

"The youngest is Kea Leestel, our resident rock thrower. Second is the eldest; young Sehrea. They are allies in our plight."

"Leestel..." King Clarje muttered, "you are the niece of

Miyune Leestel?"

"I'm no niece of that witch." I said, "She kidnapped me."

"And do we know the reason she did that?"

Sehrea stepped forward. "We hail from somewhere else entirely. I don't know where; the only people who do are Miyune and Loshki. Miyune held Kea as a hostage, seeking to coerce our people into acting as her army."

King Clarje turned yet again. "Mermadak, have you ascertained what people Miyune is after?"

Mermadak shook his head. "I believe they're something along the lines of a hidden society, linked to the abandoned temples."

"What steps must we take to learn the truth?"

"We start by doing ourselves a service; destroy the empire of Lord Keras, and Lady Miyune."

My eyes lit up... this was going perfect!

"What request have you of me?" King Clarje asked.

"Let the knights of Sohal, led by Lathimian, take up their quest through Hadia. I would join them, if it is good to you, My King."

"Do what you must, Mermadak."

King Clarje looked to Lathimian. "I trust you, however, I would have you defer to Mermadak should anything crucial to the nation arise."

"Of course, King Clarje. I won't let you down."

"I'm sure you will not."

You could tell something was weighing on King Clarje's mind. We were fortunate, and he opted to tell us what that something was.

"Keras is in Hadia as we speak." he said.

"I know." Mermadak replied.

"Scheming, plotting our downfall."

"Naturally."

"Him, and..."

"I know."

Lathimian cut in. "Him and Nothaniir?"

All the bright emotions in the room fled out. A dark air was all that remained. King Clarje's voice grew dire. "What do you know of Nothaniir?"

"Not much. I only know his name because of the young ones."

"And what of you two?" asked the King.

"We know he's the master of Keras, and Miyune." I said.

"And if I may add," Arsaphi said, "I think it's worth considering that Miyune married Keras for his connection to Nothaniir."

I'd never considered such a thing... but the idea did sound right, right enough to consider truth.

"I haven't thought about it that way." Mermadak admitted.

He tossed Lathimian an eye, who looked away. "How should I have known? She never answered to anyone in the past."

Lathimian looked higher away yet. "It still bothers me... Miyune accepting someone else as a master. That's not her."

"All these things will come to light one day." King Clarje said, "But for now, we work with what we do not know. We move towards the day we do know. Lathimian?"

"Yes?"

"Be careful, be *very* careful. *Nothaniir,* is not a name to be used lightly. His followers are everywhere in the shadows; from powerful men, to weak men. They bring *slow,* painful deaths, to *any* who reveal the name."

"They make examples?"

"Precisely. I do not want you to become an example."

"I won't, trust me."

"So I will. May fortune smile upon your quest, Lathimian. May it smile upon all of you, and all the way to the ends of Lathine."

"It will, My Lord." Mermadak said, "I'm sure of it."

We left the castle, and went back to the outskirts, to the company.

"Has this been everything you hoped for?" Sehrea asked me.

"It really has been... I'm just shocked at how much real good is out there."

"I'm just happy to see we found a purpose, after so long."

"Me too."

Bonds that strengthened over the course of our quest meant the world to me. If only all the love I felt, and all the friendships that I forged, didn't make things so much more painful down the line...

"You really want to go there first?" I heard Lathimian say, later on.

"I do." Mermadak said, "There's nothing I'd rather do than pester Lord Keras. Let's make a nuisance of ourselves."

So, they wanted to challenge Lord Keras head on? Looks like Mermadak and Lathimian weren't the cowering sort. They were determined to bring justice, and I respected them deeply for that. Mutual respect was one of the pillars to the friendships we would all build; friendships that would last a lifetime, and sprout roots at the center of my heart. Given how my feelings attached themselves to my core, it was no wonder why the future would hurt so much. A question would always arise inside my head, in the years to come.

"Why couldn't we all just get along like we used to?"

I don't think that question would ever leave me...

CHAPTER 24

It was interesting to see how Sehrea interacted with the company. You would have thought she'd be drawn to Lathimian, Arsaphi, or Breovit, right? Well, turns out that wasn't the case! Instead, she was drawn to Mermadak. She even started taking extra lessons on the spear from him. Each time they trained, I made sure to keep my distance. I didn't hold anything against Mermadak, I just felt too anxious about the thought of mingling with him freely, is all. If only I'd never gone through with Keras' mission...

When I watched her train with him, it all began to make sense. At first glance, both of them were calm and refrained people that bore little real emotion. I wager Mermadak had a past worth forgetting of his own. When they fought, however, that's when some of their old selves broke free. Sehrea had once been as fierce a person as you could imagine, that I knew. I coupled that with my first hand knowledge of how fierce Mermadak was in combat. Everything considered, I didn't have issue understanding how they got along so well, because the more I watched them, the more they reminded me of one another.

Lathimian stopped their training. He shared words with Mermadak, then made his way over to me.

"Still having fun?"

"More than I've ever had. I love this sort of peace. Why

do you ask?"

"Eh, should I know? It's just a conversation starter. Anyways, me and a few others are going into town."

"I'm guessing me and Sehrea are staying back here?"

"Right. You, Sehrea, Mermadak, and another few."

"Mermadak's not joining? Isn't that the town where Keras is?"

"It is." Lathimian said, "But we can't show our cards yet. Mermadak's too big to play stealth. Once we know for sure where Keras is, and what he's doing, then the big man'll march in."

"Alright, that sounds good."

"'Course it does! It's one of my plans."

Lathimian took his company out. I watched the clouds pass by in the meantime, and gave Sehrea an occasional glance. Sweating off stress seemed to work for her. It made me squirm how intense she was getting with Mermadak. I didn't like to think of the past, and how she'd used to be. Mermadak was all too willing to go along with what she wanted, and however intensely she wanted to train. He seemed to think it was healthy for her, which I didn't disagree with.

Soon, someone in camp spoke out loud enough for us all to hear. "He's back!"

Mermadak left Sehrea, and went to speak with the re-turners. Right away, another company was concocted! It was much like the first company that had went out, save for Arsaphi, who was swapped out with Merma-dak. I was happy to have Arsaphi around, even if I didn't plan on interacting with him. Sometimes, just a person's face made all the difference. I was more than content to lay alone, and keep watching the clouds go by. Sehrea seemed to think something similar; she came over, and laid alongside me.

"Mermadak feels that good or bad, things will get messy."

"Why am I not surprised?"

"But let's say it doesn't, and the world rests in peace. What do you envision yourself doing, for the rest of your life onwards?"

"I barely know what to envision myself doing tomorrow."

She chuckled, which caused me to as well.

"I mean it." I said.

"I know, I feel the same way."

We laid back, and looked to the sky until sleep reaped us. For the next two days, we lazed around in the same way. In the meantime, Lathimian and Mermadak would come back to camp with one set of men, and then set right back out with another. I could only imagine how on edge Keras must have felt.

"We're learning of his connections." Mermadak told Sehrea, who told me.

"We're making him uncomfortable." Breovit said.

"I'm just happy they haven't sent out a force to kill us yet." Lathimian grinned, later yet.

I think that was a joke... but I wasn't sure, because who ever knew with Lathimian?

"Could they send out a strong enough force?" I asked.

Lathimian's eyes crawled out to Mermadak. "I'm going to say *no,* a strong *no.*"

"And I guess there's the knights in town too." I said.

"A strong *no* at it's finest."

Two days after, I was awaken before even the sun had risen. A cold, moist air reigned, that tried hard to lull me back to sleep.

Lathimian's face emerged from the shadows. "Let's get up and at 'em, Kea, we've got Keras on the run."

"We have to follow him... don't we?"

"Everyone else but me said 'yes'. 'Here I thought we'd get a little shut-eye."

Curses... I hated waking up early. We ended up following Keras from a great distance away, as a precaution, because Lathimian felt so confident in his tracking abilities. As a matter of fact, not even once did we see Keras in the horizon! It didn't matter if we were looking down from hilltops, or mountains! Even Mermadak was impressed, and made a habit of picking Lathimian's brain. Soon, we crossed back into Sohal. I had a sour feeling from the get-go, about where Keras could have been going. Lathimian seemed to sense this.

"I'll send you back to Muinflor." he offered.

"..."

"You want to go back there, I know you do."

"You're right, but I can't. I want to see this through with you all, if you'll let me."

"Alright, as long as you're sure."

"I'm sure."

"I won't bother asking Sehrea." he said.

I chuckled. We both knew what she'd say, something like 'whatever Kea wants, is good enough for me'. It wasn't until Sciruthon was upon us, that we came to see Lord Keras' company in the furthest distance. We saw them enter into the city. To think, I was beginning to wonder if Lathimian had lost them! Anyways; Lathimian, Mermadak, and Arsaphi, pulled away to think. When they came out of discussion, Lathimian approached me.

"The best way to keep you safe, is to keep you close."

"So you're taking me in too?"

He grimaced, and clicked off one side of his mouth. "'Don't see a good way around it."

"That's fine by me."

One last stroll in Sciruthon sounded appropriate... even if I hated the idea. There was a piece of my heart that couldn't help but be drawn to the place.

"Don't let your cloaks down." he'd go on to tell Sehrea and I.

We nodded.

Arsaphi came up alongside us. "They'll be fine, Lathimian, I'll keep an eye on them."

"Two?"

"Where would the other one be going!?!"

We were going to enter Sciruthon in little waves, that much I knew. Lathimian went out with a few men for wave one, and ere it began.

"What exactly was his plan? I didn't hear much earlier." Sehrea said.

Arsaphi turned to her. "His first objective is to get in touch with the knights, and have them on their feet; then he's going on a scavenger hunt. He's after a multitude of records."

It was a smart move by Lathimian to bring all hands he could on deck. Miyune had Sciruthon on lockdown, after all. A fight was more than possible, if not probable. It didn't help that they'd gone and provoked Keras just a few days before.

Arsaphi, Sehrea, and I, ended up as part of the third wave. We didn't head into town long after Lathimian himself, so we were able to catch up before he made much progress. Everyone stayed in the shadows, which made sense... except, of course, for none other than Lathimian. No doubts about it, he had a flair for the dramatic! He strolled down Sciruthon's moonlit roads, and didn't bother to put his hood up. Whatever was going through his head, I could only imagine. Paranoia aside, I guess his feelings of safety made some sense. There was a knight down every street, after all, in addition to all our men in the shadows.

Lathimian had too much swagger to him, and you could tell he knew the town well. He must have had a lot of encounters with Miyune in the past; there was no way he'd just memorized map routes, or something like that. He took all the shortcuts and backroads I would have taken.

Lathimian was smart, and kept a distance from Miyune's palace. He also kept distance from Loshki's house for good measure. He hit up four buildings, and vanished inside two of them for extended periods of time. In the end, he seemed to have gotten what he was after! He grinned as a means of telling us so, and brushed twice at his left shoulder, which meant it was time to go! We made our way through town, one more time.

"A good start is something, but means nothing with a bad ending." Sehrea said.

Her nerves weren't easing; if anything, she seemed to be getting more tense. I couldn't have agreed any more with such uneasiness. A fight could have broken out at any second! Being in Sciruthon brought a lot of tough memories to mind, so my own nerves weren't doing much better. Once Lathimian neared the outskirts, I repeated a little mantra in my head.

Just a little bit more...

I could even see the end in sight. Being so close made my heart flutter.

Just a little bit more...

Please God, please.

Just a little bit more...

He'd done it, he'd outsmarted Miyune! Now he only had a few more steps to go!

Just a little bit more...

We were *so* close, which made what happened next all the more gut-wrenching.

I could barely breathe anymore. As if the mission going up in flames wasn't bad enough, now Lathimian's safety was in jeopardy! I don't know what I would have done if I hadn't had Sehrea to calm me down. I can't say for sure that I wouldn't have done something stupid, nor can I say I wouldn't have panicked so loud that I gave away my location.

Lahsahn ahneo lahsahn ahneo lahsahn.

When I came back to the present, my eyes fell upon a figure standing parallel to Lathimian. Lathimian caught on, and turned to meet his stalker, and there... stood Loshki. Right away, the light from above became stifled by thick, dark clouds.

"Be ready to run, Kea. Trust in what he'd want." Sehrea whispered.

She already knew this was a bloody battle waiting to happen. I didn't have the heart to run while Lathimian, Arsaphi, and the others, suffered for my sake. I was resolved to turn myself over as a peace offering if need be. I watched on my toes as Lathimian and Loshki exchanged glances, Lathimian doing it in his own strange way, of course. I'd wager the shadows was littered with fighters; some for Lathimian, and some for Loshki. Sehrea pulled me into a tight crevice between some old crates and a rundown home. Nobody could spot us there, but we could still get a good view. I was happy we got off our feet, and to our knees. My shaking had gotten bad again, I would have collapsed if I'd had to stand much longer.

My hearing went into overdrive, which let me make out faint words. My eyes went to work, which let me see that Loshki didn't seem angry, not in the slightest!

"Sure you don't want to stay for ale and company, heh, Lathimian?"

"Mmmm... ordinarily, yes, but I hear Miyune doesn't need the likes of us for company anymore. She's got that shiny new someone."

Loshki laughed, it was the first time I'd ever heard a real laugh from him.

Sehrea's lips graced my ear. "Is this real or an act?"

"I don't know, but it feels real."

"Your work never fails to impress." we heard Loshki say.

Lathimian was nonchalant. "I try, buuuut I'm just so talented, so it makes sense."

When the clouds rolled by, and the moonlight returned, a dark smirk rolled off Loshki's lips. "I could give you better training than even General Febrithien." he said.

"I'm not going to doubt you could teach me a thing or two."

"You know what Miyune thinks of you." Loshki said.

"Unfortunately."

This marked the first time I'd ever heard him drop the *"Lady Miyune"* bit, far as I could remember.

"'Used to be me she'd vent to," Loshki said, "I know better than anyone."

Lathimian grinned, and looked to the stars. "Then you *really* catch my drift."

"You know she'd move heaven and Lathine to have

you."

"I know."

"Pay's good."

"I know that too."

"What do you say? 'Worth considering?"

Lathimian grinned again. He was too comfortable, sort of like Miyune. "I'm not a very good mercenary, and I find executions a little silly."

"You already do those things, accept it."

"Does it treat you well?" Lathimian asked, "The insanity of life and death? Does it help you sleep, like a bedtime story?"

"I keep it out of mind."

"It's not for me."

"It could be."

"I know, I just won't let it."

Loshki seemed to be understanding. "That offer won't die, no matter how many times we *cross* paths."

Some sort of mutual respect existed for one another... in a weird way.

"I'll keep it in mind."

Loshki started to walk away. Lathimian only got a few steps off, before Loshki stopped again. Lathimian seemed to know... and glued himself to where he stood.

"You lucked out, that I didn't kill you." Loshki said.

"I know."

"Be more careful, blood's going to be everywhere."

"I will."

That didn't sound right. What was Lathimian not telling me? Loshki left without another word. Lathimian continued to the plains, in no particular rush. You would have never guessed he was in the middle of a mission. How was he so calm?

Sehrea and I followed right behind. I ran up beside him, where he beat me to the punch with words.

"Me and Loshki get along face to face." he said.

"You still don't seem big on him, even though he seems big on you."

"Well, that's because he can't take *no* for an answer. He wants me to join with them, just like Miyune does. 'Doesn't stop him from going behind my back to get me killed, though."

I cringed at the thought. In turn, he tried to be more upbeat.

"We'd do well if we sat down for tea." he joked, "That's all that really matters."

"Where are we off to now?" Sehrea asked, as she ran along his left.

At the same moment, Mermadak walked up on his right. Something wasn't right with Mermadak's face. He looked... conflicted?

"Back to the east." Mermadak said, "I'll see every last one of them behind bars, or under graves."

His eyes started to burn like embers. You could tell he'd meant every last word he'd said... Why was he so infuriated, all of a sudden? What could have sparked him so?

CHAPTER 25

Sehrea, Lathimian, and I, sat around a pot of stew. He poured it into bowls with a ladle, and served us first.

"What are the Legion's like?" Sehrea asked.

Lathimian poured himself a serving, while I pigged down on my own. "Organized chaos." he said, "They'd be a little more fun if I could pull a Jerthian."

"He's the best." Sehrea remarked, "You shouldn't set your bar that high."

"Nah, I could take him."

"Now you're making stuff up."

"No way," he said, "I've literally never lost to him, that's a fact."

"Should I-...?"

He cut her off. "'Neeeever fought him and not won, that says all you need to know."

"Um... you've never actually fought him, have you?"

He started to devour his bowl. "Can you believe how good a cook I am?"

It felt good to mess around, and be a kid; watching others be at ease really did the trick for me. Sehrea, however, wasn't content to just leave me out.

She leaned into my ear. *"Ah liih neo nayeh uhiih ooeo oofah koh tsoo."*

I chuckled.

"I'm calling you out on that one." Lathimian said, "That's cheating."

Sehrea had more to say in our tongue, but resisted. That alone made me laugh.

"Anyways-" Lathimian started to say.

Out of nowhere, a sound shutdown our fun and games... We heard a scream!

Lathimian was on his feet before we could turn our heads. He put a hand on our backs, and sent us to the ground.

"Stay down!"

There was something wrong in his voice. My head shot around to see what was going on. What I caught sight of was our own men; all pulling shining blades, sharp lances, mighty axes, and powerful bows! One and the same, they all rushed into the distance. Out of thin air, foes emerged aplenty, and bashed against our lines! I saw Mermadak burst onto the scene, and Arsaphi too! Breovit was about to, before Lathimian grabbed hold of him.

"Babysit the kids!" Lathimian said, never one to resist a stupid joke.

Breovit backtracked towards us. He kept his eyes set on the fight. You could tell he wanted to get in on the action.

"I'm sorry." Sehrea said.

"Don't be." he said, "You're part of the team, 'course I'll do what I have to for you two."

Enemies flooded in by the dozen! It must have been the full blown wrath of Lord Keras! It's a good thing we had Mermadak; everyone, *everyone,* could tell Mermadak was the greatest hand at work. I loved Lathimian, I liked Arsaphi, Breovit was a good friend, and I respected Loshki; but *none* of them could *even compare* to Mermadak. He swatted men left and right, he held men by the throat while thrashing other men. There wasn't a single enemy that wasn't actively trying to avoid him!

"They want to surround us." Breovit said.

Mermadak's might was like the coming of God. Single-handedly, he kept the front line together, albeit only by a thin margin. Lathimian was always on the defensive, so he wasn't helping the cause much. Arsaphi was downing men at a good rate, but he just couldn't inflict the raw might Mermadak had. Consequently, three, no, four enemies broke through!

"Kill them!" Lathimian screamed, *"Kill them!"*

Breovit dragged us to Lolagis, and pulled me up onto him. For whatever reason, Sehrea didn't hop on too.

"I'll jump up if we have to!"

Breovit shot her idea. "No! You have-"

"Don't worry, trust me!"

Breovit turned back, to see two of the men left. They were close, which left no more time for arguing. Breovit ran out to meet them! He launched the first strike, which was deflected, and then the man he'd struck at took hold of him! Breovit gave the man a crossguard to the mouth, then guarded against a blow from the second man. Breovit was fast as the wind! He bombarded the second man, knocked him down, then spun back around to entertain the first enemy-...!

Out of nowhere, a spear popped into the first enemy's side. The man grabbed at the spear, staggered, and let a wail. He was lucky the throw hadn't been strong, or well placed. I looked to my right, and saw what I'd thought I'd seen; Sehrea had thrown the spear! She'd been keeping it hidden inside her cloak! Mermadak must have helped her pull that weaponry off.

Breovit turned back to the second man, deflected a blow, then got in a deep cut! He pulled his blade from the man's side, and blood sliced out with it. After kicking the man back, he lunged forward with a stab through the mouth; red gushed long after the man fell dead. Next, Breovit spun right around, and fended off a blow from the weakened first man! He countered, knocked the man to a knee, then pierced him one more time. In turn, the man dropped his weapon, began to scream, and then got put down. Breovit pulled out Sehrea's little throwing spear, wiped it off in the dirt, and brought it back to her.

"Every bit makes a difference." he said, as he turned for a look at the main battle.

"I can only hope so." she said.

We watched the company force the enemy into retreat; that was when riders on horseback started to show in the near distance! I think we hadn't noticed sooner because we'd all been too focused on the fight at hand.

"They don't know when to give up." Breovit grumbled.

"Are they knights coming to help us!?!" I clamored, desperate for optimism.

He shook his head. Curses! That couldn't be good! Our archers did great work, and cut down a hoard of men before they could reach us. In the meantime, Breovit went and grabbed himself a horse.

"Get on Lolagis." he said.

This time, Sehrea did as he said.

He didn't mince words. "There's no way our lines'll stop every last one of them."

Lathimian pulled the lines back towards us. There was no way he'd be able to get to us in time, so Breovit made a call, and had us start riding off. It was good Breovit made the call he did, because we'd have been as good as dead if we'd stayed to hold our ground. Horsemen were slinging off arrows, and thrusting lances everywhere.

"*Zeon,* Lolagis, *zeon!*" Sehrea reassured her steed.

We started on a straightway, which was fortunate; it quickly faded away into a claustrophobic region laden with rocks, however, which was *extremely* unfortunate. It started to become clear how much room Sehrea had for improvement as a rider. She couldn't navigate tight spaces well, which meant Breovit was forced to slow down, and get behind us.

"No matter what, keep going." he told us.

Sehrea nodded, and continued to crawl her way through the rocky tundra. Breovit rode back, to meet a trio of riders. He forced them to slow, and bought us time; that was for sure. He caught one man off guard, and slew him from his horse, then he and the other two swung around blades. One of the enemies chose to slew Breovit's horse, which caused Breovit to be slung to the ground. Rather than trying to finish him, the riders continued pursuit after us.

I shook Sehrea's shoulder. "Horses! They're still after us!!!"

"Is Breovit alive?!?"

"Yes, but his horse isn't! He can't help us anymore!"

Sehrea spun her brown haired head to see what I did; two men were close behind! What's worse is that we were *long* out of distance for any aid.

Sehrea lashed out. "*Vehoh!*"

"Lolagis is faster than them, right? We can do this, can't we!?!"

Our terrain kept getting worse, and worse. It didn't matter how fast Lolagis was, if Sehrea wasn't able to guide him well. I turned my head back to see that we'd... lost one of our followers? He must have spun out, I guess?

"One down!" I told Sehrea.

Regardless, pressure continued to mount on her face.

"Hiih nee... ah... rahsah."

She rambled one panicked thing after another.

"Hiih nee ah rahsah..."

"Yaheen!"

"Hiih, hiih..."

"Zvah!"

Her head turned back to see that the last rider was right on our tail! What laid up next was a brutal stretch of inclining rock; behind it was plains, straight plains...

She knew what I knew well; that she wouldn't be able to guide Lolagis through the rocks. She jumped down, and I beside her. She grabbed Lolagis' reigns, and led us up the slope.

"Don't look back," she cried, "keep going! Don't look back!"

I snuck a peek anyways. Our enemy jumped from his horse, and pulled a ruined blade! Sehrea wouldn't let go of the firm grip she had on me, and kept dragging me on.

"Keep running, just keep running!"

Death made it's way into my heart, and I felt the creeping truth; that there was no escaping this man. We were losing ground on foot, just like we had on horse. Sehrea took her first look back. She gave up any foolish hope left of outrunning him, and knew we'd have no choice but to act. I saw her reach into her cloak; it looks like she was going to try seizing fate. I didn't doubt that her gamble had a chance to work, but that didn't mean I liked our chances.

In an instant, she stopped dead in her tracks, and spun around! She was a half second from letting a spear fly, before something fell out of nowhere! From overtop the rock wall, Lathimian jumped down with a monstrous blow! He sent the enemy crashing down the slope, and then he himself stumbled right behind.

At the bottom of the slope, our attacker roared. "*'You really that eager to die!?!"*

"You're going to have to get a little more creative; I've been told worse things, by much better people."

How could Lathimian keep so calm, even in times like these?

Sehrea ran her hand along the flustered Lolagis, and calmed him down. "*Lneel koh ee Lolagis, lneel ehoh!"*

We gave a look down to the bottom, to Lathimian. He motioned for us to go on, and paid us no more mind. Sehrea grabbed me by the hand, and forced me along. Lathimian had said before, that no matter what, Sehrea and I must live. He believed the knowledge in our heads was the single greatest asset of the company. Sehrea, of course, was all too willing to agree with that sentiment, because it helped her to keep me safe. At least if Lathimian couldn't pull through in this fight, his efforts wouldn't be in vain...

Steel scorched the air. Once we got to the plains, Sehrea and I knew there was no way for anyone to catch us, so we let down our urgency. I turned back, and watched what became of Lathimian. Like always, he went straight to the defensive, and deterred one powerful blow after another. It made sense, since his defense was so good, but such a gameplan also seemed like a weakness. I don't think he had any good moves for changing the flow of battle.

A punch flew out of nowhere, and hit Lathimian clean in the face! He stumbled to a knee, and pulled out a quick reaction to fend off a deathblow. Lathimian managed to wrap the tip of his blade around, and stab the enemy in the side! If only the enemy's armor wasn't so good, if only Lathimian had managed to get some juice on the thrust; in the end, his stab didn't do much damage.

Lathimian was pulled by the collar, smashed against stone, and put into a chokehold! Lathimian threw two frantic punches at the man's face; the second in particular had power behind it, and dazed the man for just a second. A second was all Lathimian needed. Lathimian worked the crossguard of his weapon inwards, and bashed it straight into the man's jaw. A nasty *"crunch"* met Sehrea and I, all the way up high. Red gleamed from the man's mouth. Lathimian tried to punch with his other hand, only to have his fist caught! The enemy took hold of Lathimian, and flung him into the ground. Lathimian pounced back up, and deflect a quick strike with the armor plate on his left arm. Still, weak or not, the blow carried stress with it, and caused Lathimian to let out a loud grunt.

Lathimian grabbed the man's weapon, and they struggled for possession. It was weird, because Lathimian didn't seem to be trying as much as the other man for control of the weapon. It became apparent why, when all of a sudden, Lathimian let go! In turn, the enemy flew backwards! Lathimian lept forward, and launched the enemy's weapon away with a swing of the sword. Lathimian kicked the man's face, and so ensued another *"crunch!"*. Not about to give up, the attacker sprung, and tried to grab Lathimian, except Lathimian was too quick. He swung his sword... and took the man's hand off! It flew two dozen feet, and painted the rocks with it's contents.

Even with everything I'd seen, all the gore, all the

pain... I still had to look away, and try hard not to throw up. Sehrea was just as mortified. I turned back, expecting the fight to be over... but no, the man was still going!

Sehrea started to sprint down the slope, and I did the same. Our enemy was intent on fighting to his dying breath! Lathimian grabbed him, and threw him against a wall of stone, and then did it a second time for good measure. Seeped from top to bottom in blood, the enemy limped away; he grabbed a knife that was hidden inside his clothing, and made one last leap at Lathimian! Lathimian was too keen for party tricks. He grabbed the man's wrist before the stab could be laid, and bent it backwards until control of the knife was relinquished. Once the knife fell down, Lathimian let up some, thinking the fight was over...

The attacker fell to his knees, and crawled away. Lathimian stayed a step behind him. All of a sudden, the man lept up, grabbed a boulder, and tried to come down with it! Lathimian did what he had to, and stabbed the man clean through the wrist. Horrible, horrible screams met our ears. The attacker grabbed at his wrist, and fell to his knees. Blood spewed in storm, and stained the landscape.

Now at Lathimian's side, Sehrea and I watched the man whimper in a pool of fresh blood. His armor, his clothes... even his hair was wine red. There was no point in trying to fight anymore, and so he gave up. He laid down, and waited to die. Lathimian kneeled beside him.

"Do something before you go. Don't let this be in vain."

"No..." the man cackled, "it is in vain... all of it."

"Then make something that isn't."

Coughing up blood, the man laughed. "You don't understand the world."

Lathimian didn't look like he was going to try anymore. He pulled up his sword, intent on putting the man down... and that's when the man surprised us.

"In my left pocket, is our... mission statement."

Lathimian reached down. Not only did he come up with a piece of paper, but bright eyes! He must have gotten good intel!

"He... abandoned us at the start of the fight." the man said, "Our boss... he abandoned us. He's a liar, he's a coward... make him pay."

Lathimian tried to speak, but the man cut him off. On the verge of death, all the man could do was spit a mantra.

"Make him pay."

"Make him pay."

"Make him pay..."

At last, he fell back and died. Lathimian stepped away, and wiped off the droplets of blood on his face.

"That didn't feel so hot..." he said, stretching out his left wrist.

Sehrea stepped up, and wiped him clean with the overhang of her sleeves.

"but it might lead to something worthwhile." he said, "It'll be worth it."

"Do you really feel it will?" Sehrea asked.

Her face made it clear that she wouldn't accept anything but straight answers.

Lathimian obliged. "If I said how good I felt about this, you'd think I was lying. Keras, Miyune, and Loshki, are going down, guaranteed. I'd bet my life on it."

"Then that's good enough for me. I'm sure that's good enough for Kea too."

"Of course!"

Yes... I'd made the mistake of not trusting enough in the past, but I wouldn't make that mistake anymore! If he said things were under control, then I had no reason to waste my time worrying.

CHAPTER 26

We rode back to camp, and hoped to find that most of the party still remained. Even from a distance, you could tell what a bloodbath there had been. Bodies contaminated the horizon. Red dominated what had once been green. Our numbers had been decimated, and many of those that remained were wounded.

We hoped off our horses. Lathimian didn't bother with us anymore, instead he went straight to Arsaphi and Mermadak. It was good to see the both of them still alive. My heart weighed like brick, and I fell to my knees. Such a countless number of good men, all dead... all because I'd insisted on a venture, because I'd sent Sehrea out to try and start this all in the first place. Just this morning I'd been sure that only good had come of this quest, but now I wondered whether or not I should have ever started it in the first place.

Sehrea pulled me off the ground, she wasn't content to let me writhe. "There's no time to wail, and cry." she said, "Their deaths are only in vain if we don't press on, so we have to keep going."

As I got further away from the control of my people, from a doctrine ruled by fear; the more lost I felt. At least Sehrea felt more and more confident with every passing day... She was right; I needed to stay strong, at least for now. I went to see to the wounded men, and hoped I could prove useful in some manner. None of the injuries seemed to be too dire, so that was good. There was some bad ones, of course, but none that would lead to death. That was... all we could hope for, I guess. I helped wrap up wounds, and do any little thing I could. Not too long after, I spotted Breovit!

I ran up, and flung myself around him. "Thank goodness you're still alive!"

He laughed, and put an arm around me. "I was always going to be fine, I'm just happy you're fine."

"Somehow..."

I let go of him, and saw he was standing in an awkward manner.

"Did you hurt your leg?"

"Why do you ask, are you calling me a wimp?"

I chuckled. "I'm sorry..."

"You should be, I've-"

"...that your leg got hurt. I can tell, it's pretty obvious."

He shrugged, like it was nothing. "I don't want you to worry about it, it's no big deal."

"Alright... just lay down, please? Let me get you a pillow so you can rest, I'd feel better if you did."

"How could I say no? You're one of a kind, Kea, thank you."

"No, thank you."

I got him a little pillow, and had him rest. There wasn't anything else I could do for the other wounded men that hadn't already been done, so I sought after Lathimian.

He didn't sugarcoat any of his words, or even his tone. "It's only going to get more dangerous from here on out." he said.

I could tell what he was getting at.

"I understand..." I said.

"Once we reach the next town, I'll send you and Sehrea

out with a few knights. It's important word gets back to Muinflor. Can I trust you two?"

"Of course, of course... anything we can do to help."

That's precisely what happened, but first, we laid the fallen to rest. We buried them one by one, set up markers to stand as testament to their bravery, and then pressed on. At the next town we reached, Lathimian pulled Sehrea and I off to the side.

He clicked, and then spoke to us. "This is it, for now." he said.

He'd been clicking a lot since the attack, I could tell he was on edge. Was he overwhelmed with sorrow about what had happened? Was he mortified about what could happen?

"Thank you for all you've done." Sehrea said.

I wasn't sure how to express my gratitude. I stood by, wordless, as Mermadak approached Sehrea.

"The two of you are welcome in Hadia, anytime."

"Thank you," she said, "I'll keep that in mind."

"Seek me out if you find there are anymore mysteries to uncover."

"Of course, thank you."

Arsaphi gave me a pat on the head. "Hang in there, Kea."

"Of course, of course. I will."

"Do your best, 'promise me that?"

"Yes, yes, I promise. Thank you, Arsaphi."

"We should be thanking you."

...Sehrea, I, and two other knights, slipped from the company. A few days of good travel ensued. There really wasn't much to say of our travel, I spent most of it lazing around, or in a daze. We were at an inn, one morning, when I was awakened to find Sehrea standing beside my bed.

"We're going out for food." she said, "I'll bring you something back."

I nodded, and smiled. "Thank you, Sehrea; love you."

"Love you too."

She left, so I locked the door, and returned to bed. I was elated to go back to sleep. I don't know how long passed. A time later, the sound of footsteps awoke me; someone was right outside my room! I was sure it was just Sehrea, back with breakfast, so I didn't think anything of it. If it wasn't Sehrea, it must have just been a random passerby, right? I raised my eyes, and awaited a call to open the door. To my shock, the door crashed open!

There, in the door's wake, stood Loshki. My heart started to race. I was mortified at the prospect of being on his bad side.

"Turns out you're safe, huh?"

He was in an alright mood, thank goodness...

"Lady Miyune's starting to get scared about you, Leestel."

Dread pierced my body, even if it didn't show. My ability to put up masks kicked back into gear, just like old times.

"Of course I'm fine! I just want to see the world is all. Miyune should be patient, I'll be back soon."

Loshki got gruff, and serious.

"You've been gone awhile as is." he said, "You're already the first person to burn her patience."

I couldn't imagine he wanted to play games, but I guess there was no harm in trying.

"Did I really?" I said.

"Seems you did, let's get a move on."

So much for trying... Loshki started to make his way out, which left me to run along and follow beside him.

There was no way I could escape, so there was no point in being difficult; the last thing I wanted to do was dawdle, and risk drawing Sehrea into this mess.

One of Miyune's carriages stood at the ready, right outside of the inn. I hopped in the back of the carriage, and Loshki kicked the company at a rabid pace. We were moving with as much haste as we had when Mermadak was on our trail! I sulked through every moment of our journey back to Sciruthon, because of how close I'd been to escaping once and for all...

We made it back to Sciruthon in lightning time. Loshki's last act before leaving me, was to lead me through the front doors. I looked like a mess, but I didn't care. I went straight to the dining hall, where I found Keras and Miyune having dinner.

Miyune's eyes slithered upon me. "My dearest Kea," she said, "how was your adventure with Lathimian?"

Curses... I wonder how she knew. There was *no way* I'd been spotted when I was in Sciruthon last. Was there a turncoat in Lathimian's midst? Or was Loshki just that good?

"You should ask him yourself." I said, taking a seat.

Best to play things calm, right?

"You haven't missed much, Kea." Miyune went on to say.

"Isn't that lovely."

"Now, if you don't step back into the fray? Only then might you miss something truly special."

I wondered what she meant by that. Regardless, it made sense she wanted me back on her side. Having songs to dazzle nobles with was quite a tool; that tool had helped her make all sorts of progress in the past, albeit I imagined it couldn't help her for much longer. She was as good as a dead woman walking. All I needed to do at this point was make sure she didn't bring me down with her.

"One day soon, we will have the might to overthrow it all, Kea." so she said, "King Clarje of Hadia, King Neromas of Sohal, the houses of Elratheo, and even King Metifell of Dial; all of it."

This woman was insane! I didn't want to upset her, but how couldn't I at least snicker at someone who thought ruling the world was so simple?

"Giggle now if you wish, Kea, but you'll soon see what comes to pass."

"As you say, Miyu."

An attendant rolled out a platter of food for me. I started eating. Miyune made small talk with me like nothing had ever happened, whereas Keras never talked to me at all. I bet he didn't trust me; if that wasn't the case, then he just didn't like me. I didn't blame him if he just didn't like me, it's not like I knew how to connect with people all that well.

"I only wished Loshki had gotten you here sooner, my dear. I would have liked to incorporate you into today's plans."

"Oh, how will I ever go on with my life now? What'll you two be up to today? Banquet, torture session, a stroll around town, a party?"

I'm sure they'd found the corpse in the cellar by now. Did they know I'd gone down there? I wondered. Maybe giving them hints about knowledge I had wasn't a good idea; albeit, if she already knew, then it didn't matter. If she didn't know, she'd probably just think that inclusion of words was me being snarky.

Her face didn't give anything away. "Drinks with

nobles." she said, arising to her feet, "Well then, Kea, we must be off. I hope you have a splendid evening."

Miyune conjoined arms with Keras, and the two made their way out. I left the dining hall moments after them, and flew to the second story. I went into one of the guest rooms, and looked down at the courtyard through a window. There was something I wanted to do, but I couldn't do, until I was *absolutely sure* Miyune and Keras were gone. My eyes followed them out of the courtyard, then deep into town. Now, I could see them no longer... so I ran from the room, and started to roll downstairs.

On my trek downwards, a familiar force tickled at my spine. A faint face came alongside my own, one made of black and red.

"You led them to death." it said.

I scoffed.

"You are the harbinger of death."

Again, I scoffed. I wasn't a harbinger of anything! I wasn't the foretold Miracle Maiden! I was just a stupid kid, graced by ill fate! I bit my lips, wiped away at the sweat on my face, and then wiped away at my neck. For whatever reason, my neck wouldn't stop streaming sweat, so I kept wiping it. I battled dizzyness, and a sudden loss of vision, as I made my way downstairs.

Miyune's home had many windows, and the day was at it's brightest, so there was no reason the first flight should have been dark when I got down there. All that graced the first story was a red light with no source. It looked like night had arisen, and the moon had begun to bleed. I'd been through worse; I ignored the new atmosphere, and pressed on to Miyune's room.

"*Hypocrite...*" it said, as I entered her room.

I wanted to vomit... I fell to a knee, and took a moment to breathe. What on Lathine was wrong with me? A minute passed before I felt any better. At last, I got up, walked over to Miyune's drawers, and pillaged out her key.

"*Theif...*" I heard, once I took the key.

"*Accept the truth.*" was it's last words, before I got back up to the locked room on the second floor.

Something wasn't right with me... why was I standing in front of the door, motionless? Why wasn't I acting? How long had I been standing there for? I guess I'd zoned out hard. My vision was now back in full. I brought my hand down to the keyhole, only to find it colored with blood. A burning sensation ran all across my neck. I threw up my clean hand to rub it, and when it came down, it too was now drenched in blood.

"Zehn yeh, Lahthiihneh...?"

I put the hand to my neck one more time.

"*Zvah!*"

My throat seemed to have stopped bleeding awhile ago. It must have been quite the sight when it was going, because my whole neck was lathered in semi-dry blood. I couldn't begin to guess whether it was an act of possession, or my own rising insanity. I put the key in the keyhole, and unlocked the door one more time.

Focus

Focus

Focus...

My head raced. What had come of Sehrea? Was she alright? Thoughts of what could have befallen her only worsened how I was feeling. Honestly, it's a miracle I didn't pass out...

"Leave this place, and I will leave you." it said.

I hadn't opened the door yet. Who knows how long I'd

been standing for, after unlocking it?

"Leave this place, and I will leave you."

Giving in wouldn't do me any good, so I pushed the door open, picked up my feet, and went in. Once I entered, the world returned to normal, and the things that had been on my back went away. I was left to open up the cabinet in peace, and see what I could find. What I found first read as follows...

"Lord Keras,

our attack on the company of Lathimian ended in vain, they yet live. Neither could we take the child. My Lord, they seek to bring down the rule of the Unsaid One, Mermadak is crushing his allies with an iron fist. Please relate this to the Unsaid One, and ask him what course of action we will take. His kingship is so close to reality, and cannot be trounced now. Mermadak and Lathimian must die.

-Death to all who oppose us."

Was this what Miyune meant, when she said I might miss something *"truly special"*? All the new letters ended up like the one I'd just read; vague, but insightful. I found letters of alliances Miyune and Keras had recently formed, as well as new schemes they had raised. It wasn't until some twenty minutes later, that a paper really strangled my attention span.

"Lady Miyune, I wish to warn you of the investigation formed by Lathimian of Sohal, and Mermadak of Hadia. It now seems they've sent men to Dial to look into what truths might be unearthed. It is quite possible they will learn the truth of your servant, Loshki. Please act with caution. Your faithful servant is glad to give what he can, blessed be you."

Loshki, Loshki, Loshki... what secrets did you have to hide? I guess he wasn't the straightforward mercenary he seemed to be.

CHAPTER 27

After lurking around, I had trouble getting to sleep. It didn't help that I hadn't eaten much while dining with Miyune and Keras. Needless to say, my first night back didn't result in much peace. What could have come of Sehrea? That thought loomed over my head all night. Bed was giving me no comfort, so I was more than eager to leave when sunrise hit. I went to the dining hall, hoping delicious food would take my worries away. There, the hands of fate delivered me to Miyune. Her posture was perfect, she had her signature cutting eyes, and of course, there was a bottle of wine sitting around... you know, her usual setup.

Her eyes laid on me from the get-go. "My dear Kea, is a late rise no longer to your liking?"

"I'm just hungry is all."

As much as I wanted to leave, I couldn't bring myself to. That would look all kinds of suspicious. I guess there was no choice but to bear down, and take a seat at the table...

"There's something important I feel you have yet to learn, my dear."

I kicked back, and tried to play casual.

"And what's that?" I said.

"That mothers have a way of knowing the secrets their daughters keep."

She sure knew how to make me squeamish...

"What mother lets their daughter roam the country alone? That's my first question."

"Do I, or do I not, keep an elite guard at your disposal? Kea, I only wish you did not make such a habit of running off, and throwing fits. If that were the case, it would be quite easy to protect you properly."

I slouched low in my chair, and got rambunctious in my reply. "You're not protecting me, you're imprisoning me."

Her new grin seemed forced. Was she unsure of what card to play? Was she wondering what I really knew? What I'd spilled to Lathimian? Something about this spat wasn't as one sided as usual. Maybe, just maybe... I was getting a little ground to stand on. There was all the reason in the world to think this when she started to take slow sips from her goblet, which seemed to be her way of buying time.

When her glass came down, words joined it. "Keras and I will soon be attending a grand banquet to the south."

"You want me to sing?"

"Yes, Kea, if you would."

"My time would be better spent working with Loshki. I still have many things to learn of this land."

Being to the south wasn't a bad idea, since I'd be close to Muinflor... maybe I could escape to there, one last time. That aside, I still didn't want to join. Who knew what she might have had up her sleeve?

"Nobody values your time and education more than I, Kea. I will personally assure you that."

I tried to roll with her words, and see if I could sneak a win. "Alright, thank you for your understanding."

She wasn't about to let this go. "Kea, if you want to be an adult, be an adult. These games of pretend are worn and tired. Can we not be honest if nothing else?"

"Says the woman who built an empire off lies and corruption."

"I don't lie to you, Kea."

"No, you don't tell outright lies."

Her elegance faded away into something dark. "Kea, I try to work with you."

Before she could continue on, I caught sight of her left hand. She was clutching her goblet in a violent, claw-like manner.

"Regardless of whatever you think, I can honestly say I have tried." she reiterated.

I wanted to go off on her... but knew it was in my best interest to keep calm. I didn't want to get made an example of. Regardless, I didn't keep my calm as well as I should have.

"To scar me, or break my sanity?"

"Kea-"

"You pry information, use me for politics... and send me out to murder."

"If you wish to be nothing more than an ally, so be it, Kehah."

My blood boiled, anger started to leak from the cellar within. "I'm not even that, I'm just a puppet!"

She hid her emotions behind her goblet; I just wish I knew which emotions those were. She didn't reply. An attendant came out to give me a platter of food. I ignored Miyune, and started to eat.

"Tell me something, Kehah..." Miyune said, pouring a glass of wine.

She filled it to the brim, and then pushed it my way. "How is Sehrea?"

Maybe if I acted swiftly, I could kill her here and now.

After all, the attendant had given me a knife for my food. I downed the glass of wine in moments; when she leaned in to pour me some more, I glanced at the butter knife, and thought about trying. I couldn't stop thinking about it... but I chickened out. What could I really do with a dinky butter knife? She was older, and thus stronger, and the attendants would have been out in moments if I did something. Sehrea could have done it, I bet, but not me.

I didn't know what else to do but down another glass out of spite. "How would I know? I'm too busy being here."

I pushed the glass forward.

Miyune repeated the process, and filled it again. "I hope she's safe..." she said, pushing the glass back my way, "It is such a dangerous world, after all, Kehah."

"I'm sure she's fine."

Stress started to wind a knot in my stomach.

"Have you lost your appetite, Kehah? Are you alright?"

"Just a headache, don't sweat it."

She looked to me with sad eyes. "You should rest after you eat, my dear. Take time to be at peace, and think of what is good for you. Think of what is good for your growth as a person, and those you love."

Zvah... that had to be a threat.

She rose from her seat, and gave me a little wave. "I'll be passing on, Kehah. Please enjoy your day."

After the door closed, my skin began to tingle. Shortness of breath found me. She couldn't really have Sehrea... could she?

A familiar voice tickled inside my ear. "Go save her." it said, "You *know* where she is."

My teeth crunched, and coarse words slithered out. ***"Leave, me, alone..."***

"Save her Kehah."

"Leave... me... alone."

"Kehah."

I couldn't keep myself together, so I ran out; it followed me all the way out of the palace.

"Kehah..."

It wouldn't stop saying my name.

"Kehah, Kehah, Kehah..."

There was rarely anyone up at this hour. I was able to move through town without issue. Hopefully a lack of issues would continue, namely; once I reached Loshki's house. I had to get the key to the cellar, and make sure Sehrea wasn't down there. I doubted Loshki would be at his house, since he always started his day so early, but even if he was home, I was determined to figure something out.

I was fortunate, because the voice inside my head was quick to leave. If only it wasn't just as quick to return... It emerged again when I got to the garbage pile behind Loshki's home. A familiar pair of red eyes manifested; it chose to take a spectral form, both dark as night, and blurred as the wind. What on Lathine was it thinking? All it did was walk around me, and stare.

"Kehah... *KehaH*... **KeHah**... KehAh... *KeHaH*."

It wouldn't stop crying my name. It's voice got more demented with every pass it made around me. I'd be lying if I said that experience made ignoring it easy. By the time I'd uncovered the house's crawl space, the voice had already put me on the verge of a breakdown. My heart blazed, and seared. I was terrified to go down into the dark, knowing it would follow me.

"Go down there Kehah, *go down there Kehah.*"

I had to push through, for Sehrea. I couldn't give up.

My feet kicked down through the opening, and brought me into the darkness, or, to what should have been darkness, at least. The *presence* fell in front of me, and stared straight into my eyes. It's bright red eyes were torn open, and it's jaw was unhinged. It was deathly thin, with pale skin, long black hair, claws, and sharp teeth. It looked like a human, in a lot of ways. It tilted it's head, and did nothing but stare at me. I froze with fear.

Light began to fade from it's eyes. I couldn't make it out, just it's silhouette... and now, as the last bit of light left it, I couldn't even see a silhouette anymore. All that let me know it was near was the soft crunching of footsteps around me.

"Zvah..."

Saliva pounded down my throat. My breaths got so loud that even the twisted laughs around me couldn't drown them out. Footsteps continued to echo, and just kept getting faster. As a means of not screaming, I buried my face into the ground. I couldn't acknowledge what was with me... I couldn't, *I couldn't,* **I couldn't.**

I laid there, and kept thinking to myself *"Oh God... how did it ever come to this?"*

This life was anything but what I would have hoped for. It's a good thing I was realistic, and knew wishing for a better life meant nothing at all. All that matters is working with the hand you're given, and being a product of your will, as opposed to circumstance. I wiped away my tears, and picked my head up. Dirt, grime, and myriads of garbage met me; I struggled through it all, one inch at a time.

"It's finding something stronger than your fear, that's all bravery is." so Mermadak had said.

Yes, yes... I didn't have to look hard to find that something; for me, that something was Sehrea. She was that something that made the pain of living worthwhile. My heart did everything it could to hold together for both our sakes. I wasn't sure what to look for... but awhile passed, I finally bumped into a latch. I pulled on it, and crawled through. I looked up to see... that I was at the bottom of an outhouse like toilet. Vulgarities would have been slinging from my mouth aplenty if not for how suddenly the entity harassing me vanished. That alone put me in too good of a mood to swear.

I made quick work of finding out how Sehrea had gotten to the top... now if only strength was a skill of mine. She'd put dents in the wall to use as footholes! It was difficult for me to work with... but I managed to make decent progress. My muscles began to ache as I climbed. Right under the way out was when exhaustion hit.

"Zvah... zvah, zvah!"

I struggled for the last few inches, and managed to throw myself through! My body crashed into the floor on the other side. From there, I picked myself up, and took a quick look through Loshki's home, to make sure he wasn't in. It turned out he was gone, thank goodness! My feet staggered to the kitchen, and stumbled into the pantry. I pushed the flour aside, got the cellar key, put the flour back, and got going.

CHAPTER 28

Anxiety carouseled up my spine, while goosebumps ran down my fingertips. I couldn't imagine how anyone could go into the abyss under Miyune's palace, alone, and not feel terrified. My hands started to tremble from the moment I walked into the palace. What would a wise person have done to vent fear? Well, I didn't know... What I ended up doing, was tapping at my side, but my rythmic tapping was quick to develop into a full fledged song. Bruises would greet me later, but that was the last thing on my mind...

Curse it all, had I zoned out again? Was I bleeding? I looked up, to see I was now in front of the cellar door. Drips started to leave my right hand, which made my heart drop. I looked down... and didn't see anything. My hand went to my forehead, and brought down something colorless. Alright, I was just sweating, that's fine... no big deal. Something loud banged from the otherside of the door, which made me jump out of my skin. It must have been a spirit at work...

"It's just Lathimian trying to save you." I lied, to soothe myself.

Oh, wait... that thunderstorm sound was just my breathing. My hands weren't doing any better; they shook worse than a feather on the wind. They got the key into the keyhole though, so I guess that's all that mattered.

"Open it, Kea!" I scolded myself, "Open it! You can do this, Kea..."

I put the key in my pocket, and pushed the door open. Right away, a blast of energy rubbed my bones. A bad feeling gripped me. Was something dark watching me, or had I let something dark out? Did it have to do with what Sehrea and I had encountered last time? Something... *was here with me,* that's all I knew.

"Hold in there Kea, hold in there, hold in there Kea..."

I couldn't risk someone prancing upon the open door; I closed it, and welcomed the darkness. Nobody would be able to hear me if I screamed, so if there was someone down here with me... then there was no telling what could happen. I pressed through total darkness, down into the abyss, and saw a faint light at the bottom. Everything began to spin, and it took all I had just to keep my balance.

Now, the cellar smelt like a rotted corpse, which made my headache worse. I had to keep both hands on the wall just to stay on my feet. I made my way down extremely slow, because I might have died if I lost my balance and tumbled all the way down.

There was a figure under the light. Was it the advisor of my father? No, no, it couldn't be! It wasn't in the right position! My feet continued down, with no lack of caution. My eyes stayed sharp, and I was ready to bolt at any moment, if I had to.

"Sehrea!?!" I echoed down the steps.

That's when the figure moved, and turned to me. It was her! My tears flew down the stairs before my feet ever could. She didn't just have binds on her arms and legs; but also a gag in her mouth. She was trying to scream something, but I couldn't tell what. She kept shaking me off, but of course I wasn't about to go away! As my first act, I freed her from the gag.

"Miyune's sick!" I screamed, "That witch'll...!!!"

Cold entered my heart, like I'd never felt before; it went beyond a skipped heartbeat.

"My, my..." a voice echoed, "what do you wish to do to me, my dear?"

So that's why Sehrea's eyes had been shooting past me... towards the top of the stairs. Even if I knew what she was looking at, I still couldn't accept it.

"Continue on, Kehah." Miyune giggled, "Continue on. You know I love your voice."

I couldn't hold back any longer, and thrusted my face her way. *"You witch!!! Fah nohoo naheh gveo viih! Rahsah ahn seoviih!"*

I don't know how I should have felt. Her face didn't change!

"Now do you understand what playing games in an adult laden world does, Kehah?"

Saliva flew with every word I screamed. "You don't deserve to call me that!"

Bearing a candle, Miyune leaned against the wall. She was as calm as ever. It was unsettling to look at how her face flickered in the dark. How could the cellar be beneath her, how could she pay this nightmare of a place no mind?

"Let's make a deal." she said.

My heart was screaming, my veins were popping, and my hands were shaking. Even still, nothing meant more to me than Sehrea's safety, so I bore down, and took a moment to breath.

"Let's hear it." I finally said.

"Stay with me, and do what you would in times

passed. Can you still be my perfect little niece? If you stay true to your word, Sehrea's life will become every bit as luxurious as yours. We will give her a room on the second flight, and allow her to wander the palace as she pleases. Aren't I quite generous, Kehah?"

As much as I wanted to tell Miyune to go dig her grave... I couldn't. Sehrea's life depended on my actions.

"I'll take it, unchain her immediately."

"See? You can act like a princess after all."

Her eyes stayed upon me a good while, and all went to silence. I guess that was her way of claiming victory. She didn't have any qualms about rubbing it in my face...

"I'll get Loshki, and we'll sort this all out." Miyune said.

She left to whence she'd came. Sehrea wasn't excited about safety, or the prospect of luxury.

"You can't sacrifice yourself for me. Just get out of here, go back to Muinflor."

"I can't do that! How could I just leave you!?!"

Neither of us had the heart for anymore words, instead, I held her. My eyes stayed closed until Loshki arrived.

"Good for you, Leestel." he said.

I think that was him applauding me for braving it, getting the cellar key, and coming all the way down into the abyss. You'd have thought he'd be mad I'd broken into his house! Regardless, he undid Sehrea's binds. All's well that ends well, I guess? He began to lead us up the steps... and that's when curiosity took me. I stopped in my tracks. Loshki was here, after all, which meant no harm could befall me. With that in mind, I had a spurt of bravery.

"Loshki?"

"Yes, Milady Leestel?"

"If you knew... just in theory, where this hallway goes

on to, could you tell me?"

"I'm afraid I can't. You're smart for not going down there."

For better or for worse, I'd probably never know what laid at the end. Loshki led us out, I gave him the key, and then he locked the door one last time.

He held the key in front of his face. "I'm putting this somewhere you'll never find. Don't think of what else could be down there, Milady Leestel. You shouldn't see."

"I understand..."

My nerves began to settle. Loshki led us to the bathroom, and then left us. There, a handful of maids flourished around Sehrea; they held up all sorts of clothes to see how she'd look in them. Sehrea seemed a little taken by surprise, you could tell high society wasn't part of her blood. It wasn't long until they settled on a pair of clothes for her. She took them, then went into the bathroom to clean up, and change. Maids went in with her after she finished. When she finally came out, she had a shine to her! Pretty frills and bright colors looked good on her, even if it was weird for me to see. Miyune stayed true to her word, and gave Sehrea a room on the second story.

"The maids are at your service." Miyune told her, "Let them know whenever you have a wish."

"I will."

I could tell Sehrea was fiery about this whole ordeal, she was doing good at suppressing it.

"Is there anything else I can bless you with, my dear?"

Sehrea shook her head.

Miyune looked to me. "Then, the both of you, please enjoy your time together."

"Alright. Thank you, Miyu."

I didn't want to be a kiss up, but I just couldn't risk getting on Miyune's bad side.

Lashing back at her was out of the question. Even just getting a little passive aggressive sounded dangerous. I will admit, it was hard to not at least mumble something under my breath as she walked away.

"What fate does God hold for us?" Sehrea wondered, "Why does it happen in this way?"

She went over, and fell back on her new bed. I saw her face elate the moment she touched it.

"I'll admit, this is wonderful."

I threw myself beside her. "Everything material here is wonderful. Miyune knows the physical world better than anyone."

Like usual, neither of us said a word. Neither of us seemed to know who we should be, or what we should believe in... so I guess it made sense we never knew what to say.

"Let's go along with her games." Sehrea said, "Justice will reign in the long run, we must buy time in the present."

"I couldn't agree more... whatever it takes."

Yes, Lathimian would be here to rain vengeance any day now...

CHAPTER 29

I wanted to stay with Sehrea for every second of every day, if only reality would accept that wish... Sehrea wasn't allowed to leave the palace, and that was understandable. I had a letter I needed to send to Muinflor, so I rushed through town, and hoped to make my errand quick. My letter would let Muinflor know that Sehrea and I been taken, and everything that had happened since. My feet didn't stop until they were back in the palace again. Sehrea had been in the study, so I ran to there, fearing something could have happened in the short time I'd been out. I was happy to see that wasn't the case; she was still in there, reading away.

"You look panicked, Kea."

"It's nothing, don't worry about it."

We went back to studying. At first, we didn't find anything that could help us. All we found was good tales of days passed, such as the tale of Queen Siegliss, and her faithful knight, Vesoleth. Not long after, we found information on the Break of Lathine, which was the first war to ever engulf Lathine. The Break of Lathine was from the time of the Dark Priest, Thirivu, who King Neromas said gave the prophecy of the Miracle Maiden. His beliefs were very much the same as my people's.

Were Sehrea and I descended from him, or was our people just stupid enough to go along with his madness? Who could say? All I knew is that he seemed to view the

Miracle Maiden as death itself. According to him, I was as good as the devil, or, as good as the devil to all who opposed him, at least. He was also from the same point in time as the tactician Lathiris, which I found interesting.

We had just finished studying a book containing knowledge of Thirivu, when Miyune appeared in the doorway.

"How I do love a studious spirit, I was much the same as you two. With that thought aside; dinner is prepared, will you both join?"

"Yes." I said, feeling like we had to, "Thank you for letting us know."

"Of course, my dear."

Miyune left us. Sehrea and I rose to our feet.

"This whole thing is odd, very, very odd..." Sehrea said.

"I know, this life is just one crazy mess."

"Agreed."

Sehrea and I took a moment to pick up after ourselves. We'd been snacking all day thus far. I could tell Sehrea enjoyed being waited on, even if she didn't want to admit it. We went to the dining hall right after. Platters were laid upon the table, four in total. They were for Sehrea, Miyune, Keras, and I, no doubt, except; Keras had yet to arrive, only Miyune was there.

We took seats, and Sehrea demolished her food before I could blink. She looked good, everything considered. My eating exploits had been far more embarrassing during my first while at the palace.

"I'm happy to see you enjoy our food so." Miyune said, taking note of Sehrea's gusto.

"It's excellent," Sehrea said, "you must be very proud of your attendants."

"They are the finest."

"I see that."

Us three continued to eat, and it seemed nobody felt like speaking anymore. We just needed to buy time, and keep on her good side for a little while longer; that's what my gut told me.

"Do you ever find banquets interesting?" I asked, off the top of my head, "Is it always the same old people?"

"It is interesting at first." Miyu said, "When you are just starting out, you'll find a rush in your skin. You find yourself looking to go farther, and farther. I relished the rise up the ladder, however, matters become dull when you reach the height of your power. It is a nuisance to see the same faces time and time again."

"I can only imagine how stale you must find them nowadays." Sehrea said.

"I quite hate them, but I must endure them all the same."

Miyune tilted her glass towards me, and spoke. "Actually, that reminds me..."

"Yes?" I said.

"Keras and I have that banquet to the south. It turns out our host, Lord Ruvaen, is quite the lover of music. He is even holding an event the second day of our arrival. There will be many musicians, songstresses, and entertainers. I would not force your hand, of course, but merely ask once more whether or not you wish to join."

Her eyes told me to say yes. She had Sehrea as collateral, so I didn't have a choice.

"Sure," I said, "I will."

"Wonderful."

"Will we be attending the event you speak of?" I asked.

"I was not planning on it. In all seriousness, I am quite in reverence of your singing. Nothing else compares, so I have no interest in listening to others."

"Ah... I ask, because I'd be interested in joining his little event."

She grinned, I could tell she hadn't expected me to feel that way. "Would you now? If you would like to, then you absolutely may; no doubt Lord Ruvaen will allow you to participate upon hearing your voice."

"Yes, I'm sure he will."

Miyune turned to Sehrea. "I would be very much appreciative if you could keep an eye on the palace in the meantime. It would be quite good for you to have time to adjust to this domain."

"I have no complaints. It's excellent here... heavenly, even."

You could tell she enjoyed the plush beds, silk sheets, and endless array of delicacies that being part of Miyune's house entailed.

"Wonderful then, Sehrea, I am quite glad to hear that."

A creak pierced the air, drowning out the sound of silverware. My head spun back, to see Keras entering the room. I wondered what part he had to play in all this. By logic, he was the most powerful person in the room, but by my eyes, it looked like Miyune was! I imagined he didn't like all the shenanigans Miyu was running.

"I can tell I'm no longer single." he said.

It was hard to tell whether he was serious, or joking; his voice was always so dry...

"Do you not love the feeling?" Miyune said.

"I don't know."

He took a seat, and began to eat. He and Miyune made small talk, albeit he never said a word to Sehrea or I; in fact, he never talked to me to begin with. I bet he didn't trust me, let alone Sehrea. It's good for our sakes that Miyune had quite the leash around him.

"Kea will be joining us to the home of Lord Ruvaen. She will also sing a song for the honor of our house." Miyu told him, "Isn't that exciting?"

"I would think she'd be weary from her last trip."

"I am more than ready to wander the land, and learn more." I said.

"What did you learn on your last trip?" he said, dropping eyes upon me.

"Nothing I'm sure you don't already know." I said, "Sohal and Hadia are seeking to act against the underworld. They even plan to go into Dial, and investigate the truth about Loshki. That's left me wondering, is he from Dial?"

Keras wasn't willing to show cards.

Miyune, however, was game. "He is, except we do not like to remember that time in his life. It was quite difficult for him."

"I see... that makes sense. I guess all that matters is the work he does in the present."

"Precisely." Miyu commended me, before turning to Keras, "Is she not becoming quite wise?"

"Yes... she is gaining wisdom. Wisdom and knowledge is a powerful tool."

He didn't trust us, there was no way! As to why Miyune was still big on me, I could only imagine. If not for what she'd done to Sehrea, I might have considered opening up, and reaching out to her. Now, all I cared about was putting her behind bars; I even cared about that more than the better world I'd always dreamed of. Bringing her to justice was just a way of venting all the emotions I had, I'll admit. I had a lot of emotions, which must have been why my desire to sentence her had gotten so great.

Was it right to put your morals aside for the greater

good? I don't think I could say it was, at least in my case...
because in my case, it was just revenge; it was just a
selfish way of making myself feel better. I know that was
bad. I know things like that made me no better than the
people I sought to inflict *"justice"* upon...

CHAPTER 30

A good while passed.

Sehrea looked to me with sad eyes. "Do you really think they're alright?"

I didn't know what to say.

"If something did happen to them all..." she went on to say, "Sohal and Hadia would be pushed to drastic action. It seems either way, fate's bound to bring something here shortly."

"Do you believe in fate?" I asked her.

"I use it moreso to mean *'something that is bound to happen'*, but no, I don't believe in it like we used to."

"Do you believe anything we grew up with?"

She shook her head. "We were washed of reason from birth, forced to adopt something made from the head of man. Sometimes I reminisce, but I'll never go back."

"That makes sense."

"It has to. What else do I have to cling to, Kehah? I want to soul-search once this is all through."

"Me too, everything that's happened since I was taken has just made me more confused than I started."

"Me as well."

I slid a hand through my hair... I hated thinking about how much I didn't know!

Sehrea sighed, and got up. "I'm going to bathe out, and try to relax."

"That sounds good. I've been sort of craving treats

from town; I'll be back with some before you get out, alright?"

"That sounds good, be safe."

"I'll be fine. In a weird sort of way, we're safer in Sciruthon than anywhere else."

"I know... and it's things like that which only confuse me more. Miyune keeps us so safe, so fed, so well served."

"Whether or not she needs us as hostages, the lengths she goes to still doesn't make sense." I agreed.

After a quick hug, we parted ways. I kicked through the palace, out the gate, and towards the street where the sweets vendors always lined up. On the way there, a pair of footsteps began to take up residence behind me. Before running could even be contemplated, the footsteps slipped up beside me. It was a knight!

"Kea Leestel, correct?"

"Possibly?"

He kept a hand over his mouth, and peered cautiously around. "I was set up to keep an eye on the palace, for the next time you left. You have a visitor from Muinflor, who's hoping to speak with you."

"You said from Muinflor?"

I wasn't about to trust this man outright.

"Yes, in reply to the letter you sent."

Alright, maybe I should trust him outright... nobody could have known about that letter except Muinflor.

"Go to the knight's headquarters. Miyune's guards are always watching, I must be going."

"Thank you."

So much for just making a quick sweets run! My little feet crossed through back alleys, dark corners, and on to the knight's of Sciruthon's headquarters. There, a knight nodded to me at the door, and let me in. When I entered,

I was met by the definition of simplistic; the room had boring wood floors, boring plain walls, a few windows, some tables, and chairs. It was nice to see the knight's acted in a humble manner. There was about four men sitting at one of the table's, and their eyes in particular fell upon me. Something about one of them felt familiar... I stared for a few seconds, and tried to see if I could remember why.

"General Tranel!" I finally cried.

He gave me a nod. "Looks like I owe an apology to the man who got you. You see, I thought you'd just think *'stranger danger'*, and not come."

"That is what I thought at first." I admitted.

Tranel grinned. "Then I'm partially right." he said.

All of a sudden, a different demeanor took him. "Are you ready to talk about more serious things?"

"I am." I said, taking a seat, "I want to hear everything you can tell me, bar none."

"You're smart to say that, because there's no way around it. There's a lot of things to go over."

He threw his arms on the table, and stammered around. He didn't seem sure where to start.

"I-I... I... here, I'm not the right one for a synopsis, but I'll do my best. Lathimian is holed up in Hadia with Mermadak, working through issues."

"Will he be back soon?"

"Hard to say, but Muinflor needs him before it acts, and that's why I'm here. We'll take you back to Muinflor. There's no point for you to stay around here if you don't have to."

"I can't, Miyune has my sister."

Tranel grumbled under his breath, and began to pull at the hairs on his chin. "That complicates things. Forget everything I said, because there is a reason to stay here."

"Correct, I can't leave until she's freed."

Tranel nodded. "Of course not, she's family. You've got to be there for her."

"Yes, exactly!"

"And this is where thing's get really difficult, because I'm not in a position to lead any liberation."

"I understand."

"And let's say I did? Things would get messy, quick. There's no such thing as a *'clean stomp'* of Keras and Miyune."

"At least not until Lathimian returns?"

"Yes. When it starts, it's going to hit fast. There's going to be raids all over Sohal. This is going to be the sort of thing the average person goes to bed during, and hears of the next morning when all's said and done, if at all. If we don't take every single person we can in the hierarchy of Miyune and Keras, then others will just rise through the ranks to take their places."

"Something so grandscale... is that really necessary? How could their empire be so strong?"

"They're a shadow government, is what they are. They may as well be the fifth nation of Lathine."

"You're kidding..."

"I wish. Intel says they were close to acting. If they'd had just a little more time, we'd be engulfed in cival war without end. We still might be if we don't move quick."

"Unbelievable..."

"You've seen Miyune up close, I'm sure you understand that she knows how to keep things in the dark."

"Unfortunately... and, speaking of what I've learned up close, you're all going to Dial too, right? Or sending some men out there, or something?"

"How do you know that?"

"There's a locked room in Miyune's palace that I sneak into a lot. She keeps loads of important letters there. One of them tells how you'll be sending men to Dial to investigate."

"Then the men are going to get a warning, immediately."

"Miyune's scared you'll learn about her chief guard. I can't imagine what he could be hiding."

"Yes, Loshki, if I'm right?"

"Yes, General. Miyune told me that Loshki's from Dial, and has a tough past, but that's all she'd say. Loshki himself has told me he's been a mercenary since he was young, so he's probably wanted in Dial."

"I'll get that sent to Lathimian immediately."

I set my head down, feeling uneasy about my next line of thinking. "What about the one they call *Nothaniir?* Has anyone found him?"

Tranel pulled at his beard again. "Nothing, we have absolutely nothing. Anyone we find is too terrified to bring him up, or doesn't know where he is."

"How terrified?"

"They'd rather kill themselves than speak; in fact, one man did kill himself, 'stabbed his throat through. There's a stigma surrounding the name. Anyone who flaunts it is said to later reach a grisly death by Nothaniir's own hands."

"Miyune can be brutal as well. Now that I think of it, that's probably where she gets it from."

"You're on the right line of thinking." Tranel said, "I guess what I'm really here to say, is we need you to be patient a little longer. Me being here is proof of what's going to happen."

"Alright, I can do that. That's already what Sehrea and I assumed."

"Then you made a good call. Don't get in Miyune's way, don't worry about unraveling secrets, don't worry about any of it; you're bystanders now. I want you to stay safe, the end'll come soon."

"I got it. Thank you, General Tranel."

"Don't thank me, just keep safe."

It's a good thing he got to me when he did. If he'd been just a day and a half later, he would have missed me! Keras, Miyune, and I, were on the verge of heading out for the banquet to the north, for the banquet of some man named Ruvaen. In retrospect, I should have asked General Tranel about Lord Ruvaen. I should have picked his mind to see if it knew something. Retrospect aside, I hurried back to the palace as fast as I could. Sehrea was probably nervous about how long I'd been gone for. She ended up being in the study, and could tell something had happened.

"Are you alright, Kea?" she asked.

I closed the door behind me. "I just spoke with General Tranel."

"What? Really? What did he say!?!"

"Mostly what we already knew; to be patient. He's up here, because it's almost time to act. They're on the precipice of ending this."

"That's good to hear. I'm not sure how long things would stay peaceful for, if we were to stay here indefinitely."

Something warped her face.

"What is it?" I asked.

"I listened in on Keras and Miyune, while you were gone."

"What did you hear?"

"What we already knew; Keras doesn't trust us. He doesn't like playing around with us. He feels we're traitors to their will."

"I mean... he's not wrong."

"Precisely my point, Kea. How long will Miyune choose to overlook the facts for?"

"I see your point, that's why I've been kissing up to her. We have to put our egos away for a little while longer. No more snooping around, no more sass... we just have to be patient."

"If that's what Muinflor wants, then I couldn't agree more."

"Excellent."

CHAPTER 31

"Please be careful, Kea."

Sehrea's eyes were big and sad.

I tried to reassure her. "I'll be fine, trust me."

"She knows they hailed me as the Miracle Maiden in your absence, so... just be *very* careful."

"I don't understand what you mean."

"As long as she has one of us, our father will most likely see that as enough. I'm worried she'll make an example of one of us, to keep the other in line."

"I've never even considered that... but, the two of us together are too valuable."

"That's true. With both of us, she might be able to press the King into bringing out our people as an army."

"Quite possibly."

Neither of us knew what else to say, so things got quite. It was one of the longer silences we'd had in awhile, which was saying something. Silence didn't end until a shadow popped in the doorway.

"Are you ready to take leave, young one?" Miyune asked.

I turned to her, and nodded. "Ready as I can be."

"Good. What a responsible young lady you are, Kea."

Neither Sehrea or I had anything we were comfortable saying with Miyune right there. I left without uttering another word.

Miyune gave Sehrea a gentle wave. "Please enjoy yourself." she said.

I doubt there would be many more times Miyune's kindness to my sister outweighed my own, if any. Together, Miyune and I made our way to the outskirts. On the outskirts, we found carriages waiting. It surprised me how quiet she ended up being through the rest of the day. She left me be, and didn't say a word, nor did she share a carriage with me. I was relieved to have a carriage to myself. Should I have considered this a good thing, her sudden silence? Or was it a bad thing? It was different, at least. Her silence remained for the duration of our trip to the south.

Now, I had no Sehrea, no Lathimian, no Arsaphi, no Breovit... and Miyune seemed to have given up on me. In loneliness was where the phantoms found me. Like always, when I felt most isolated, they got to me. Miyune gave me my own inn room every night, which seemed to please that which follows.

"Stop running..." it said, endlessly, *"stop running, stop running, stop running."*

I wondered if it knew what it was talking about.

Each morning of the trip, I went out, and tried to find breakfast. Most of the people I saw around were stained with mud, and tattered clothes. People were breaking their backs on physical labor, left and right. There was homeless men sprawled all over the streets, who seemed to be waiting on death, and it came to mind how much I'd ignored these sorts of details in the past. I'd always been so focused on Miyune, on bringing an end to her tyranny, or solving my own problems... but was either of those missions what really mattered? That thought was yet another thing to plop on the pile of questions I didn't have an answer to.

Lots of rambling came from my mind over the course of the venture; I'd had way too much free time on my hands. Finally, on the day of the banquet, we reached the home of Lord Ruvaen.

"Welcome!" a guard greeted, "To the home of Lord Ruvaen!"

I was surprised to see who stepped in front of me, and took charge... Keras! I shot a quick glance at Miyune. She wasn't paying any of this much mind.

"Blessed be this house." Keras greeted, as we pushed by, and entered.

For some reason, a feeling of déjà vu gnawed at my bones. Lord Ruvaen's castle was quite plain in nature, as opposed to the paradise of sights that was Miyune's palace; granted, that's not to say his home wasn't still incredible in it's own right. Few people that have ever lived would have turned it down.

Keras led us much like Lathimian would, in the aspect that he knew too well what he was doing. He didn't have Lathimian's bearings, so the fact it looked like he did put me on edge. Keras must have been here before. Beyond that, something else gripped the air. I flinched when a shadow flew away from the corner of my sight. Was it... a spirit? I kept watching the shadows, and confirmed something was hiding, but what I found wasn't a phantom. There were humans hiding in the shadows, and in dark rooms! I pressed my face into Miyune's arm, and played it off like a loving child. In actuality, I did this so nobody could see my mouth.

"Miyu?" I said, "There's people hiding in the corners."

She stopped, and kissed me on the forehead. Her lips stayed against me, so nobody could see her own mouth.

"Call it a test, Kea. Walk on and pay it no mind, you are

quite safe."

"Alright."

That set my fears at ease, even if it didn't stop me from sneaking peeks. My eyes kept inking over into dark rooms that had been left open, and to the shadows that loomed. My continued diligence was out of curiosity, more than anything else. If Miyune was confident in our safety, then there was no reason to fret. Either way, we ended up before a pair of great doors, decorated from top to bottom with crimson red, vibrant yellows, and fine dark accents. Red and yellow with darkness mixed in was the prototypical color scheme of Sohal.

Two guards stood at the door. They opened it up, and there I saw the greatest dining hall I'd ever laid eyes on. It's marble flooring had the most intricate design imaginable. It's abundant chandeliers were each big as a house, with the beauty of the moon! Tables spun like branches, while statues pranced about, and food accompanied drinks all over. Back to statues... each one looked crazed. It was odd, because they reminded me of the statues my father had.

Keras went to the grandest of all the tables. Again, like Lathimian, he just *knew* where to go. He took a seat, I sat at his left hand, and Miyune sat at my left hand. In turn, people of eloquent garb and beautiful hues began to take places around the table. All eyes looked to Keras, and Miyune, which served to show how prominent they were. Even amongst nobles they were noble.

Keras sat tall, and proud, and then addressed the table. "It is an honor to be here, and see you all."

He gave a little talk, while Miyune stayed back. She held down good posture, played the role of a submissive wife, and did nothing more. It was odd to see that turn of events. There must have been something unknown at work, because Keras wasn't half Miyune's equal in terms of bending others to their will.

Keras's speech was quick to end. Everyone went silent. For a second, I thought nobody was going to reply. Imagine giving a tandem like Keras and Miyune the cold shoulder! That was when a shadow moved over me, and passed on to Keras. Everyone was looking to said shadow; he bore a golden crown, a well kept beard, and fine, silk-like hair. His hair had a natural sway to it, so he looked quite regal as a result. Just like you couldn't fake the level of looks Miyune had, neither could you fake the sort of sway he had.

He looked to Keras. "My old, old friend... father time hit you hard! Turns out you could attend after all, huh? I'm glad, aren't you glad?"

Keras rose to his feet, nodded out of respect, and then shook the man's hand. "Both glad, and honored."

This would have been a good time for Miyune to join the game, right? I was surprised when she didn't. My eyes stayed on Keras' *old friend*, and tried to decipher him. He was quick to return my curiosity.

"Surely you can't raise a child this fast, can you?" he said.

"She is the niece of my eternal love." Keras told.

I could tell something was lingering in the man's head... I felt like he was the sort of person I shouldn't mess around with. My head turned from him, and I pretended to be fascinated with the room around me.

"This is the one blessed with the gift of old tongue, and songs like starlight?"

Keras turned to me. "Gift us, Kea."

I blew a smile from cheek to cheek. "Of course, of

course!"

This was probably my audition for the event, yet I couldn't have felt any less pressured. I was confident my singing would more than speak for itself.

"Ah rooiih lahsah gahme soo fah kehl liihreen

Ah lahiih koh yaiih ahn dkah zluh seev

Zen meo ah twih koh ehreen, tohreht, vah ee"

Just a few lines should have been more than enough. My eyes opened to see a bewildered crowd. Mouths gaped open, and eyes were amazed.

"Ruvaen, she's quite gifted, isn't she?" Keras said to the man from before.

Well, now I knew who Lord Ruvaen was... although, I'd already guessed as much.

"Yes, she really is. I'd do a fair bit to get someone of that caliber in my own house."

After those words, a smug little grin enveloped Miyune's face. Sass about me must have been running amok in her head.

"I'm enlisting her talents, Keras." Ruvaen said, "There's nothing you can say about it. Now, I know you'll hate me; but I had to move the event back a day. You'll still let her join, right? You know she'd fit perfectly!"

"Allow me a sec-"

I cut Keras off. "Uncle Keras, Uncle Keras! I would be more than happy to!"

Keras knew how much I liked to laze. I'm sure he hadn't expected me to actually go through with the event. He couldn't get anything more than a *"Really?"* out, before Ruvaen shut him down.

"It'd be good for you, Keras, and you know it. You don't get out enough anymore. We'll kick back with a few bottles, *the good stuff,* and unwind. You still like to unwind, right?"

"I-..."

Ruvaen continued to put words in Keras' mouth. "Of course you do! It'll be good for you."

Keras pretended to think it over, but I could tell he was just getting Miyu's thoughts.

Miyune poured herself another glass. "If Kea wishes to, we absolutely will."

"'Wonderful woman, Keras. Your taste is unparalleled."

"Couldn't agree more."

Ruvaen clapped. "You'll stay with me, you'll all stay with me. We'll have some good times, like the old times. How about it, Keras? This'll be good."

"I hope so." Miyune muttered to me, "Can't be any worse than the wine..."

Keras and Ruvaen continued to talk. Everyone else went back to socializing. As a result, no eyes were upon Miyune and I. She set her glass down, and nudged it to me. I lifted up for a sip; it was awful! Figures that Miyune would only give me the garbage stuff...

As far as banquets went, this one turned out being pretty alright. I had some fun... Keras went off with Lord Ruvaen to do their own thing, and steal attention, which meant Miyune and I were left alone. We shared some food, shared some wine... and just talked. We didn't talk about anything serious, or anything dire; instead, we just talked about silly, normal, everyday things. It was nice to concern myself with trivialities for a change, except I couldn't help but feel guilty the whole time Miyu and I spoke. I couldn't look into her eyes, because the simple truth was that I was a no-good backstabber.

I wonder what would have happened, if in the beginning, I'd been a little better... I thought back to the first time I'd met her; when she'd raised me from the ground. She'd fed me well, cleaned me up, and given me a nice bed to rest upon. She could have thrown me into the cellar, and thought nothing more, but that wasn't what she did.

I'd always been taught by my people, by their doctrine, from birth on, *"It's justice against evil, it's us against them."*

Yes, it was us against the worlds we'd one day venture out to seize... Those of other worlds were ultimate evil, so my people always said. I'd never believed such doctrine, but somewhere deep down, I knew such teachings had worked their way into my soul. After fourteen years of being brought up one way, it was hard to follow any other way, no matter how hard I tried. I wonder if I could have helped Miyune, had I been a different person. Perhaps having faith, and reaching out with my heart, was all I had to do all along? I guess I'd never know what could have been. In the end, all that matters is what I chose to do. I chose to act with the cold hand of justice... like I was bred to.

CHAPTER 32

Miyune had packed me a beautiful dress, perfect for performing! I put it on, and the bright leggings that went with it. Miyune did my hair, and many things after.

"Do you like the shade, Kea?" she asked, as she did my lips.

I looked into a mirror, and saw that it was good.

"I do." I said.

"Do you like this, Kea?" she asked, later on, as she did my eyes.

"It's beautiful. You do really well, I mean it."

She did my skin too.

"How bright do you want to go?"

"As bright as you can." I said, "I'm curious what my skin can hold."

"We'll have you glistening like a star." she said, "It only takes a skilled hand."

I was impressed. She frilled me up, and did my makeup better than any of her attendants ever had! My heart weighed more and more as our time together waned. I had fun doing girly things with her... it hurt to know what a backstabber I was. I think she was beginning to pick up on the fact I had something bubbling in my head. By the time we finished, it was too late for her to bring it up. We left, and went straight to the town's opera house; it was a stunning building that reached up into the heavens, and ranged far as a castle. We entered, and saw seats were lined up by the hundreds... no, thousands! There was also an *enormous* red curtain, that veiled what must have been a just as *colossal* stage. Miyune gave me a warm rub on the head. She kneeled halfway down, and looked into my eyes.

"Go ahead, hurry along backstage." she said, "Lord Ruvaen and his attendants will be back there. If there is anything else you need, please let them know."

"Of course... thank you, Miyu."

"Do not worry, Kea."

I felt lost, like an infant in the dark. I wanted to cry, and would have too... but I didn't want to ruin all the work Miyune had spent on my face. I shoved my emotions aside, and went backstage. I couldn't get anymore than a few steps deep backstage, before Lord Ruvaen's eyes fell upon me.

"Chocolate, warm milk, applesauce, teddy bear? Anything to cool the nerves?"

Curses... I guess I had to go along with the baby treatment.

"I am good, absolutely good!"

"Good, good. Feel like being my finishing act?" he said.

"Yes, of course! That's fine."

Lord Ruvaen turned around. He seemed to be looking for someone. Finally, he found who he'd wanted, and pointed to said person. I saw a shaved man, with dark skin, and a thin build. He must have been somewhere in his fourties.

"Jerameel. Get him for your needs, any of them."

"Alright, thank you."

Lord Ruvaen passed on, and I found myself a seat. I watched all the other performers, and all the fancy things they had going in their acts. I hadn't even thought about pairing some flavor with my singing... Every other songstress I saw had some sort of routine, some sort of flair.

"Stupid Kea." I muttered.

I should have thought about bringing something else to the party. I did, of course, have a trump card locked away, but did I really want to pull it out? I pondered over what to do. Minutes later, an attendant walked up to me.

"A gift, from Lord Ruvaen." said the attendant.

She handed me a tray with milk, and cookies.

"Thank you." I said, faking a smile.

Curse Ruvaen. It annoyed me how he was treating me like a toddler. In protest, I munched away at the cookies in a very angry manner! I munched away, drank the milk, and continued to wonder what should be done about my act. In the midst of my thinking, another handful of performers entered the backstage. There was a few jesters among them, a man with an instrument, and a few more songstresses... or, were they dancers? Either way.

A sharp accent flew at me. "Aaaaw, how cute." a woman said.

"Where do you hail from?" asked someone at her side.

"I have no home, I merely wander."

Since the makeup added a few years, I went with an older voice than usual.

"Ah, I'm so very sorry to hear that."

"You should take Dial as a home if you ever wish." said the second, while fiddling with large, hoopy earings, "King Metifell has a great taste for the arts."

I liked where this was going!

"Do you know King Metifell personally?" I asked.

"Personally? I would not say that. I have spoken to him on an occasion or two."

"Have you performed for him many times?"

"'Fair few times, yes."

Interesting...

"Lord Ruvaen wishes to become chummy with nobles of Dial, that is what I hear. That is why many in attendance are of Dial." said the first.

"Are they really?"

"Yes."

"So..." I began, "if I wished to make a name for myself in Dial, this would be a good place to start?"

"Yes, it would be quite a great place to start."

"We-..." the second started to say, before the first pulled her away.

"That's our cue, come now!"

They passed on, and I listened to their song. It was mediocre at best. If King Metifell would listen to something like *that,* then my songs would *kill* him! In a good way... of course. My feet kicked over to the dark skinned man, Jerameel. He had a big smile on his wrinkled face.

"How can I help you, young one?"

"I was hoping you could get me large streamers, do you think you could?"

"Of course, Miss Leestel, without a doubt!"

Relief left my lips. "Thank you. Now, are there any good players of the flute, or drums, around here?"

"Quite a few." he said.

I opened my mouth, but he spoke before I could get words out.

"I'll get you with the best of the best."

Out of gratitude, my head bowed to my hips. "Thank you, Jerameel. I am grateful."

"Don't think a thing of it."

He got me together with a good drummer, then he

brought over a man who specialized in not just flutes, but also flute-like instruments. Jerameel went off to get what I needed; in the meantime, I collaborated with the two players of instruments Jerameel had gifted me. I ran them through any and everything I needed of them. They appreciated my knowledge of music, and we discussed the routine for some hour. They knew it like clockwork by the time we stopped.

Another act ended, so my eyes flew around the backstage. Was Jerameel back yet? He'd... been gone a long time. Two hours had passed! Curses. Anxiety knocked on the door, because there wasn't many people left to go onstage before me. What on Lathine would I do if Jerameel didn't get back in time? I started pacing holes in the floor.

"Sorry I'm late!" I finally heard.

My head spun to see Jerameel! Thank goodness!

"It's fine!" I said, "I'm just happy you made it!"

He had a large basket in tow, and handed it off to me. "'Got everything I could find you."

The basket was loaded to the brim with streamers! I had my pick from a sea of them.

"Wonderful, Jerameel! Thank you!"

"Anything I can do to help."

I took a seat, and went through the basket to find the best streamers for my part. It was hard to chose, because all the streamers Jerameel had brought me were beautiful. I wanted my act to be perfect, which hurt my decisiveness. High society events were a great time for making connections, and so that considered, I was determined to nail every aspect of my act!

Time unraveled; the final act before me finished, and left. I couldn't have been any more ready. I made my way onstage, in a solemn state of mind. I stood center stage, closed my eyes, and put my head down. I did this until the soft praise from the previous act died out. Confusion wrapped around the crowd, because I wasn't moving. At long last, I snapped behind my back, and that served as a cue to the drummer. His soft sounds started to echo through the opera house, then the flute master started in synch with my singing.

"Ah naheo neh kahsahs neo meesh zahlah

Ah rooiih lahsah gahme soo fah kehl lihreen"

A massive streamer twirled out from behind my back; I started with just the one. At the same time, the sound of music sped up.

"Ah ooyoo ehmihn yaiih eon dahiih nayeh"

Out spun the second streamer, and ere continued my slow dance, to a still rather slow song.

"Ee vah zehn sah yoon uhiih fehl"

Right on time, both musicians kicked their beats to another level. From this point onwards, the music kept getting more *exciting,* and *faster* with every line I gave. My movements played along with the new pace. A blur of pink and blue gusted like a hurricane. *Speed, speed, speed...* everything I did kept speeding up. Adrenaline rushed through my blood with each spin, and I loved every second of it. A bad spin would ruin my act, and yet fear still couldn't find me. There was no room for fear, no room for even the thought of failure!

Dancing felt good, singing felt great, and twirling was a throwback. I don't remember much of my act, though... if not from adrenaline, then because of how at ease dancing put me. For the most part, my eyes stayed closed for the duration of the dance, which might have been part of the reason why it went by so quick. I kept them closed as much for looks, as I did out of fear. I feared the crowd would fade away, and be replaced by the people I'd once known. I was scared I'd see my parents... the fire, the blood, the corpses; all of it.

"Soo fah ziihf neh kahehn fiih ah sahn vliih fah beo"

Without another word, it ended... My eyes opened to see the reality I'd created. Cheers fluttered from left to right. It was hard not to mistake it all for the screams of torture I'd used to hear, which made my feet start to quiver. I bowed low, and spun a streamer one last time. Echoes beat the building from corner to corner. It was like an army was shooting down a battle cry! I didn't bother to give Miyune or Keras a look. I already knew Miyune would be happy, because my performances would give her another tool to play around with. I went backstage, where Jerameel's wrinkled face was smiling from end to end.

He ran over, and gave me a celebratory hug. "Brilliant, Ms. Leestel, brilliant!"

"I can only hope so. I want to perform in Dial someday, so I'll have to be."

I'd said that hoping he had some connections of his own.

"Well, I'll tell you this," Jerameel said, "if you're ever in Sinliir; *go to the castle!* I'll personally give Metifell the 'ol heads up."

Sinliir was the capital of Dial!

"Do you know the King?"

"Unfortunately," Jerameel joked, "thanks to my skill as a forger. I'm the best of the best! Swords, armor, axes, you name it! I've always got him calling my name."

His eyes were bolstered with pride.

"I can do anything." he said, "If Lady Miyune ever needs

a forger, you know where to send her!"

In retrospect, this day might have been the true beginning of all that would occur, albeit, there were many days that could be said of. There were many reasons for me to think this, in days long passed. Cheif of all the reasons was a reason I'd yet to see; a reason I'd see in just a few short days.

Time continued to spin one hand after another, it just wouldn't stop spinning... who alive could stop the hemorrhaging of Lathine? I wish there had been someone who could heal the bleeding, but there wasn't.

CHAPTER 33

Keras and Miyune left me alone during our return to Sciruthon. As a result, those days were uneventful, with no stories to tell. Back on the doorsteps of Sciruthon, I did my best not to get too hopeful. It was hard not to let fantasies of knights swarming the city get the best of me. I wanted to see Sehrea at Lathimian's side, free and safe.

I'd been crowned as the Miracle Maiden, and anointed by men as an envoy of God... as one with a penchant for miracles. I prayed that today of all days, such a thing could prove true.

A mix of emotions bubbled in my head. We moved into town, and made our way through. It was never a good sign when I could feel every pass of blood inside me... but that was exactly what I felt. Town turned out to be just how we'd left it; simplistic, and clean. Soon, the palace came into view. There was no reason to think anything had taken hold of fate, and swayed the path of the world, at least... until Loshki emerged from the shadows. You could tell something wasn't right.

Keras snapped. "Loshki! What's happened!"

Loshki threw his head towards the palace. "It's been compromised."

"Then why are you standing around!?!"

I saw another face emerge from the shadows. I saw Lathimian! Aloofness and bravado ran down his chiseled cheeks.

Loshki turned to him. "'You really want to do this? 'You really that eager to die?"

Loshki made a slow walk towards Lathimian... but didn't pull a weapon.

Lathimian had a smug little grin on his face.

"No," he replied, "not since I went through that whole 'gloom and doom' teen phase."

Loshki... *laughed* at this! What on Lathine was going on here!?!

"Kill him, Loshki!" Keras cried, "Kill him! Kill him!!!"

Why was Miyune so calm? All of a sudden, Lathimian's men swarmed! Swords were drawn, lances were extended, and axes were brought high! I saw Arsaphi, Breovit, all of them! Loshki sneered at the sight.

"Loshki!" Keras roared, "How could this happen!?! **HOW!**"

I would have never guessed what Loshki said next, never, not in a million years!

"Because I sold you out." he said.

Keras' entire face dropped. He was even more stunned than me!

"Loshki-...! No-... *Curse you!!!*"

Loshki stood, cross armed, tall and proud. He couldn't have seemed any less scared of Keras.

"I'm not in any better shape than you, but 'least now I'm off death row. 'What you want me to say, My Lord?"

"TRAITOR!!! Curse you! Curse you all!"

Men with swords rushed in, and men with bows followed. Lathimian's men took hold of Keras and Miyune... and I thought my heart was going to give out.

He'd... *done it.*

He'd really done it...

I wouldn't be sent back to the abyss...

Lathimian had won, we'd won! Right? This was it? Ultimate victory!?! Loshki nodded to Lathimian, who nodded back. Knights took Loshki away, followed by Keras. Keras flailed every inch of the way, and screamed one vulgar thing after another; it didn't take an astute mind to know why he was so emotional... Loshki had just brought up the topic of *"death row"*, after all.

Miyune was taken next, and the guards were gentle with her. On her way out, she turned her head to me. I wasn't sure how to feel, nor what to think. I'd expected a plea for help, or something like that, except that's not what she did. She did nothing at all, nothing; there was no emotion on her, *none.* No despair hugged her face, no sadness warped her eyes, no anger devoured her. She looked back to me, and I to her, and nothing was exchanged... except for one thing, one small thing as she turned away from me. I could swear, for the slightest hint of a second, I'd caught sight of a grin... the same grin she'd always give when she'd won. Could I have seen her wrong? Everything happened so quick... so I guess I must have.

Even if I hadn't seen it wrong, it was probably just her way of messing with me one last time, right?

It took me a moment to realize I'd spaced out. When I came back to reality, Sehrea was standing before me! Warmth exuded from her like a bright lamp. Her eyes held all the words she couldn't bring herself to say, which worked for me, because I couldn't bring myself to say anything either! I buried myself into her arms, and if I'd gotten my way, I would have never let go.

Lathimian stood alongside us, and rubbed my head. "This is as much your triumph as anyone else's."

"This could've only happened with you." I said, "I can't

take credit."

Lathimian grinned, and looked away. "Weeeeell, you're not wrong."

I appreciated how lighthearted he always was. He was the sort of man to bright up any dark, which is what people really needed in dire times.

"Speaking of taking," Lathimian said, "I'm bringing the both of you to Muinflor. Things'll be different for you two there. All the things that hurt you will be long gone."

Relief blasted through Sehrea's lips.

"And Sehrea?" Lathimian said.

"Yes?"

"Found your horse."

She pounced like a cat. Even being freed couldn't have brought such a twinkle to her eye.

"Lolagis!?!"

Lathimian really wasn't one to pass up a stale joke. "You have any others?"

He hissed at Breovit, and pointed to Sehrea. "You there, whatever your name is! Take her to Lolagis."

"Oh, come on Lath, that's just cold."

Breovit gave Lathimian a little shove on the way by, and the both of them smiled. I watched as Breovit led Sehrea into Miyune's courtyard; looks like Miyune had kept even Lolagis at arm's reach...

Lathimian looked to the palace with me. "You want to go in?" he asked, "One last time?"

Yes, one last time... why not? We worked our way to the palace, where I spotted three of Lathimian's men keeping watch atop the wall. There was four knights at the gate, when we reached it. Once they opened the gate for us, I counted another three men in the courtyard.

Lathimian had really come prepared, no doubts there!

We entered, and saw a knight in every hall we went down, which set me at ease. For a change, walking around the palace felt good; for once, I could relish in it's beauty. It was nice to let myself feel, and think. My thoughts were soon interrupted by a familiar face. General Tranel popped around a corner!

"Everything go alright?" he said.

"Peachy dandy." Lathimian replied, "Any luck on the door?"

"There's no opening it without the key." Tranel told, "The hallway's too narrow, you'll never get a big enough battering ram in there."

Lathimian clicked off one side of his mouth. "Of course not... We'll just leave it be for now, General, 'come back to it later."

Again, here was Lathimian acting like an equal to a superior. He was never haughty, or insidious about it; instead, he was just good at keeping things casual. All of his joking to Breovit aside, he always treated those under him as equals too. It was good to see people of power that weren't puffed with pride, and didn't treat their decrees like the word of God.

"Good, good..." Tranel said, "I was thinking the same."

I guess the truth of what laid inside the cellar would have to wait... We stayed in town for a few days, so Lathimian could see to loose ends. He kept nothing short of the entire town under the tightest lockdown I'd ever seen! Him and General Tranel were notified if so much as an eyelash fell; better yet, they kept the prisoners *far* away from me. I never had to see *any* of them, though there was one I did want to speak with.

Loshki was held in a cell, in the Knight's of Sciruthon's

headquarters. I was allowed in, and waltzed to his bars, where I found him doing push-ups. He gave me an eye, then popped to his feet.

"Lady Leestel."

"'*Kea*', is fine…"

"Guilty?"

"H-, I…"

"It's written on your face. You've looked unsure for awhile now, about who you should be, and all that deep stuff."

"You don't… hate me?"

"I don't hate anyone. Business is business, we all do what we have to do."

"Alright…"

"'You want answers, or meaning?"

"Both, I guess."

He grinned, finding this whole thing amusing. "Remember what I told you, way back? About building up all the talents you can, for the time when you do know?"

"Yes…"

"I'd still tell you to hold dear to that. Kea, you're just a kid, a kid in a wide, wide world. Don't grow up too fast. 'You ask anyone what they want at fourteen, and it'll be different than what they want at twenty four. Don't lock your life away so young."

"Thank you, Loshki…"

A silence ensued, I think he wanted me to say something for a change.

"Will you be alright?" I asked.

He'd done nothing but act with respect, and teach me well. He'd been brave enough to liberate me from my homeworld, so I was truly grateful. His liberation of me was something I could probably never repay. If he'd just been a little bit less brave, or a little bit less determined in his training... I'd probably still be back in the dark, being beaten by my father's advisor.

"'Wager the rest of my days will be in a cell." he said, "'Not scared of that, wouldn't mind the peace and solitude, wouldn't mind not being ordered around anymore. I'll have my life, can't ask for much more, eh?"

"I guess so..."

"Don't sell your mind to people locked away. Don't bring yourself down with thoughts of me, or Miyune. Don't waste your life, you're better than that."

"Thank you Loshki, for everything... I *really,* really mean it."

He nodded, and then I left. That was probably the last time I'd ever see him again...

CHAPTER 34;
FINALE

Why did the voices torment I, and I alone? They awoke me in the dead of night, but left Sehrea to sleep in peace just a dozen feet away. Looks like this was just the way I'd have to remember my first night back in Muinflor...

"This is no end." they said.

I didn't doubt they were right.

"There is no end."

Why on Lathine were they speaking? They never spoke when others were around! In the end, I guess it didn't matter, since I wasn't about to do anything. I prayed the day never arose when I was foolish enough to open my eyes, and test what haunts me.

It continued to speak to me... the whisper that preys on weary hearts.

"Eo nahkeh nahiih."

Like always, I kept my head down, and battled through. This marked the first time I realized how therapeutic the heat of it's breath, and the cold of it's hair was. Yes, I know that sounds crazy... My tense skin began to soothe, and my restlessness was replaced with drowsiness. Had this thing always helped me with my anxieties so? Was I just now noticing? Or, was it just familiarity that set me at ease, in an unfamiliar time? I guess there was no saying for sure. All I could say, is that this one time, I enjoyed the voice's presence.

After hearing a knock on the door that next morning, I opened up to see Lathimian!

"Did your meeting with King Neromas fare well?" Sehrea asked him, her mouth stuffed with food.

"It did." Lathimian said.

It was clear he was keeping something to himself.

He answered before I could open my mouth. "Looks like you'll be going to the Yearlies without me." he said to Sehrea.

That must have been it...

"Then we will stay in Muinflor." Sehrea said, "It would be dangerous for us to venture without you."

"No, you should still go, King Neromas even arranged you your own guard. Call it a *'thank you'*, if you will."

"Our own guard?" I choked out, "That's generous, but how long for?"

"Well, he intended it to be for the Yearly run, buuuut if you got a little lost, I'm sure he wouldn't mind."

Sehrea looked concerned. She could tell something new was brewing in my head. Fears aside, she still seemed accepting of whatever I'd decided.

"Do what you will." her eyes all but said, *"I'll follow you through anything."*

Lathimian didn't ask questions, instead he left us to our own machinations. There should have been no room for harm to befall us, after all, since we'd have our own guard, and I'm sure Lathimian knew that.

"I have something else for you." Lathimian said.

"What's that?" Sehrea asked.

"Breovit." he said, "He's supposed to go with me, but I owe you two and him both a favor."

"Really?" I squeaked.

I loved the thought of having a familiar face around.

Sehrea did something between a nod and a bow. "Thank you, Lathimian. We appreciate it, really, but are you sure you'll be fine without him? He's loyal, and helpful; I can't imagine you want to be without his aid."

"Well, you got me there, but my party is already loaded. I'm not worried."

"Thank you, Lathimian." I said, nodding like Sehrea had.

Lathimian held back a smile. "Breovit won't admit it, but he wants to fight in the Yearlies. 'Thought I'd cut him some slack."

"I couldn't agree more!" I said, "You should definitely, definitely do that!"

Next afternoon, Sehrea and I heard a knock on the door. Again, it was Lathimian! Lathimian led us through Muinflor, and out one of it's gates. We caught sight of a little group, whom Breovit was amongst.

Breovit walked over to see us, then set his eyes on Sehrea and I.

"You both ready for fun?"

"I don't think I know how." I said, only half joking.

"We're very excited," Sehrea said, "both of us, truly."

"Good," Breovit said, "good…"

He turned to Lathimian. "I'd greet you, Sir Holy Lord High Highness, but you wouldn't know who I am."

"Naaaaah, you're the pride of the company! Dare I say it; every man, woman, and child, for the next hundred generations will know your name."

"No Lathimian, I'm not joining Cavala."

"You know, now that you mention it, we do have a few spots open. I don't suppose-"

Breovit nudged Sehrea and I towards the rest of the

company, and cut Lathimian off. "I don't think so, not happening."

"You'll come around!" Lathimian called, "You know you want to!"

"No," Breovit called back, "I want to win! I'll join Teran if anything!"

"You won't win anything there! Jerthian's washed!"

"He's in his prime!"

Lathimian grinned, and disappeared into Muinflor.

"What did he mean by all that?" Sehrea asked.

"You know he's a Legion fighter, right?" Breovit replied.

"Of course."

"His team needs a few more fighters to fill out their squad with, so Lathimian's been trying to recruit me for awhile now."

"It would be fun to watch if you did join." I said.

"Probably." he admitted.

"I bet you would really like to fight in the Yearlies too." Sehrea said.

"Planning on it, if that's fine with you two."

Alright... so Lathimian was right, and Breovit had wanted to fight after all!

"Of course that's fine!" I said.

"Hopefully I'll have some good showings, that'll get me some good offers when the Legions roll around."

There were thirteen Yearlies each year, all held in the time of Senitheera. Senitheera was one of the four months of the year, by the calendar of Lathine. Sehrea was excited to see what a Yearly was like, so I stayed upbeat, for her sake.

Yes... I'd let my own problems fade away, and just worry about having fun with my sister. That was a good idea, right? Thanks to the guard, we made it to the first Yearly of the thirteen without issue; it was hosted in a town by the name of "Tenamayu". When we entered, Breovit broke from the shadows.

"We're staying close," he said, "for caution's sake."

"I appreciate your forethought." Sehrea remarked.

I couldn't help but agree with his idea, after I saw the dense streets of Tenamayu. There was no open space anywhere, none!

Breovit grinned. "Lathimian told me this is you two's first Yearly Run. You're both in for a treat."

Here I'd thought the atmosphere of a Legion was something special, and yet this city's energy was twice as great! Breovit led us to Tenamayu's fighting grounds, which was outside of town. We three found decent seats, and the fighting began soon after. I ended up turning into *that* person at an event... you know, *that* person? *That* person, that ends up paying more attention to fans, vendors, and weird things like that, than the actual event? There was just so much excitement in the crowd, so much heart! I loved the feeling of unity everyone had, and finally understood why Yearlies were held in such high esteem.

It felt like the number of combatants who fought in the tourney was endless, which explained why the event spanned two days. Naturally, we came back the second day. Finals was nearing, Breovit had already been knocked out, and now the crowd was in a frenzy.

"I've never seen anything like it!" one man said.

"Who'd have ever guessed it!?!" said another.

I kept hearing things like that.

Sehrea nudged Breovit, who was sitting beside her. "What do they mean?"

"Just what they say; that this fight is unbelievable. First off, you've got the hottest prodigy in decades, Inen, and then pitted against him you've got a mystery man *nobody* has ever heard of, Kyniro. Kyniro even bounced a man by the name of Themazar last round, which proves he's no slouch. Themazar has won four Yearlies in the past."

"That's odd nobody's ever heard of him..." I muttered.

At the heart of the arena stood one of the officials of the event; he began to call out to the heavens. "For the first fighter of circle one, Kyniro, of Zahn-...ehlahk...estrahkahn!"

"That can't be an actual place." Breovit remarked.

"You've never heard of it?" I asked.

He shook his head. "Never. 'Bet he's not from Sohal, at the very least."

I watched as Kyniro ran onto the field. He had shoulder height pitch black hair, and just as dark armor.

"To oppose him," the official called, "Inen, of Novira!"

Out ran a young man... a very young man, at least compared to the other fighters. Words like *"prodigy"* do seem to assume youth, so I guess I shouldn't have been surprised. Other fighters were called to wage their own battles, and then Inen and Kyniro went to fighting!

Inen fought like a rabid beast, while Kyniro fended him off with a level of finesse I'd *never* seen before. Inen only got to launch off a handful of blows, before Kyniro slipped in a match ending stab! Kyniro reminded me of Lathimian, in the sense that he just *knew* everything Inen would try. It was no surprise to me when Kyniro's cold and calculated style of play resulted in him being crowned champion of the Yearly of Tenamayu...

I didn't mention all of this for no reason. I wonder

what the world would have been like, if someone had stopped Kyniro. Kyniro's crowning as champion of Tenamayu might have been the true beginning to all that would become.

...On route to the second Yearly, the company took a break. Sehrea and I laid on our backs, and watched the clouds go by. An endless sea of plains served as a lush background. We listened to the birds chatter, made shapes out of clouds, talked, rested, and talked some more. I tried to enjoy myself, but couldn't... because what we were doing reminded me too much of what I'd do with Miyu. Some hurts ran too deep; I don't think the pain the past brought me would ever go away, not fully.

Sehrea spoke out of the blue. "It's fine to be a kid, there's nothing wrong with that."

I used to be such a convincing face... why couldn't I muster that anymore?

"Yes, yes of course." I said, "I'm fine, don't worry."

She wasn't wrong about anything she'd said, but it was just too hard for me to put everything aside, and live like I really wanted to.

During the first round of Yearly number three, Sehrea stepped out for sweets. I looked to the skies, and fell deep into thought. I couldn't stop doubting everything I'd ever heard, and now I couldn't stop doubting everything I'd ever believed.

What kicked me back to reality was the voice of a man. An aura surrounded his voice... I felt the weight of people long passed, and events that had fallen to history. His voice was like the rebirth of it all. What do I mean by that, you ask? Well, I don't know... those words just came to me, I guess. Maybe I was going crazy. I looked to find the owner of the voice, which was hard to do, given the roars, and cheers, of the tens of thousands in attendance. Fate was willing, and I heard the man's voice again. It was a fiery sort of voice, and I could tell it belonged to a young soul.

"Any worthwhile fighter doesn't go out there and lose round one." it said.

I glanced up, through my outstretched bangs. Turns out, the owner of the voice was sitting right in front of me! He had a thin, brown beard, and floppy hair that was bound to fall down to eyebrow length in the heat of battle. In terms of muscle, his physique was reminiscent of Loshki's! Muscle like that, at such a young age, took an uncountable amount of training, and immeasurable resolve!

"Competitors are always going to fail more than they succeed." Breovit told him, "Remember that, and remember to keep that spunk of yours. It'll serve you well."

A grin left the young man. "That's a reminder I'm fortunate not to need. I'll topple anything that 'should' come. Legendary fighters? Fate? You name it, I'll stomp it!"

At that moment, Breovit's name was called.

Breovit hopped up, and started to take the field, then he called back at the young man. "Never let anyone take that spirit!"

"Count on it!"

Hearing from someone that thought so little of fate irked me, because I was desperate to think the same.

"Fate..." I hissed, not bothering to mask my real voice, "nobody can tame fate."

Hate for my people had culminated into those words; I hated everything about them! I hated their reverence of fate! I turned my sights to the ground, and tried to get a grip on myself. Fourteen years of bottling anger was taking it's toll, and the demon within me was ready to take shape.

It took some time before the young man's eyes fell upon me. "Was that you?" he asked.

A moment passed.

I decided I should keep speaking, since I'd started our little chat in the first place. "Fate cannot be toppled... that's all I meant to say."

It just couldn't, right? Here I'd always said I didn't believe any of my people's teachings, and yet I still bowed to fate like a god. Was there no escape from the chains my people had put around my heart after all?

"You sound mature for someone so young." he said, "What's your name, kid? I'm Kr-..."

"As if it matters."

Why was I so angry? He was taken back by my sharpness, but still chuckled. I don't know what had overtaken me, all I knew is that I couldn't help but keep my eyes locked to the ground. His curious eyes stayed upon me. My night black bangs held guard to my eyes, so I'm sure he was curious to see what I really looked like.

"As if?" he said, "I-..."

My lips cut him off. "Best wishes. Please enjoy your day, pay me no mind..."

I started to depart from him.

"Kid! Hey...!"

No doubt he wanted an answer or two. I kept on going.

"How obnoxious..." I grumbled.

Why had I grumbled? Anger was a cause, sure, but I think knowing I'd blown the chance to learn something was also to blame. Maybe I was sour because I felt I'd never escape my people, not in the ways that mattered...

My head was unraveling more than ever. I was in the greatest peace I'd ever had, so why did I feel so miserable? What did that say about me? In no way was I pioneering the sort of world I wanted; a world founded by compassion, and love. If I couldn't do that, then what right did I have to dream of a better world in the first place? Is that even still what I *really* wanted? I think that was the sentiment I still believed in, but I wasn't sure anymore.

Miyune and Keras being in chains only meant so much. There was yet legions of people suffering, starving, homeless... How could I be so selfish as to call this a time of peace? Nothaniir was still out there! There was still questions to get from whomever, or whatever he was! He, she, or it, was bound to replace Miyune and Keras. Cut off one head, and another will arise, right? That is the way of the world.

Yes, yes, this wasn't the time to rest, or doubt! I'd never have gotten close to Lathimian, or Sehrea, if my people really had put chains around my heart. I'd learned to start trusting... and that made all the difference in the world.

As long as I continued to hold faith that truth would find me, and kept close to Sehrea, things would be fine. Some pains never do heal, but that doesn't make us slaves to them. I wouldn't let myself become a slave to the past!

This world would yet bloom.

With a little action on my part, things would be alright. That line of thinking had brought me to where I was now; a road that differed from any I could have ever imagined, after living all those years in the dark. What I started to learn is how there was no one road in life.

Out before us all, lays an endless sea of roads. We have no right to pretend in such things as *'fate'*, to pretend that our lives are shackled, set in stone. I'd begun to learn the ways of the world, and would only learn more through all that would occur... through occurrences that nobody could have predicted, not even the voices in the night.

"*Eo nahkeh nahiih.*"

Soon after this tale you now know, the world would dawn anew, but before that, here I wait...

before the *Eclipse,*
before the *Betrayal,*
before... the *High General.*

Made in the USA
San Bernardino, CA
01 March 2020

65030336R00163